After about half an hour—but it felt like about three hours—Suzy looked at her watch and said in a great fake voice that she didn't know it had gotten so late. I caught Lisa looking at my face, and her eyes looked as if she had a lot of things to say, but wasn't going to.

"Yeah, it is late," I said, agreeing with Suzy that it was time to go.

"It's impossible during the week," she said to me, but not meeting my eyes. "I mean, I'm so busy—but next weekend; for sure. Do you want me to bring you anything?"

I shook my head, knowing that my voice would shake if I tried to use it.

"When are you going home?" Lisa asked.

I shrugged, to say I didn't know.

"I bet you're looking forward to that," Lisa said.

I pushed the ends of my mouth out into a smile to show that, yes, I was.

Finally they left. I unclenched my teeth, unclenched the muscles around my eyes, which had been holding the tears back. . . .

IZZY, WILLY-NILLY

Cynthia Voigt

FAWCETT JUNIPER • NEW YORK

RLI: $\dfrac{\text{VL: 5 \& up}}{\text{IL: 6 \& up}}$

A Fawcett Juniper Book
Published by Ballantine Books
Copyright © 1986 by Cynthia Voigt

All rights reserved under International and Pan-American Copyright Conventions. Published in the United States by Ballantine Books, a division of Random House, Inc., New York, and simultaneously in Canada by Random House of Canada Limited, Toronto.

Library of Congress Catalog Card Number: 85-22933

ISBN 0-449-70214-6

This edition published by arrangement with Atheneum Publishers, a division of The Scribner Book Companies, Inc.

Manufactured in the United States of America

First Ballantine Books Edition: April 1987
Fourteenth Printing: September 1991

For JESSICA,
who is old-fashioned nice,
new-fangled nice,
and a pleasure to have around

I'd like to thank Dwight Fortier, MD,
for answering my questions
and clarifying the possibilities,
not to mention enriching
my vocabulary.

1

"Isobel? I'm afraid we're going to have to take it off."

"Take it off, take it off," I sang, like a vamp song; but I don't think I actually did, and I know my laughter stayed locked inside my head. I think my voice did too.

"Isobel. Can you hear me?"

I didn't know. I didn't think so.

It was my leg. I went to sleep.

"Izzy," I said, finally figuring out what was wrong. "My name's Izzy." Nobody ever called me Isobel. I felt better, then. I didn't open my eyes, but now that the disturbing, frightening feeling that something was wrong was explained, I relaxed.

Except that nobody here called me Izzy, I remembered that. Here, where everything was bright white, or cold metal, or pale plastic, where voices seemed to echo strangely, here they called me Isobel. Doctors and nurses, and there had been a policeman—why had there been a policeman in my room?—all calling me Isobel. I didn't correct them. It didn't seem so important at the time.

Except my parents, sometimes they called me Izzy,

although most of the time they called me old baby names, Pumpkin and Angel, Sweetheart, Lamb. Remembering their voices, I drifted back to sleep. Pumpkin and Angel, Sweetheart, Lamb.

The next time, I was really awake. I knew where I was. Before I could stop them, my eyes opened.

I was still attached to an IV, this time clear liquid, not one of the red bottles of somebody else's blood. My mother sat in a chair near the metal crib sides of the bed. She looked terrible. She was dressed all right, but her face looked terrible. Her eyes were closed. Beside her sat my father, broad-shouldered, his hair still white-blond from the summer sun.

A nurse turned the pages of the chart that hung from the foot of the bed. The only sound in the room was the rustling of papers. Before the nurse could see me, I closed my eyes again.

What, I asked, is a nice girl like me doing in a place like this?

A nice girl—that's just exactly what I was. Am.

Most of the people I know don't want to be just nice. They want to be interesting, or exciting, romantic, terrific—something special. I don't think I ever wanted to be more than nice. Nice suited me: pretty but nowhere near beautiful; popular enough, with girls and with boys; although no jock, I could give somebody a respectable game of tennis, and I was one of only three sophomores on the school cheerleading squad. A B student, except for Latin where, for some reason, I got a few A's, I did the work I was told to do and didn't mind school: just a nice person, easy to get along with, fun to have around. I usually got jokes although I seldom made them. I often tried to make peace in quarrels although I took part in my share of them. I liked people, liked doing things with people, liked being with people. Like.

And here I was in the hospital, surrounded by the unhappy silence of my parents, with—

I had awakened once before, I didn't know how many days ago. Against the backdrop of my closed eyelids I could replay that day. Like a TV rerun. Of "Mary Tyler Moore" or something. Like "M*A*S*H?" No, it was like a soap opera, like I'd been tossed into the script of one of the soaps, where I didn't belong. Nice girls are too dull for the soaps. I wasn't wild about being dull, but there wasn't much I could do about that, even if I wanted to; and I didn't, not really anyway, want to do anything about it. I liked myself pretty much exactly the way I was.

That other day, the soap opera day, I was in the same bed, in the same room, and it was morning. There was blue sky outside the one window. I had an IV attached to my left arm, only that one dripped blood. I didn't feel like moving, because the only part of me that didn't hurt was my right hand, and my mother was holding onto that with both hands. She looked pretty terrible that day, too. My mother doesn't really look like herself to me without her makeup on. Not that she wears so much, but it makes her eyes look a darker brown, and it shades in the bones of her face and gives color to her skin. My father was there too, that day, and he came to stand behind my mother when I woke up. My father looks like someone in an Ingmar Bergman movie. That day he looked like the hero in an Ingmar Bergman movie.

"I'm sorry," I said to them.

That made my father angry. "Don't you ever apologize," he said. When my father gets angry, his blue eyes turn icy and his voice would freeze hell over, that's what the twins say anyway. Then either Jack turns to Joel and says, "I guess you'd know about that, hunh?" or Joel turns to Jack and says the same thing, and they laugh. The twins weren't there, that day, and I didn't feel much like laughing, so my father just stood there being angry.

"Ever," he repeated. "It's that little bas—"

"Hendrik," my mother stopped him.

I was beginning to feel terrible, pains all over my body, and my head throbbed, and I tightened my grip on my mother's hand. I liked the way her engagement ring cut into my fingers. She asked my father to get the nurse and stayed there, holding my hand, until the nurse gave me a shot.

The surgeon came first, that day. He was short and bald. He stood at the foot of the bed, never looking at me, while he told me. I already knew that my right leg was broken, because it was held up in the air with pulleys and wires. I had to lie flat and the blankets covering my right leg made a kind of tent that hid the doorway. The surgeon stood to the left of that tent. He told me that my left leg was broken too, a simple fracture. He asked me if I could move my toes. After I showed him, I wanted him to say something approving, like, "That's good." He didn't say anything though, Dr. Carstairs. He just "hmmed" and made a note. Then he told me about contusions and bruising "of the upper torso," which he sounded pretty bored with. After that, he moved around the IV stand so he was next to my bed, opposite to where my parents were. Even though he moved closer, he didn't get any closer.

"Now that leg," he said, sounding more interested, "that leg's had severe bone and muscle trauma. Multiple fracture of tibula and fibula, a closed fracture of the femur." I looked at my parents, hoping they would explain, but they were just staring at Dr. Carstairs, the way kids stare at a teacher who is really angry at them, silent and . . . waiting for what they already know.

"That sounds serious," I said. My voice squeaked a little.

Dr. Carstairs agreed. "Yes. It is. The time that elapsed between the accident and when you finally were admitted here did you no good at all. No good at all. You'd have been a lot better off if you'd gotten in right away. I avulsed the

debride tissue, tried to align the bones. .   ." It was as if
he was talking in a foreign language, but I got the general
message: Things were pretty bad with my right leg.

"We've got you stabilized," Dr. Carstairs told me, "and
we'll keep the leg pinned up." He indicated the blanket
tent. "You're young, you're healthy." I didn't understand
why he was telling me this. He waited for me to say
something, or ask a question.

"I see," I said. "Thank you."

The expression that crossed his face was like a teacher
who thinks you're going to have the right answer and you
don't.

"Isobel," he said.

I was getting frightened, so I didn't correct him.

"There's a strong possibility that the right leg won't
heal."

My mother's hand tightened. I swallowed, and asked,
"You mean, like, I'd have a limp?" I hoped he wasn't
talking about a brace, but I didn't want to mention that.

"The leg may well have to be amputated," Dr. Carstairs
said. "In twenty-five percent of cases this severe, the limb
has to come off."

"But why?" I asked. "It feels all right."

"I doubt that you feel anything at all," he said. He was
right, but at least it didn't hurt, which was, frankly, about all
I cared about. "Isobel," he started again. I felt my eyes
getting bigger and bigger, just waiting for him to say
whatever he was going to say. "We can't predict how much
tissue necrosis there will be, and that leads, of course, to the
danger of infection."

I swallowed again and tried to look attentive. I was
frightened and I hurt and my heart was beating up in my
throat. I concentrated on behaving well, because then things
would have a better chance of turning out all right.

"You must stay absolutely quiet while we see what the
leg is going to do," Dr. Carstairs told me sternly.

"I will," I told him. "How long—"

"Nobody can predict. You've been given plenty of antibiotics and all we can do now is wait and see. But if you feel at all funny—feverish or dizzy—you must say so right away. Will you do that?"

"I will," I promised.

"We'll see how it goes," he said. He nodded to my parents and left the room.

When bad news comes, you don't believe it right away. Not really. Or anyway, I didn't. I didn't even know, then, not really, what I was doing in the hospital. I'd been in a car wreck, but I couldn't remember that. I only knew it. Dr. Carstair's words washed over me, like icy water, and froze my brain. None of it made sense, so I didn't believe in it. I concentrated on not crying, which was hard because I really felt like crying.

The policeman came in the late afternoon. I'd spent most of the day asleep. My father had gone home to take care of Francie but my mother stayed, just sitting in that chair. She didn't talk much to me, but I didn't need her to talk to me. I just needed her to be there.

The police officer appeared from behind the tent. He was in uniform, blue jacket and blue trousers. The policeman introduced himself. I said hello. He stood there, turning his hat around in his hands. "I'll only take a couple of minutes." He tried to smile. He had a pleasant, round face, and he looked young. I tried to smile back. "You sure are a lucky young lady," he said. "I was the first one there and— You sure look a lot better today. Afternoon, Mrs. Lingard," he said to my mother.

"Officer Thoms was at the scene," she told me. She reached out for my hand again. "I imagine he wants to ask you how it happened."

By then I knew the accident had been the night before, and they had called my parents from the hospital. It's only twenty minutes to the hospital from our house outside of town, and my parents had come right down.

"I don't remember," I said to the officer. "I'm sorry, I just don't remember."

He nodded. "Not to worry. That often happens, or so they tell me. I'm sort of new at the job. It'll come back to you. Your friend doesn't remember either."

"Marco?" I did remember that, then. I don't know how I knew I'd been out with Marco Griggers that night, but I knew it. "Is he all right?"

"Yeah. He is. I gotta admit, Isobel, when I first saw you— You must have been there an hour or more and I thought—" He tried another smile, and this one worked. I guessed he really had been worried. "You sure are lucky, that's all I can say. Look, you just concentrate on getting better, and I'll get back in touch with you in a couple of weeks—if that's all right with you?" he asked my mother.

"Of course."

"I didn't expect you to remember," he told me again. "Mostly, I just wanted to see you. I've got a daughter myself—and a son. Much younger than you," he said. He flushed, as if embarrassed, and turned to leave.

"Can I ask you one thing though?" he asked from the doorway, looking around the tent.

"Sure," I said.

"Would you have been driving? Or messing around with the steering wheel? I mean, if you were steering and he was working the accelerator, you know?"

"Me? Driving? I'm only fifteen," I said to him. My father would skin me alive if he caught me doing any kind of driving before I was even old enough for a permit. I sort of wanted to tell Officer Thoms that, because I thought he'd like to hear about a parent who was so strict, but I was too tired to find the words. I'd never even steered a car, in my life.

"I didn't think so," he said.

After he'd gone, my mother stood up. I could hear activity in the hall beyond the door, carts rolling, I thought. My mother leaned over the crib railings. She held onto my hand but she didn't touch any other part of me. "I ought to go home," she said. "I can stay, though, if you want me to?"

"It's OK. You look like you could use some sleep. You look terrible," I told her. She had her face where I could see it without moving my head and she didn't mind my telling her that.

"I feel terrible," she said. "You don't look too terrific yourself," she said, which was about the first normal-sounding thing she'd said all day. "I'll be back first thing in the morning. If you want me, want company or anything, they'll call us. Even in the middle of the night. You know that, Sweetheart, don't you?"

I knew that.

"I'd rather stay, but—I'll be no use to anyone if I don't get some sleep. A good mother would stay."

That made me want to laugh, but I knew it would hurt if I did. I felt better when she talked that way, and when she brushed her hand over my forehead, it felt like she had pulled her love up over me like a blanket and tucked it in around my shoulders. "You get some sleep too, Pumpkin. You need it. There will be somebody in the room with you, all night, so you sleep too."

I watched her walk to the door. She pulled it open and looked back at me. "A good mother would stay here, reading aloud to you. Something uplifting," she said.

I smiled at her, to let her know I was all right. I closed my eyes and thought about the fictitious good mother my mother talked about, who would fight off Indians at the cabin door and be as with-it as Barbara Walters, who baked pineapple upside-down cakes and never got bored with what her children were telling her. This good mother was some mix of a best friend and Supreme Court Judge, with a lot of fairy godmother thrown in, not to mention the glamour of Jackie Onassis and the saintliness of Mother Teresa. The twins teased her about this good mother, and I was old enough now to understand. Francie, who was only ten, was too young. So when my mother admitted that a good mother would start up a troop of Girl Scouts in Newton, Francie really thought that was what she was going to do.

I drifted off to sleep. They woke me up, throughout the night, to take my temperature and my blood pressure. I didn't sleep all that well with some stranger sitting in a chair by my bed, watching me. I remember that. I remember how long the night seemed, and how much I wanted the sky to get light and the night to be over. I remember how much I wanted to go home.

Once I did fall really asleep, but then I dreamed. In my dream, I was sitting in a car—front seat by the window, the suicide seat—and it was going toward a tree. The car seemed to be going very slowly, but I knew it was going much too fast. I screamed and tried to back away from the big tree with its cloud of branches. I didn't have my seat belt done up. I pulled my legs up and shoved with my hands against the dashboard to push myself away from the tree. But the back of the seat held me trapped. There wasn't anybody driving the car, even though it was being driven. There was just the filmy darkness cut by the headlights and the tree trunk coming at me and that helpless feeling nightmares have, when you can't move your body the way your brain tells you to. Even in my dream I thought it was funny that I screamed, because I'm not a screamer.

I woke up to the dim light from the open doorway and somebody bending over me, to wrap the blood pressure strap around my right arm and put a thermometer into my mouth. "There now, open your mouth, that's good." The voice was soft. "Isobel? That's a good girl. You can go back to sleep in a minute."

I didn't think I would, but I did. I wondered if my dream

was what had actually happened; but the tree, I remembered, was on the wrong side of the road. In the colorless night of my dream, the tree trunk rushed toward me, bright white under the car lights, thick and tall, every groove on the bark etched clear. It came after me and something threw me at it.

"It was an elm," I said, opening my eyes. There was daylight in the room and a pale blue sky showed through the window. My mother turned around from the window. "Mom? Was it an elm?"

"What? Was what an elm? How do you feel, Lamb, do you feel all right?" She put her cool hand on my forehead. She had her makeup on, eyes and lips, and her brown hair was neatly combed, the spray holding its waves in place. Seeing her, looking the way she normally did, made me feel better. Everything was going to be all right, everything was going to get back to normal.

I saw my leg, or, rather, the length of my leg, hoisted by the knee and hanging from pulleys under its concealing blanket. I moved the toes on my left leg. I stretched my shoulders without moving my arms. I took a deep breath, against my ribs. I turned my head on the pillow and looked at the locker in the room, then I turned it the other way and saw a plastic jug on my night table. I thought I might like a drink of water.

"Daddy had to go to the office," my mother told me. "He's coming by later."

"I had a dream."

"Francie sends her love. She even wanted to have me bring you Pierre." Pierre is a stuffed frog, about Francie's favorite stuffed animal.

"Is today Monday? Today's Monday, isn't it?"

"So you wouldn't be lonely, she said. She's really upset, as you can imagine. The twins say hello and—they're going to try to get home this weekend, if you can have visitors."

"Can I? Has anybody called?"

"I don't think anybody hasn't called. I've got a list a mile long. I'm keeping a list."

That didn't surprise me. "What time is it?"

"Around nine."

"History," I said. My first period class was History and everybody in the class would be sitting in the assigned seats, probably envying me for not being there.

"If it's not your friends on the phone, it's your relatives," my mother said. "I'm tempted to rip it out of the wall, really I am. Someday I'm going to do that. And you'll all wonder why."

"A good mother would let her kids have their own phone," I told her. This was our normal kind of conversation, which made the night seem very far away.

"Don't you wish you had a good mother?" She gave me her usual answer to that kind of remark. "What did you dream?"

"It doesn't matter."

"It was an elm, Sweetheart," my mother said. Her eyes watched my face carefully as she told me this. "Did you dream about the accident?"

I didn't know.

"But it was on the wrong side of the road."

"Your car was on the wrong side of the road."

Then the dream made sense. My mother waited. I had a sudden, frightening question: "Why don't I have to go to the bathroom?"

At that, my mother smiled; she knew what I was thinking and she knew what she wanted to say. She sat down in the chair and leaned forward, looking pretty. "They've run a tube called a catheter directly up into your bladder. There's a sack at the other end." She watched my face. "Don't think about it too precisely, Izzy, just be glad they know how to do it." One of my mother's volunteer positions is at the hospital, where she does publicity work. She's an upbeat person and loves stories about the miracles of modern medicine. My father is much more practical and serious. He's a tax man, with offices in the center of town. Our whole family, even my mother, used Dad's office as a way-station—or so he said, grousing the way he does when he really is pleased—between shopping trips and dentist appointments. It was like an "extension of the living room," he groused. "What are my clients supposed to think?"

As I thought of the twins, I thought of Francie, too, and how much she loved Pierre. "Tell Francie that—I'd love it if Pierre could spend the night with me," I said to my mother. "Tell her I'd take good care of him."

"You aren't paralyzed, or anything," my mother told me. "It's just precisely what Dr. Carstairs told you."

Then I remembered what Dr. Carstairs had told me. "I didn't like him," I said quickly.

"He's the best around," my mother said. "You know your father, nothing but the best." She didn't like him either, I could tell from the way she'd answered. But I also knew that my father would have personally sprung a child molester from prison if he was a better surgeon.

Dr. Epstein, my pediatrician, came into my room that morning. My mother said his name, surprised. "Saul." He rested his hand on her arm for a minute. He was reassuring her. "And you, young lady."

Dr. Epstein has always been my doctor. He's easy to talk to, because he fixes his funny little eyes on you and waits to hear what you have to say. His face, even hidden behind the beard he wears, always looks interested and sympathetic and amused, all at once. He always knows what to do and what to say. That morning, all he said was, "Well, young lady, you certainly gave us a busy weekend." His eyes kind of checked me over, and he didn't seem displeased with what he saw.

"Saul was here Saturday night," my mother explained.

"To hold your father's hand," Dr. Epstein explained.

"Your father was holding your mother's hand, so I held his. You look more perky today."

I giggled. It didn't hurt. "I guess I am."

"Then I'll go look in on my other patients and see you again. Soon," he promised me. That was something to look forward to. "I had appendicitis last night," he told us. "Do you know how long it's been since I had appendicitis? No, of course not, how could you."

He didn't wait for us to answer any of his questions. I looked at my mother and she looked back at me. I didn't need to say what I was thinking, because I knew she was thinking the same thing. Certainly she said it often enough. "What a good doctor. What a good man he is."

My father came by on his lunch hour and again after work, when my mother had gone home to be with Francie. My father didn't talk to me; he just sat in the chair, being there, as the sky outside the window got dark. I didn't want to talk. I was feeling tired again, and weak, and I told myself that that was always the way it was when you were sick. You always felt best in the morning and worst in the evening. I watched my father, who was studying papers from his attaché case. The nurses came and went, taking my temperature, taking my blood pressure, giving me shots. Every now and then my father would look up and see me. Our eyes would meet and he would nod and look back to his papers. He was keeping an eye on things, taking care of me.

It was after he had gone home and a nurse was sitting in the dim light that I began to remember. They were right, I thought, it does all come back to you.

2

It was the Wednesday before that when Marco had asked me out, to the football team's post-game party. I thought at first he was just going to offer to drive me home in his orange VW bug and I thought I'd accept. The late bus takes everybody who has a practice, or an activity, or detention, so it goes all over Newton and takes hours. Besides, Marco was a senior, the first senior who'd asked me to do anything. He was a notorious flirt, but I couldn't see what harm driving home with him would do. As a tenth grader, I might date seniors. There were other seniors I'd rather have had notice me, like Tony Marcel, but Marco was a beginning.

When he asked me, instead, if I wanted to go to the post-game party on Saturday, I was really surprised. I didn't sound surprised, though. I kept cool, even though I was the first of my friends to be asked out by a senior.

"I guess so," I said.

Marco grinned. He's a grinner, probably because, while he's not handsome, his stocky body and sort of pushed-in features make him cute. Cute and grinning go well together. I grin some myself, sometimes. "I'll pick you up at eight."

14

"I'll have to ask my parents."

"Ask your parents? What are you, a kid?"

I didn't answer that. I knew that trick boys have, that way of getting you to act like they want you to by telling you if you were grown up you would. I could see by his face that he was waiting for me to apologize and act embarrassed, so I just kept quiet. I made sure he couldn't see what I was thinking, though.

"How will I know if Mommy and Daddy will let you out?" he finally asked.

I thought for a minute of just walking away from him, but I wanted to go to the party. These post-game parties weren't a big deal, just get-togethers for the team and other seniors, but it was a good chance to let them see me, outside of school. Marco finally figured out that he wasn't going to get an answer to that crack either so he said, "OK, I'll check with you tomorrow, or sometime. You're a cool chick, aren't you, Izzy?"

That made me laugh. "Maybe I am," I said, not minding it a bit if he thought I was.

My parents didn't much want me to go out with Marco. They didn't know him, or anything about him, except that he was a senior and played football. He hadn't been a friend of the twins'. "Won't all the kids there be older than you?" my mother asked.

"I'm fifteen, Mom."

I knew what she was thinking. The twins were only one year beyond being seniors, and while we're not the kind of family who tells one another *everything*, my parents knew enough about what went on to be glad to stay up all night the night of the twins' prom and to serve a bang-up breakfast at four in the morning, with lots of coffee, and not to mind how many people slept over the rest of the night at our house. I had heard about things my parents didn't know, because the twins talked to me more than to them. I suspected there were things I didn't know, too. But my mother didn't say what she was thinking. She just looked at my father, at the other end of the table. My father didn't say anything either.

At that point, I discovered how much I wanted to go. More than anything. "I'm not a little kid," I said. "I know how to take care of myself. You just don't want me to grow up, you say you trust me but you're only saying that." I was working myself up. It has been a while since I'd worked myself up. During ninth grade, there wasn't anything we didn't fight about. It seemed like they were always misunderstanding what I meant. All last year, we fought a lot, especially at dinner. But they seemed to have calmed down and tenth grade was going along pretty easily. "You think I can't handle myself so you're not going to let me go and—"

"Nobody said you couldn't go," my mother corrected me.

"Then I can?"

"I guess so. But I wish you wouldn't. If it helps, you could tell him I won't let you go out with older boys yet."

"Great, that would be great, wouldn't it," I asked sarcastically. "That would just about kill any chance of anybody asking me out again. You can't *do* that, Mom. You wouldn't do that, would you?"

"No, I wouldn't. But I'd like to."

I ran around the table hugging everybody. When I called Suzy and Lisa that night, they were jealous, but happy for me. I would have felt the same way if it had been one of my friends, not me. "What'll you do if he tries something?" they both asked me, and I told them what I thought I'd do. "What if he's drinking?" they asked. I reminded them that I had the twins to educate me. Neither of them had an older brother. "What are you going to wear?" "Who do you think will be there?" "You're so lucky, Izzy." At that point, I decided that I should play it cool, as if it happened every day; I didn't want to be the center of a lot of conversation the next day, like some ninth grader going out on her first date, or something. "I don't know," I said. "I don't think Marco's so great."

In fact, I didn't even like him much. One thing I always like in a boy is a slender neck, and Marco had a thick neck, just a chunk connecting his shoulders to his head. But you didn't have to be wildly in love with someone to go to a party with him.

The party was at John Wintersize's house. His parents had sensibly fled the scene, so we had the whole downstairs to ourselves. There was dancing, Ping-Pong, and talk. Sodas and beer were in the kitchen, along with big boxes of chips and pretzels. I fitted in all right and I had a good time.

Marco and I split up pretty soon after we got there. I danced with a lot of people and sat in on a lot of conversations. Mostly, it was the boys who decided what the conversations were about, because it was the boys, not their dates, who were friends. Every now and then, Marco would come sit down with me, or dance with me. As the night went on he'd try putting his arm around me, but it was just fooling around, not as if he was really interested, not as if he was likely to try anything later. It was just so he'd look good to his friends. I didn't mind because it showed everyone that I wasn't a kid, even if I was the only sophomore there.

The music played continuously and the lights in the room where we were dancing were turned off. The air smelled of beer and smoke, some of which—to my inexperienced nose—seemed suspiciously sweet. I didn't say anything. The subject didn't come up.

Tony Marcel was there, but I didn't know who with. He never tried to talk to me and didn't ask me to dance. A couple of times I went into the kitchen when I knew he was there to say, "Hey" to him, just in passing. I didn't want him to think I was like half the girls in my class, just falling to pieces whenever he came into view. But I wanted him to know I was there.

"Hey Izzy, how's it going?" he would answer.

"Fine," I'd say. Then I'd move back to another room.

I had to be home by one, my parents said, which meant one-fifteen at the latest. I didn't mind that. I was having fun, but I didn't feel entirely at ease: I couldn't really relax with them, not the way I could with my friends. Marco pretended to be surprised when I went and got him from the group sitting on a long sofa watching Ping-Pong games, but he'd said, "Yes, sir," to my father when he'd picked me up, so I knew he was faking.

"That's what I get for cradle-robbing." He made a joke. It was, I thought, a pretty predictable joke and not very funny, and I pretended I hadn't heard it.

But he didn't get up. He just sat there, grinning at everybody. I didn't know quite what to do. Anybody who knows me knows I keep to my curfews and not just because my parents won't accept excuses. "Hey, are you trying to get me grounded or something?" I laughed. I wanted to be home on time, but I wasn't about to make a scene or anything. I didn't want to make that mistake. I figured the best thing was to treat it like a joke.

Somebody said Marco couldn't get up, he'd been sitting there swilling all night. Everybody laughed. Marco laughed too and raised his can of beer as if he were making a toast.

"I'll take you home, Izzy," Tony said.

I thought—I don't know what I thought—I thought that was a great idea. I didn't say anything, of course, but I wouldn't have minded that one bit.

"Hey man, you trying to move in on my date?" Marco asked. He lurched up.

And there I was, almost with two seniors fighting over me. I remember thinking that and reminding myself that neither one of them was really thinking about me at all.

Somebody else suggested that Marco should have some

coffee before he got behind the wheel, but Marco said he'd only been drinking beer and everyone knew you couldn't get drunk on beer. He didn't want any coffee, he said, because his evening wasn't finished yet, wasn't anywhere near finished, just because it was time to put the children to bed. He was going to be right back, he said.

"If it's inconvenient for you, I can always call my parents," I suggested, in a sweet and sincere and naive voice. Everybody thought that was pretty funny, except Marco. He began to get angry, which wasn't cool at all, which made him even angrier.

I began to wonder if he wasn't drunker than he was acting, but by then we were almost at the door. Tony and John and a couple of girls were moving with us. The girl with Tony was another senior, who worked with him on the paper, Deborah—never Debby—dark and pretty and smart and funny. She was looking at me, but she didn't say anything.

"You all right, man?" John asked Marco.

"Never better. For Christ's sake, it's only a couple of miles."

The air outside the door was black and cold, refreshing. I was a little nervous about Marco, but—you just don't ask somebody else's date to take you home unless your date really can't, unless you want the reputation of being more trouble than it's worth to take you out.

"OK, Izzy?" Tony asked me. He didn't look really worried, just as if he wanted to reassure me. I couldn't believe the way he was really looking at me, and I grinned at him. I thought that someday, probably not right away, but sooner or later, Tony Marcel was going to ask me out. I knew that, the way you sometimes do, the way you sometimes feel things click into place. Seniors or not, boys were just boys, and they all acted the way boys did. So I grinned at him and did a little dance inside my heart, and said, "I'm OK."

In his car, heading down along the dark roads, Marco asked me if I'd had a good time. I told him I had. He said maybe we might do it again sometime, and I laughed inside myself. He was checking me out, to be sure I'd say I'd go out with him again. "You'll have to ask me and see, won't you?" I teased.

"You're a cool kid," he said.

But he was driving too fast and slipping through stop signs without stopping, and I didn't feel at all cool. VW bugs, I reminded myself, always feel as if they're going faster than they are. Marco had both hands on the wheel, and he leaned forward, concentrating hard, harder than he should have had to. He stayed in the middle of the road, with the center line running under the center of the car. I didn't say anything, because at night you can see lights coming, and it was only a couple of miles anyway. I just wanted to get home, I couldn't wait to get home. I just wanted to be back home and shutting the door on this part of the evening. I sat quiet.

I don't know how fast he was going, or why he decided on a long straight stretch to play the swerving game, swinging the car from side to side of the two-lane road, his arms swinging the steering wheel from one side to the other. The white center line shone under the headlights, sweeping under the belly of the car and then off to my side, then under again and off to the driver's side. I felt the weight of the car swing out of control before I heard Marco's voice, cursing, and I watched the tree—an elm—rise up at me. The car lights had swung off of it by the time the tree got to me. That was all I remembered. I remembered everything.

By the time I knew I remembered, I couldn't seem to stay clearheaded long enough to tell anyone about it. Faces floated sometimes above my bed when I opened my eyes. It seemed as if time wasn't passing at all, I was always half-waking up and a face was always floating there. It felt as if I was trapped in some single moment of time that would never finish itself, just the way I'd been trapped in Marco's car when the tree was coming at me.

"Isobel? I'm afraid we're going to have to take it off."

That was Dr. Carstairs's voice, I knew. Sure enough, it was Dr. Carstairs's face floating there. That was the last time I saw him, or heard him. He disappeared from my life, taking half of my right leg with him.

3

I felt fine.

The noise that woke me was a nurse lowering the crib sides of the bed, a quiet clanking of metal. The nurse stood between me and the window. I was in my same room, bright now with sunlight. I saw the flat ceiling and the right-angle corners where walls met. I heard the busy quietness of the hospital all around me. I had slept deeply and I felt good. The tent was gone, the IV was gone, I didn't hurt anywhere.

The nurse moved and I saw my mother, her make-up on, her suit crisp-looking, fresh, her blouse a dusky yellow and the sunlight streaming in behind her. She was reading a book. I felt a smile begin in my heart and spread up over my face.

"You're awake," the nurse said. "Isobel is awake," she said across the room. But my mother had already gotten up.

"Hi," I said.

"Hello, Angel. How do you feel?"

"Fine." That didn't do justice to how I felt. "I feel good."

Inside my head, I saw this little person, a miniature Izzy in a leotard, kind of smoky blue, to match my eyes. The little Izzy raised her hands over her head and did a back flip, landing with her arms stretched out and her back arched, like Mary Lou Retton. That was a joke because I couldn't do a back flip to save my life, I couldn't even do a good back dive off of a board—but it was just exactly how I felt.

"What day is it?" I asked.

"Wednesday, and it's . . ." My mother reached out her wrist to look at the time. ". . . almost eleven. Dad's coming by at lunchtime."

"Can I sit up?" I asked.

The nurse fiddled with the bed, until I was about half-sitting up, then showed me how to work the buttons myself.

"Well." My mother just stood there for a minute. I knew how she felt: as if we ought to be talking madly, but there wasn't really anything to say because we were both feeling so good because I was feeling good. "Is there anything you want?" my mother asked.

I couldn't think of anything more to want. I shook my head no. Then I realized. "I'm hungry."

"Hungry?" she asked.

But the nurse answered, "Dr. Epstein said she might be."

"If it's all right," my mother said. "What would you like?"

I considered that. Steak sounded good, or a hamburger and fries. "Pizza."

"She'll be on a light diet for a couple of days," the nurse said.

I think my mother must have read my mind, because she took over then, asking what I could have to eat, ordering eggs and toast and fruit. I hadn't realized until I had a chance to eat how hungry I was, shaky-hungry, as if I'd been on a fast. "Milk?" she asked me. I nodded, going along with whatever she decided.

When the hospital table had been rolled over, and I had myself sitting entirely up, and the tray of food had been

placed in front of me—I was confused for a minute. It was
as if I had forgotten how to eat. My mother fussed around,
pouring the milk into the glass, shaking the knife and fork
and spoon out of their plastic wrapping, tearing the corner
off the salt and pepper papers to flavor the boiled eggs that
she had already taken out of the shell for me. The meal
came all in bowls, a bowl of eggs, a bowl of prunes, a bowl
of applesauce. The toast, with its pats of wrapped butter,
was the only thing not in a bowl.

I drank down about half of the milk. It slid down my
throat like liquid silk and I could feel my brain clearing
almost as soon as it was in my stomach. Then I turned to the
rest of my breakfast.

I started with the eggs. Scrambled eggs are the only kind
I really like, usually, but these eggs—with the rich yolk
mixed in over the silky whites, with salt and pepper and just
a touch of butter—I had never before realized how good
eggs could taste. I'd never noticed how the different flavors
of different foods filled up my mouth. I finished with the last
of the milk, feeling it slide down my throat.

The nurse came back with a little paper cup in her hand,
like a table favor at a doll's birthday party. Two little dark
pellets sat in the cup. She handed them to me, with a glass
of water: "Stool softeners."

That was about all I wanted to hear about that, so I
swallowed them quickly. I grabbed the last piece of toast off
the tray as she lifted it away. "What's with her?" I asked.

"Maybe she's had a bad day. Or maybe she's just that
way. How do you feel about a shampoo in the next day or
two?"

I put my hands up to my hair. It felt dirty to my fingers,
and my scalp did too. But it felt so good to raise my arms
and put my fingers into my hair that I took a little time over
it. "How would we do that?"

"I don't know, but we'll figure out something."

I began to think of things I needed. "Could you bring me

my radio?" I asked. My mother took her notebook out of her purse and wrote that down. My mother is a well-organized person, as well as the prettiest mother I know, and she is forever making lists, then checking things off. "I've got down nightgowns and toothbrush already," she told me. "There must be more. A bathrobe?"

"Can I have a TV?"

"They said they'd deliver it sometime today. We've arranged to have you keep the single room, unless you want a roommate?"

"No. I don't think so. Do you think I should?"

"Not necessarily," my mother said. "It's a matter of whether or not you'll get bored on your own."

"I guess I better have my books here, and I'd better get the assignments."

"Oh, I think we can wait awhile on that. You'll have to stay in the hospital for a while—until—until—"

"Until it heals," I said, because she was having trouble thinking of how to end her sentence. She looked at me, considering. I'm old enough to know what that considering look means, when she's trying to be objective about one of her own children. "Did they say how long that would be?"

"A couple of weeks. But then, with your other leg in a cast—"

I could see that I'd be pretty much immobilized. "I guess you couldn't bring my stereo, or anything."

That made her smile. "I don't think so. I've got some mail at home for you too."

"The cast'll be on for six weeks, isn't that right?" I was remembering the many casts the twins had acquired. "How about my makeup bag and hair curlers, could you bring those?"

She wrote them down.

"Can I have visitors?" I asked and then, looking around, "What about a phone?"

"They're putting it in this afternoon. I know," she said.

"I know. A good mother would have made sure it was in by now. But they'll all be in school."

"I'm going to miss Latin Club," I realized.

We had all, Lisa and Lauren and Suzy and I, joined Latin Club last year, for our activity. You need an activity for your college applications. We chose Latin Club because our Latin teacher, Mr. DePonte, was the advisor, and after a week of school there wasn't one of us who didn't have a minor crush on him. Mr. DePonte had dark hair and dark eyes, he was young, and he had a dry sense of humor. Latin Club actually turned out to be fun. We learned about the food they ate in ancient Rome, and their architecture, about the clothes they wore and getting married and divorced. We built model bridges and painted maps. At the end of the year we had a Roman feast—not Italian food, but meat marinated first then roasted in chunks over a fire and chewy flat bread—at Mr. DePonte's house. He was married and had a baby, but we liked his wife too. There were only about fifteen people in the Latin Club, and we'd decided we'd stick with it. We had already discussed what offices we'd hold in our senior year. Lisa would be president, Lauren would be the vice, Suzy would be secretary and I would be treasurer. I didn't mind missing school, but I did mind missing Latin Club.

"I'm sure they'll miss you too," my mother said.

That was such an automatic-politeness response that I looked carefully at her. "Are you worried?" I asked.

She wanted to snap back some answer, but she didn't. That worried *me*.

"I really do feel fine," I told her.

"I'll go on home and collect your things," she said. "Would you like visitors?"

"Yes."

My father came for lunch, and after he left and I'd been lying there wondering when they would hook up the TV, there was a knock on the door. A pregnant nurse came in.

She had a maternity nurse's outfit on, ballooning top and trousers and those soft-soled white shoes. She was medium height, with dirty-blonde hair held back from her face with combs.

"Hello, Isobel," she said. I didn't correct her. She sat down in the visitor's chair, resting the clipboard on what was left of her knees after her belly took its share, smiling. She had a nice smile, not bright but warm. "I'm Helen Hughes-hyphen-Pincke." I looked at her name-pin on her chest and there was her name, Hughes-Pincke. "You better call me Helen," she said.

I thought, knowing how my parents feel about kids on first name terms with adults, I'd better call her Mrs. Hughes-Pincke. Or, judging from her hyphenated name, Ms. Hughes-Pincke. "Ummn," I answered.

"Or whatever," she said. It was as if she had read my mind. "Whatever feels comfortable to you."

I just nodded. I wondered what she was doing, who she was, but I thought it would be rude to ask, so I just sat quiet, my hands on the blankets under the empty table.

Mrs. Hughes-Pincke arranged the papers on her clip-board, giving me plenty of time to look at her. "I could get you a pack of cards. They're going to bring the TV sometime today, but you can never tell what that means. It may be midnight."

"But I'll be asleep," I said.

"It was a joke," she said. "They work union hours, so it'll have to be before five. It was," she said, "a pretty poor joke."

"No, it wasn't," I said politely.

"You look much better than the last time I saw you."

"Did we meet before?"

"Not so's you'll remember. I take a look at patients I'll be working with, when they're still too sick to see me. How do you feel now?"

"I feel fine."

"You look fine, too. Oh, to be young," she said, her pen waiting. She wore a wedding ring, but no engagement ring, so I thought her husband probably didn't make very much money.

"You don't look too old," I said.

"I'm not. I'm twenty-nine," she told me, which was odd because usually adults don't volunteer their ages. "You're in tenth grade at the high school, right?"

I nodded.

We had this conversation, then, with her asking brief questions and me giving the answers. "So you got that blonde hair from your father."

"But I look more like my mother. The twins look like Daddy."

"What about Francesca?"

"Francie's only ten, but I think she's going to be tall and skinny too." I didn't know why she was so curious, but I couldn't think of why I shouldn't answer.

"How about a boyfriend, Isobel? Do you have a steady boyfriend?"

I shook my head.

"Did you ever?"

"No, not really, not yet. We all—" I stopped myself. I didn't feel like talking about this.

"Who's we all?" she asked, after a while.

"My friends and me. Suzy and Lisa and Lauren."

"Do you have a lot of friends?"

I nodded.

"Anyway, you all what?" Mrs. Hughes-Pincke returned to the subject.

I didn't know how to sidetrack her, and I knew it wasn't important, just private. "We think it's smarter to play the field."

"That makes sense. It makes more sense than I was capable of making at fifteen. Do you think kids are getting more sensible these days?"

It seemed that way to me, and to most of the people I talked to, but it wasn't polite to say that to an adult so I just shrugged. She didn't say anything then, and the time stretched out. I figured I should think of something to say, even though I still didn't know why she was there. "When are you due?" I asked her. It was question my mother asked pregnant women, even strangers waiting in a line beside her, so I knew it was all right.

"At the end of next month." She smiled. "It's a Thanksgiving baby. Do you like children?"

"Sure."

"Do you want to have children?"

"Sure." I wished she'd stop prying.

"What about a career?"

I didn't know how to answer that. I knew she thought I ought to have career plans, but I honestly didn't have anything I wanted to be, except a housewife like my mother. I thought probably if I didn't get married in college, I'd work for a year or two after college, as a secretary or airline hostess or something, and then get married. There was nothing I wanted to be, like Suzy wanted to be a vet or Lauren wanted to be a model. All of my own plans were wrapped around getting married and having a family. I thought my mother had a good life, and I knew she was happy, and I wanted to be pretty much like her when I grew up. I didn't often say that, though, because—in the first place, nobody ever asked me, not seriously, and then, it was just too much what a nice girl would think. There was one girl at school, Rosamunde Webber, who always gave wild answers when people asked her what career she was interested in. Rosamunde wasn't one of our friends, but we all had a lot of classes together, because she took Latin too and was also a member of Latin Club. She wore denim overalls and sloppy shirts, and she was a brain, and she didn't fit in. If anyone asked her what she was going to do for a career, though, she'd say spy, or movie star, or moonshiner, anything that popped into her head. I never minded having Rosamunde around, especially in a class, although I felt sorry for her because I thought she wanted to be better friends with us than she ever could be and, besides, as far as we knew she hadn't yet been asked out on a single date. But I wished right then I had one of Rosamunde's snappy answers for Mrs. Hughes-Pincke. "I don't know," I said, and I knew that would bother her, because everyone thinks all girls ought to be liberated and everything. "I'm sorry."

"Why do you apologize?" she asked.

"I don't know." I didn't know who she was, or why she was allowed to come and ask me questions.

She put her pen away. "I'll be back tomorrow." I smiled politely. "I'm here for you to talk to, if you feel like talking."

I nodded. Why did she think I would talk to a perfect stranger, when I had my friends, and my mother too?

Right after she left, the room got hectic. The man came in to hook up the TV and explain the remote control to me, my mother came in with a suitcase and a big clothing box, which she put on top of the table, and a nurse came in carrying a phone, which she placed on the night table beside me. The nurse crawled around to plug in the phone, while my mother opened up the suitcase to show me what she'd brought. The TV man held up the receipt for my mother who signed and nodded, not paying attention. She went back to the suitcase and pulled out a nightgown. Dr. Epstein put his head into the room and stopped there. The nurse stood up from behind the night table. The phone rang. "Later," Dr. Epstein said to me. My mother held up a little traveling clock she keeps in her desk drawer, in case she ever travels, I guess. "Shall I put it on the table?" I answered the phone.

"Izzy." Suzy didn't have to identify herself. "I've only got a minute. Thank God, I caught you."

Whatever Suzy was calling about was urgent. "What's up?" I asked. For all of her brains, Suzy is the emotional one, or—as she prefers—the dramatic one.

"Are you alone?"

"No." Suzy, I mouthed to my mother's inquiring expression.

"Just listen then," she said, almost whispering. "It's Marco." My hand tightened around the phone in response to some feeling I didn't even have a name for. I had trouble paying attention to what Suzy wanted to tell me because I was pushing down that feeling. "He says he's really sorry. He says to tell you he thinks he must have had a concussion because he just passed out. He says he hopes you won't try to get even with him or anything, because he says everyone who was there would get in trouble too, not just him, and he can't even remember what happened. He's really worried, Izzy. He told the police he doesn't remember what happened, just that the car must have gone out of control, but he doesn't think they believe him. Izzy? Can you hear me?"

"Sure," I said.

"He asked me, because I'm your best friend . . . he asked me if you remembered, and if the police had talked to you and what you told them. He talked to me Monday at lunch, and yesterday, and today too and . . . I feel so sorry for him, he's really worried. I mean, we stopped yesterday at McDonalds and he just sat there . . . worrying. You know? He's not such a flirt, not underneath, or, anyway, not with me. He'll be so glad I finally got hold of you. What should I tell him?"

I didn't know what to say.

"Izzy?"

"I don't know," I said.

There was a long silence on her end of the phone. I could hear school noises in the background. Suzy was calling from the pay phone outside the office. "Listen," she said. "I've got to get to Latin Club, but listen, Izzy? It wouldn't do any good, you know? I mean, it's all over now. I'll call you tonight, OK?"

"Talk to you later," I said automatically. "What is *that*?" I demanded. My mother was holding up a pink satin jacket, quilted and edged with floppy lace at the sleeves and down the front.

"It's a bed jacket." She held it up in front of her. "Believe me, it was the least fluffy one they had. It feels warm, try it on. If you don't like it I can return it. But if you're kept to your bed, they're really the most comfortable things to wear."

It looked like something out of a 1940s movie. My mother helped me put it on.

It felt pretty good, except for all that lace flopping around. My mother stepped back to study me; then she started to giggle. Every now and then my mother does that, just gets silly, as if she weren't grown up at all.

"That bad, hunh?" I asked. I flapped a hand at her, the lace waving like a flag.

"It's not really your style." She looked at the jacket with her problem-solving face on. Mom is a problem solver by nature, that's what she says anyway. Most of the things she does have problems to solve. "Does it feel all right?" I nodded. She helped me off with the jacket and then opened her purse. She took out a little pair of scissors, doubled up into a little red leather case.

"What are you doing carrying scissors in your purse?" I asked her.

"A good mother travels prepared for any contingency," she said. She sat down and got to work. "What did Suzy want?"

I sat in bed with the unopened blue box in front of me. She sat in the chair, with the pink bed jacket on her lap. She turned the jacket inside out and began snipping at the tiny stitches.

"Nothing much," I said. "Just—you know. She only had a couple of minutes before Latin Club."

I wasn't ready to put the problem before her yet. I knew what Suzy was asking me: not to tell anyone that there had been drinking at the party. Especially not to tell the police that Marco had had too much to drink. He'd probably lose his license or something. And if everyone else at the party would get in trouble too—it wasn't fair if everyone else was punished for Marco's mistake. Tony and everyone. If I ratted to the police, or to my parents.

It's not that I don't love my parents. It's just that the older I got, the more things there were that they couldn't help me with as much as my friends could, because my friends had a better idea of what was really involved, and my friends knew a lot more about me, Izzy. There were things you just couldn't tell your parents. I thought about that, watching my mother's quick hands snip the stitches that held the lace to the sleeve of the bedjacket. If I told her how Lauren always copied off of Suzy in Geometry, for tests as well as homework assignments, she wouldn't understand. Lauren's father grounds her if her grades aren't good enough for him. Her mother wouldn't care about grades but she's married to someone else and running a resort down in South Carolina, so only Lauren's stepmother is there, and she's all wrapped up in her own children. Besides, all Lauren wants is a high school diploma so she can go to modeling school; it's not as if any college was going to be lied to about her grades. But my parents would just see that Lauren was copying, cheating they'd call it. But Lauren had to, or she'd never pass. She'd done it in Algebra I, and she'd do it in Algebra II, and then she'd be finished with the math requirements. Her father made her take the college prep courses. He didn't care that she wasn't smart enough. So Lauren cheated, in everything I was pretty sure, although I only knew for certain about math.

I watched my mother fold the wide band of lace carefully

on the table. She saw me watching and smiled. "Well, it might come in handy for a Halloween costume. Or something. It's very good lace, you know."

"Nothing but the best for the Lingards," I joked. But I knew how lucky I was. My parents left me alone if I wanted them to. Suzy's mother seemed to feel she should be her daughter's best friend and kept going off into sulks if Suzy said something was none of her business, or even hinted at that.

They all said how lucky I was, and I agreed. Inside me, the miniature Izzy did a couple more impossible back flips.

"What about my radio?" I asked.

"It's in there, somewhere. I'll plug it in as soon as I finish this."

"Without the lace it'll be just right," I said. "That was nice of you, Mom."

For a minute I thought she was going to cry, but we don't do that, we Lingards, and so she didn't. "A good mother tries to think of everything," she said, instead.

"A good mother," I nagged, "would let each child have her own phone. No matter what it cost."

She bit off the final thread from the sleeve and looked at me. "A good mother would talk it over with her husband." That meant a no. It's my father who has a big thing about the dangers of living entirely separate lives. We have one TV set, in the den, and one phone line, and we always eat dinner at the same time, together.

Dr. Epstein arrived then. He rolled the table away and lowered my bed until I lay flat on my back. He checked my legs. I couldn't see what he was doing, but I answered his questions and wiggled my toes when he asked me to.

"That's good," Dr. Epstein said. He raised me back to a sitting position and fixed the pillows so I'd be comfortable. "Has Mrs. Hughes-Pincke been in yet?"

"Who is Mrs. Hughes-Pincke?" my mother asked.

"Psychological liaison nurse," he told her. My mother,

who likes doctors but doesn't trust psychiatrists, raised her eyebrows. "It's OK, Jane, it's standard practice after a trauma. It's what responsible medicine does. This isn't analysis, or therapy, or anything like that. Look, if Hendrik had an account that barely escaped bankruptcy, he'd watch it carefully for a while, wouldn't he? To see that what he expected to happen did happen, and what he expected not to happen didn't."

"If you say so, it must be all right. But I wonder—"

"It's OK, Mom. She's pregnant."

"Is she?" My mother looked at me. "When's she due?"

"Thanksgiving," I said. Then we both burst out laughing at the conversation we'd just had, because—it was just like us to have that conversation.

Dr. Epstein looked pleased with us. "Are you feeling all right, Izzy?" He really wanted to know.

"Fine. Really," I told him. "I mean, I feel so much better than I did." His eyes stayed on my face. "I mean— there are worse things, a lot worse." Kids *died* in car wrecks. One of the boys the twins went to grade school with had had cancer, one of their good friends, and that was terrible. There was a junior at school who had tripped and fallen into a campfire, and the whole side of her face—I couldn't even look at her. "Much worse," I said, thinking of it.

"And I've seen a lot of them," Dr. Epstein said, his eyes sad. "You'll start physical therapy tomorrow. Just a massage and some toe-wiggling, to start with, a little walking along the ramp. You can't afford to let your muscles get soft. We'll get you in a wheelchair pretty soon, get you out and moving around. Does that sound exciting?"

"Not exactly," I joked.

"The therapy might feel a little rough, but it's really important to do it. OK?"

"OK." I knew that whatever Dr. Epstein thought should be done was the best thing to do. I knew that he knew what should be done. I trusted him. Not just because he was a doctor, but because of the way he really talked to me, and listened, as if he really cared about me and not just about what was wrong with me.

4

When my mother left, I opened the box she'd brought. My radio played beside me. There were dozens of cards to open, messages saying *Get Well Soon* and signed *Love Ya*. The music played and sometimes I sang along, as I opened the cards. " 'I just called to say I love you,' " I'd sing, a little softer than the radio. I don't have a very good voice, but I can keep pretty much on key when I'm singing along. There was a pad with phone messages—messages from the twins, from my grandparents and aunts, from my friends and from people I didn't know were friends, and a lot of boys, too, even, "Someone named Tony—he said HI."

I read a long letter from Francie, telling me all about her life, where the handwriting got bigger and bigger so she could fill up more sheets. She numbered every sheet, all fourteen of them, even though page fourteen had only her name written in two-inch high letters on it. My mother had put in a couple of little puzzles in boxes, some stationery, and two paperback Agatha Christies—she reads mysteries and is forever telling me that they're more fun than the Harlequins I like, more interesting and more exciting and better written. People started bringing flowers into my

room, too, until the whole deep windowsill was filled, and
the nightstand too, and there were even some bowls of
flowers lined up along the wall.

Suzy called back, after supper. I turned the sound down
on the TV while we talked. "I don't know what you must
think of me," Suzy said. "I didn't even ask how you're
feeling. Can you believe I'm so—thoughtless? How are you
feeling, Izzy? Are you all right? Your Mom's told us—and I
think it's so *sad*. I mean, why should it happen to you, of all
people? But your Mom says you're feeling OK. I think
you're awfully brave, I don't know *what* I'd do if I—"

I cut her off, which is the only thing to do with Suzy
when she's rattling on. "Tell me what's happening, tell me
what's going on at school."

"You don't want your *assignments*, do you?"

"No." I had to smile at her amazement. "No, I want to
know—like, what did you do in Latin Club today."

"Nothing much." She wasn't telling the truth; I could tell
by the way she hesitated and then said something indefinite.
That's the way Suzy lies. "You missed a history test."

"Good."

"And Lauren's mother called her to say she can't have
her over Christmas, because they're so busy then, so
Lauren's pretty depressed. Remember, there was that boy
there last year, from Michigan, and they were supposed to
meet again this year?"

"Remember? How could I forget, the way she talked
about him."

"So you can imagine how she's feeling now."

"Don't tell me."

"Oh, Billy Sachs is . . . God, I thought he was going
to cry at me."

Billy Sachs has had a crush on me since we were in
seventh grade. He never bothered me with it, just sort of
wrote my name all over his notebook and stared at me
whenever we were in the same room. I didn't mind Billy.

Other boys had crushes on me too, and some of them I'd like back, sometimes, for a while, but Billy was always there. We almost never exchanged a word, which is funny, I guess, and I never would like him as a boyfriend—he isn't my type, he's one of those science types, beanpoles with thick glasses, who don't ever notice when their shirts need ironing—and I didn't know him, not at all, not as a person. But I always knew how he felt and I guessed he would be especially upset.

Suzy and I talked awhile longer, then Suzy said she had to do her homework, curse it, but had I thought of any message for Marco.

"No," I said, my eyes on the TV. "I've barely thought about it at all, since right after you called."

"But, Izzy, this is important."

"Well, I've been busy," I answered, which was true. I had to make some excuse, because you can't just tell your best friend that she's trying to bully you. Friends don't say things like that to one another.

That evening I got to change into a long flannel nightgown, and the nurse helped me off the bed and into the walker, so I could go to the bathroom. The bathroom was maybe five steps across the room, but my legs were so weak and the walker was so awkward . . .

It was hard work getting there. Really hard. So hard I was tired when I got back on the bed. "This must be the way really old people feel," I said to the nurse.

She went on settling pillows behind me. "I wouldn't know."

"I'd never thought," I said, but she didn't want to hear what I was thinking. I never had, though, thought about how it would feel to be so weak that it was hard work, really hard work, to get out of bed and into the bathroom.

The next morning I talked to my mother and Francie early. My mother only wanted to ask if I had slept well, and if it would be all right if she didn't come in until after lunch. Francie was impossible to talk to. She sounded about four years old, her voice high and squeaky, and all she would do was answer my questions. "How are you? How's school? What are you reading?" It was as if she was frightened of the telephone. I finally gave up trying.

"You're acting weird," I said.

"I don't know what I'm supposed to say," she squeaked.

My mother took the phone back to tell me her plans for the day, in case I needed to reach her.

After that, my grandparents called, both sets, one after the other, but they didn't talk long which I thought was pretty nice of them. I realized I'd forgotten to thank them for the flowers so I started to write thank-you notes, but then I wasn't sure which flowers who had sent and I didn't want to get out of bed to check the cards, so I set out one of the puzzles instead and listened to the radio. I let the rhythm of the music run along my shoulders and up my neck as I started on the edge of the puzzle.

I heard them coming down the hallway. Their high voices chattered and giggled. I couldn't hear what they were saying, but I could hear that they were a little nervous. I looked at the open door and waited.

First Suzy, then Lisa, and Lauren stood in the doorway.

For a minute, I just looked at them, too glad to do anything more than smile. The little Izzy inside my head did a couple of cartwheels. I wore the bedjacket and I had combed my hair. They looked absolutely normal, in skirts and sweaters and flats, just like always.

Lauren held my attention longest, with her tall figure, her ash blonde hair freshly washed and blown-dry to sweep back from her face—my mother says Lauren is very nearly beautiful. She has a heart-shaped face and dark, arched eyebrows she plucks carefully to keep in shape. Her eyes are so deep-blue that they look violet, large and set wide apart. She has a little Clara Bow mouth. Lauren always said that her chest was too flat and her facial bones too strong; she worried about her complexion, but she was always perfectly made up, starting with makeup base. Even at slumber parties, Lauren kept her face perfectly made up.

Just in front of her, Suzy looked plain by comparison. Ordinarily, Suzy's stylish way of dressing makes her look attractive, and her lively expressions and quick tongue make her narrow, pointed features, her thin lips and small eyes interesting. Suzy is a dishwater blonde, but she uses rinses to highlight her hair. She is constantly dieting to keep her stomach and hips in shape. Still, next to Lauren, Suzy looked plain and a little overdressed.

Whoever Lisa stands with, she looks like herself. She is the most popular of us and always has been, as well as having the best taste. Even Lauren asked Lisa's advice when we went shopping. Lisa is about my height, a little on the short side of average, and we both wear a size eight. Lisa, like Suzy, wears her hair in a flip, but she needs no rinse to bring out its color, just as she needs no makeup. Her hair is the color of the brandy my father likes to drink, and so are her eyes, a light, clear brown. Lisa is the quietest of us all, and the best listener.

My friends hesitated in the doorway, while I looked and looked at them, then Suzy led them into the room. Each one of them had something in her hands. Lauren came up and put a bouquet of flowers on the table top, then retreated to the doorway again. She didn't say anything and her face looked blank and lovely, almost as if she had been struck blind. I didn't mind her silence, because Suzy was chattering away, at about twice her normal speed.

"Our parents gave us permission to get to school late, so we could come to see you. How are you?"

"I'm really glad to see you," I said, smiling around at all of them, feeling like things were getting back to normal. Lauren's bouquet was set within a little lace paper doily, and it had thin pink ribbons hanging down from it. The flowers were pink sweetheart roses and little white patches of baby's breath. It was the kind of bouquet Shirley Temple would have carried in one of her old movies.

Suzy talked on. "History and English will just have to stumble on without us. And—if we're lucky—Math and Science too. I don't see how I can manage to stretch it out to PE, do you?" Suzy had PE last period of the day. "Oh well, maybe I can lie. How are you? My mother sends her best and, Bethy too, and"—she held out a brown paper bag—"I got these for you, because I figured you like them, and all that. Open it, Izzy."

She had gotten me two new Harlequins, and I laughed aloud. While I was taking them out and reading the covers, Suzy had been looking around my room. She brought her eyes back to me as I told her, "I haven't read either one. Thanks, Suzy, that's great."

"Good," she said.

Lisa put her eyes on my face and kept them there. Suzy and Lisa stood on opposite sides of the high hospital bed. "This is just something silly," Lisa said, handing me a box wrapped in bright red paper and tied around with a big white ribbon. It was the kind of thing Lisa always did, not only getting a present, but also wrapping it up nicely.

I unwrapped the box and then took out a stuffed cat, made of something that felt like an angora sweater, made to be floppy and cuddly. "It's great," said, cuddling it. "I love it." I sat the cat on my lap, close and warm.

"It's good to see you," I said, and it was. "It feels like ages since I've seen you," I said, and it did. "Lauren, Suzy told me about Christmas, and I'm really sorry. I think it's terrible. Did you try talking to your mother and telling her how much you want to come down? Maybe she thinks it doesn't make any difference to you, you know? Maybe if you talked to her, maybe she just doesn't understand how much you want to—"

Lauren just looked at me and shook her head. Suzy was right, she really did look unhappy, sort of pale, even with her makeup on, as if she was suffering. I hadn't known she was so serious about this boy.

But I could tell she didn't feel like talking about it. "How do you like me in a bed jacket?" I asked Suzy. "It had lace when my mother bought it, scads of lace"—I showed them with my hands where the lace had been—"hanging down. But she took it off."

"It's nice," Suzy said.

"It looks good on you," Lisa said.

The radio played softly. I didn't know what else to say to them, and they didn't say anything to me. The radio played in the background and the silence grew.

"What's going on at school?" I finally asked. I looked from Suzy to Lisa, because Lauren just stood frozen, leaning against the door frame.

"The usual," Suzy said.

"We're starting midterms. You know how that is," Lisa said.

"I guess she does." Suzy talked to Lisa, across the bed. "I don't know if I'm going to be able to make myself study for History—she makes everything so boring. Even her tests are boring, even when I know all the answers. Every time I look at that book I start to fall asleep. Really. Do you have class notes, Lisa?"

Lisa always took good notes during classes, and she always studied. She had to work for her grades, but she didn't mind working. If I'd worked as hard as Lisa, I'd have been on honor roll too, probably, but I had other things to do. Lisa played field hockey, too, but that wasn't the same kind of commitment as cheerleading, and she was always well prepared.

"You can use them if I don't need them," she offered, knowing that Suzy wouldn't take the time to copy them over.

Suzy was staring again and didn't seem to hear her.

Lisa kept on looking at my face. I wondered if I was getting a big crop of pimples or something. "How long will you have to be in here?" Lisa asked.

"About two or three more weeks, I guess." I made a face.

"You'll miss a lot of school," she observed.

"I guess so," I agreed. After a little silence, I added, "I guess the school will send me my assignments."

"That's right," Lisa said, as if it was news. "I'd forgotten it, but they do that. Or home teaching."

She didn't have anything to talk about, and neither did Suzy, and Lauren just stood there by the door saying nothing. That was odd, because we'd always talked and talked, all of us, all four together or whoever was around. We talked about everything, from nuclear war to French kissing; we could spend hours making up our faces under Lauren's direction, styling one another's hair, and just saying whatever crossed our minds. We were friends, good friends. We were old friends from seventh grade, which was when Lauren's father moved to Newton. Lisa and I had even been in the same elementary school and Suzy had come in fourth grade. Sometimes we talked over what had happened in years before. Sometimes we talked about one another. If we ever decided something was wrong about one of us, Lisa would go and tell her. It was Lisa who told me, at the start of eighth grade, that boys would like me better if I didn't always try to show off how much I knew about sports, just because I had older brothers—like me better as a girlfriend, that is. Nothing happened to any of us that we didn't talk over with our friends. And now we couldn't think of anything to say.

"I wonder what I should name this cat," I said.

Nobody had any ideas.

"I have a sort of psychologist," I said. "She's a psychological liaison nurse, whatever that means. You can imagine how my mom feels about that."

Nobody said anything. I knew, the same way that you know when a party is being a flop, that they were sorry they'd come.

"She's got one of those hyphenated names, Hughes-Pincke—with an e. She told me to call her Helen."

"Are you going to?" Lisa asked.

"My parents would kill me. You know that. They're not like your mother, Suzy."

"Speaking of whom, she asked me"—Suzy smiled, looking like herself—"if I thought I'd be more comfortable calling her by her first name, when I turn sixteen."

"Oh no," Lisa said. "What did you tell her?"

They talked across my bed.

"I didn't know what to tell her. I know what she wants me to say, of course. I mean, I know she means well, or I think she does—at least, she says she does—but I wonder sometimes if she isn't just kidding herself. The way she wants to pretend we're all really sisters."

"It's not just with you, she does it with Bethy too, doesn't she?" Lisa asked. Bethy is Suzy's older sister. Mrs. Wilkes was only married for five years before she got divorced and opened her boutique and dedicated her life to raising her girls.

"Then we'll have the three of us, just three sisters all together," Suzy said. "I wish she'd get married." She had often wished that.

"Oh well," Lisa told her, with nothing in her voice to give any indication of how she felt about it. Lisa never judges, she just listens. "She's probably worried about how he'd treat you."

Then they had run out of things to say again, and I tried to think of something else. It was hard, because I had to ignore Lauren, who was behaving so oddly. Usually, even when she was bored, she could put on a dazzling smile. She saw me looking at her then and put one on for me. I pretended to smile back and wished she'd just go out into the the hall so I could ask Lisa what was wrong with her.

"Aren't you going to get in trouble for cutting classes?" I asked Suzy.

"Naw." Her eyes came back to my face. "My mother asked your mother, on the phone, and your mother said she thought you felt well enough, so my mother gave me a note saying I have her permission, so it's a legal absense. Lisa's mom did the same, didn't she?" Lisa nodded. "And Lauren already had a dentist appointment, which is why we came today— But that reminds me," Suzy said, "it's almost ten, we'd better get going, if we're going to get to school for third period. Lisa? And Lauren's appointment's at ten, but that's just around the corner, so that's all right."

They hurried to the door. "Hey," I said from the bed. Lauren was already in the hallway, out of sight. "Thanks for the presents," I said, talking quickly. "It's great to see you. Come again, OK?" Lisa nodded, and Suzy moved out of sight. "Bring a Monopoly game or something," I suggested.

"That's a good idea," Lisa said. "See you."

She was out of sight before I could answer. The room felt empty, then, more empty than before, with only the radio playing softly. I could hear them, all talking now, as they went back down the corridor, the way voices sound when kids get out into the hallway after an exam.

I listened, until the sounds had faded away. Then I picked up the bouquet and turned it around in my hands, wondering about Lauren. There were some people who couldn't stand hospitals, because the idea of sickness and weakness and dying frightened them so much. I thought maybe Lauren was like that, which I hadn't known. Of course, we'd never been sick, except with flu and things, so we'd never have noticed. I thought that I'd like to ask Lisa about it, and maybe I'd call her up in the evening. Because I wasn't sick and I wasn't dying.

There was only the faintest smell of roses to the bouquet. I didn't know what I was supposed to do with it—since I wasn't going to a dance where I could carry it in my hand, with its ribbons trailing down. I smiled at how inappropriate the bouquet was; I didn't mind that, because it seemed very like Lauren not to figure out the appropriate thing. The stuffed cat, which I sat up on my shoulder to feel the soft fur against my neck, was a silly thing too. I opened the top Harlequin.

About thirty pages into it, I closed it and put it on the night table. I tried the other one.

I only made it through ten pages of that. I guessed maybe I was in the wrong mood for love stories. Certainly, it did seem to me that—given the odds—there couldn't be as many perfectly beautiful women as there were Harlequin books with perfectly beautiful women in them. I looked at the mystery my mother had brought, but I turned on the TV instead, without turning off the radio.

Neither of the machines was turned particularly loud, but they crowded the room with voices. I started with a movie on the TV, and as soon as the advertisements came on, I switched to a game show, and from there to a rerun of "Gilligan's Island," and then I found "Sesame Street."

I came in on one of the Grover-waiter scenes, where Grover gets everything wrong and the customer never has anything to eat. Grover is my favorite character, and he made me smile, as always.

With the TV and the radio making noise, filling the room, smiling because of Grover, I shoved the table top away from over my lap and looked at what they'd been staring at, Suzy and Lisa and Lauren.

5

The bed was elevated at the back and bent up a little for my knees, so I could sit easily. In the temperature-controlled air of the hospital, the only blanket anybody needed was a light one. I looked at my legs.

I looked at my leg.

I looked at my leg-and-a-half.

There was one long thick leg under the blanket, and one short leg. The short one looked like a monster zucchini under the blanket. After it stopped the blanket lay flat.

All of my body trembled, my heart and stomach jiggling inside my ribcage, my shoulders going back and forth like a guitar string. I was cold and afraid. I held up my hands and looked at them, to see their shaking, but it didn't look like they were shaking. I just felt like they were shaking.

I tried to swallow but I couldn't. I moved my toes back and forth. At the end of my left leg the blanket twitched, but nothing happened under the flat white blanket on the rest of the bed.

I looked at my legs and one of them had been cut off short forever.

I looked at myself and I knew exactly what Lauren felt like.

I pushed back the blankets—not to look more closely, but because I was going to throw up, or I had to go to the bathroom. I didn't want to see anybody, and I had on a long nightgown so I didn't have to see myself. I worked my leg over the side of the bed and got the bottom of the cast onto the floor. It was awkward, but I could keep some kind of balance by hanging onto the bars of the bedstead. I worked myself around until I was almost standing on my one clumsy foot, then reached out to grab the walker that waited beside the locker. Once I had that, I sort of hung over it until the wave of faintness passed. Shoving the walker ahead of me, inching along, dragging my heavy foot while I kept my weight on my arms and shoulders, I made it into the bathroom.

I bent over the sink, but I didn't have to throw up. I turned on the cold water and splashed it all over my face. Then, for the first time, I looked at myself in the mirror, the one that hung over the sink.

I looked terrible.

Turning around, leaning back against the sink while I headed the walker the other way, I got out of the bathroom and back onto the bed. My nightgown tangled down along my leg-and-a-half, but I didn't try to straighten it, I just pulled the sheet and blanket over it all. I pulled the table over again and put my forehead down on it and then covered my head with my arms.

My brain wasn't working. It was as if the little Izzy was running around and around in circles, some frantic wind-up Izzy, screeching *No, no, no.*

But it was *Yes, yes, yes.*

And I knew it.

I knew it, but I couldn't believe it.

I felt, with my forehead against the flat Formica, my arms wrapped cold around my dirty hair, as if I were sliding. I felt as if a huge long slide was slipping up past me, and I was going down it. I couldn't stop myself, and I didn't even want to. I wasn't even going down the slide particularly fast, I was just going down, and down, without any hope of stopping. Something heavy and wet and cold and gray was making me go down, pushing at the back of my bent neck and at my shoulders. At the bottom, wherever that was, something heavy and wet and cold and gray waited for me. It was softer than the ground when I hit it. I went flying off the end of the slide and fell into the gray. The gray reached up around me and closed itself over me and swallowed me up.

The words hammered down on the back of my neck. Crippled. Amputated. "Not *me*," I answered each one of them. Handicapped. "No, not *me*." Deformed. "Not me, please."

"Isobel?"

I lifted my face. A black nurse had come into the room. She gave the impression of strength, because her shoulders and arms were large, though she wasn't especially big. She had a round face and wore her hair cropped short. Her skin was very dark, with purply-black tones to the brownness, and silky smooth. Her eyes were round and flat, without any expression in them.

"Isobel Lingard?"

I nodded my head. I wanted her to go away, because I was afraid I was going to cry. We didn't cry, not the Lingards. We were brave and made jokes about things hurting, or at least the twins did, calling each other Gimp-O and Captain Hook, depending on where the injuries were. I didn't want to cry, but I was afraid I was going to.

The black nurse put her clipboard down on my table and lowered the bed flat, without asking me. She rolled the table away. She pulled down the sheet and pulled up my nightgown. She didn't say anything, just humphed and grunted. Then, "Roll over," she told me.

"I can't."

Without saying anything, she put her arms under me and rolled me over. She took away my pillow so I was lying with my cheek against the sheet. She pulled up my nightgown some more, until it was up around my armpits. I was naked under it, and I felt ashamed and helpless, but I didn't dare ask her what was going on, what was going to happen, because I thought if I moved my mouth I'd cry.

I felt her hands come down on the back of my shoulders, up under the nightgown.

"Relax, Isobel." She sounded bored. I couldn't see her because my head was facing the wrong way. All I could see was the ugly green face of the locker and the half-open door to the bathroom. "I can't work on you unless you relax." Her fingers dug into my neck.

It was a massage, I figured that out. She dug and pulled and kneaded, like she was making pizza. Her fingers hurt me.

I didn't see why she had to do that. I didn't know what else to do, though, so I just lay there, waiting for it to be over.

She worked along my arms and shoulder, then down my back. Then she worked at the uncovered part of my left leg, even on the toes, pulling them out, turning them as much as the cast would permit. She did the other leg too. Her hands grabbed at the flesh and pushed it, working it in circles. I had watched men making pizza crusts, but I had never thought before how it might feel to the dough.

When she finally stopped, I thought she'd cover me up and go away, but she hoisted me over onto my back again, and sent to work on the front muscles of my legs. I pulled down my nightgown, as far as she'd let me, and lay there with my eyes closed, waiting for her to be finished. It was a lot like being at the dentist's, when you just wait for them to finish each section of your mouth, measuring how much longer it will have to go on.

When she finally got to the right thigh I said, without opening my eyes, "Can you stop now?

She didn't even answer, and I opened my eyes to look at her. Her face was blank, all of her attention on her hands.

"I said, can you stop now please."

She shook her head. "We have to keep these muscles in shape."

My mouth trembled a little, because she wasn't paying any attention to what I asked her to do, to how I was feeling. "I don't see why," I said, thinking of all the ways I used to use my legs.

"You can't put a prosthetic device on tender skin. We have to toughen up the skin on this stump."

I didn't say another word. I just lay there with my eyes closed, wishing her away. She didn't have to hurt me. I was sure a massage didn't have to be painful.

At last, she pulled my nightgown all the way down, pulled the sheets up, pushed the buttons to set the bed back in position, and said, "I'll be back tomorrow."

She never once looked at me, at my face or eyes. I guessed if you'd finished working on the pizza dough, you wouldn't bend over and say goodbye to it. You don't talk to *things*. And that's what I was, a thing, a messed-up body.

I turned on the TV and watched women squealing with delight and disappointment on a game show, while this slick middle-aged man did kissyfaces with them. The women were mostly older and pretty bad-looking, but they all had two legs. I kept the volume up, so I wouldn't hear what I was thinking.

They dropped by some mail and a big basket of fruit from my grandmother Ingram and a round tin of homemade cookies from my grandmother Lingard who's Swedish and cooks constantly. I wasn't hungry. I read the cards. There were lots of get well messages, and the people said they hoped they'd see me soon. But they didn't know what I looked like now.

Mrs. Hughes-Pincke came in, just before lunch, and sat down in the chair she pulled up, all perky and pregnant.

"Hello, Isobel. How are you feeling today?"

"Fine," I said, turning down the volume.

"Let's turn that off so we can talk."

I turned it off.

"Do you have any questions?" she asked. "What would you like to talk about?"

There was nothing I wanted to talk about. I shrugged.

"I have to stay here," she said. "You're on my appointment sheet and I have to earn my salary." She asked questions and I answered them until finally she left.

My father came by and ate some of the fruit and cookies for lunch. My mother arrived as he was leaving. She'd bought me a needlepoint kit, for something to do with my hands. She picked through the tin of cookies, looking for the rolled kind, which are her favorites. After a while, my mother had to rush off. I turned on the TV.

Dr. Epstein came by. "You look pretty good," he told me. "How do you feel?"

"Fine," I told him. "You should have one of my grandmother's cookies."

"You're right, I should. And I will. How about you?" He held the tin out to me.

I didn't want any. Dr. Epstein stood beside the bed. He'd elevated it again, after he had checked my bandages, so I was sitting up. He picked out one of the rolled cookies and bit into it, watching my face.

I looked right back at him, because I knew by then that I could count on myself to be all right in front of other people.

"Good cookies."

"She's a good cook."

"Can I take one with me for my appendectomy?"

"As long as you don't take another one of the rolled ones. Mom really loves those."

He chose the biggest cookie, layered with raspberry jam. "Do you have any questions for me?"

I shook my head.

"OK, then, I'll see you tomorrow. Hold the fort," he said to me.

I watched TV for most of that afternoon and while I was eating my afternoon snack and while I was eating my dinner. I watched TV that night, waiting for the phone to ring, hoping that it wouldn't because I didn't have anything to talk to anyone about, wondering why it didn't.

When at last it did, a little after the nine o'clock news break, it was Suzy. As soon as she said hello and asked me how I was, I wanted to get off the phone.

"Gees, Izzy, I didn't know," she said. I kept my eyes on the screen, wondering what the Thursday night movie would be. Suzy's voice went on, into my ear. "I didn't know it was that bad. What are you going to *do*? And all."

"Ummnnh," I said. I punched at the channel changer—I never liked spy movies.

"And you're going to miss so much work." Suzy changed the subject. "How're you going to catch up? Oh well, your parents'll figure out a way."

"Yeah," I agreed, switching the channel from a sitcom. "Listen," I said, "I'm kind of busy here now."

"You are? Yeah, I am too, tons of homework, and I have to wash my hair. But what about Marco?"

I couldn't think of a thing to say.

"Izzy? You've got to let him know sometime."

I thought I was going to cry right then. Marco hadn't even sent a get-well card. I didn't want to hear from him, or anything, but I wished he wasn't so. . . . He hadn't even said he was sorry. I didn't want to talk to him, not a bit; I didn't even want to think about him; I didn't even like hearing his name. But I wished he didn't have to show me so plainly that he wasn't worth wanting to go out with, that I should never have gone out with him. Although I guessed I wasn't much better, because it wasn't as if I had wanted to go out with him, Marco, particularly. "Tell him OK," I said. "Listen I've—"

"OK what?"

"OK whatever he wants. Just tell him I don't remember anything. I've really got to go. Bye," and I dropped the receiver back into the cradle just as she started saying her happy thank-you's.

The phone rang right away, so I had to answer it. I covered my eyes with my left hand and pushed my fingers against my forehead and hoped I could sound normal enough to get rid of Suzy quickly.

But it was my mother, who talked for a couple of minutes then told me I sounded funny.

"I'm pretty tired."

"Of course, you must be. I'm sorry, Love. Just say hello to Francie—no, Francie, Izzy's tired and needs her sleep, you can only say hello. Sleep well, Angel. I'll see you tomorrow."

They were all going to see me tomorrow, and I didn't want to see any of them. I didn't want to see anybody. I didn't want tomorrow to come, because it was just going to be a repeat of today. The only thing I wanted was not to be in the hospital, not to have had my leg amputated.

I could feel tears trying to squeeze themselves up into my throat, so I got busy. I gathered up the cards and letters, leaned over, and dropped them into the wastebasket. I threw out both of the Harlequins too—tossing them up into the air and listening to the clunk they made when they landed in the trash. I pushed the table away from the bed and got myself into the bathroom. There, I scrubbed at my face with soap and hot water, then slapped cold water over it.

Crying, complaining—they never did any good anyway. I'd never been a weeper or a whiner.

Yeah, but I'd never had anything really to weep about, or whine over, before. I'd just never known, before.

I got to sleep all right, but when I woke up in the darkness of the night, there wasn't anything I could do to stop myself. I didn't know why it had happened to me, because I knew lots of girls whose dates had too much to drink and they didn't end up crippled. For life. I couldn't think of what to do with my life, what to want to do, because all the things I wanted to do required normal people—and I wasn't normal anymore. I was abnormal. I wasn't going to be able to be a cheerleader, or even to walk around. I couldn't ride my bike or play tennis—I didn't think crippled people could drive cars, not with only one leg. Not to mention dances, I wouldn't be able to dance with a boy, and besides, who would ask me to a dance with him now? Who would want to go out with a cripple?

The tears ran down by my ears and my hair got wet and cold, and I couldn't stop them any more than I could stop the thoughts I was having; but I tried not to make any noise. If anybody heard me, and came in, and saw the way I was sniveling. . . .

I wondered why I couldn't be brave, the way other people were, and I wept more. I couldn't turn on the TV to distract myself, because of the noise—or the radio either. If I didn't want someone coming in.

It was dark in my room, and I felt so all alone that I couldn't stand it. I started sobbing, really crying. I put my pillow over my head. I didn't want to be alone and abandoned here—while everybody else was asleep in his own bed—and I didn't want to be crying, but I couldn't do anything about anything.

After a long time, I went back to sleep.

It used to be, before, that when I woke up in the morning everything was fresh, and there were new chances every morning. When I woke up that Friday morning, nothing had changed. I was in the same small room being awakened so that my temperature could be taken. I waited for the usual length of time, until I was so hungry I wasn't hungry, for breakfast to arrive—the same bland and half-cold hot food on plastic plates and in plastic bowls. My mother called at the same time and asked if I thought ten o'clock would be an inconvenient time for her to come by. I told her maybe, because of people who said they'd see me tomorrow, so she said she'd come in the afternoon. The only edible thing on my breakfast tray was a piece of toast.

The same noises were there, where I couldn't see them, sometimes quiet conversation, sometimes a loud worried voice, sometimes a little kid crying or laughing. The black nurse came back and pummeled at me, rolling me over because I couldn't do it myself. Then she put me into a wheelchair and took me for a walk—covered from the waist down with a blanket. We went down the long corridor to what she called the sun room, where some kids sat around a TV set, and then back to my room, where she hefted me up onto the bed again. I didn't know why she made me do that, because she didn't say a word to me and she didn't enjoy it one bit. Mrs. Hughes-Pincke came by and made a conversation. This time she was all interested in my courses and my grades, but I didn't have much of anything to say. Dr. Epstein examined me and had a couple of cookies. He gave me an orange from the fruit basket. I got it about half-peeled before I realized I didn't want to eat anything and heaved it into the wastebasket. Another nurse came in to give me a sponge bath. They brought me lunch and the creamed chicken was tasteless, the biscuits dried out and crumbly, the milk warm. My mother came by and asked me why I hadn't started the needlepoint kit. Nobody called me up. Nobody came to see me. I knew there was a football game that evening and probably everybody was tied up with that. So I turned the light out early and lay watching the perfect people on TV, with their perfect complexions and perfect bodies acting their parts. It was a color TV, but the grayness had swallowed me up.

I wanted to go home. To my own room, in my own

house, where at least I could eat what I liked. I wanted to be
in my own bed, an old four-poster, with my stuffed animals
all over it. I thought if only I was home, it wouldn't be so
bad. At home I knew all the nighttime noises. At home I
could see the trees from my window. At home, if I was
awake in the middle of the night, I could go quietly down
the carpeted staircase and sit in the kitchen, to have a snack
or drink some hot milk or just look around at the bright
yellow cupboards and maybe listen to the radio. If anyone
came in when I was at home I'd know who they were.

If only, I thought—

If only my parents hadn't said I could go out with Marco.

If only I'd had the nerve to tell Tony I'd rather he took me
home, whatever people might say.

Or if I'd called my parents.

I remembered back and changed things—wishing I could
find magic to work it, wishing there was magic in the world
to turn back time, hoping that if I wished hard enough it
would turn out that the magic was there.

If only my leg had healed, the way seventy-five percent
of them did.

I played the scene where Marco asked me out over and
over in my mind, the way you replay a nightmare, changing
things to make everything come out all right. In the scenes I
played, I had another plan for Saturday—and even if it was
only going to the movies with my friends, I wouldn't
change those plans, not even for a senior.

If I'd had more pride, when he tried to act big and I could
see what he was doing, I would have turned him down. If
he'd seen someone else standing there at the bus stop, or if
he hadn't broken up with Carol that summer so she would
have been the one to go with him to the party.

If only I'd learned how to drive, I could have driven
myself home, but we Lingards were nice people, law-
abiding—and look what happened.

That night, I never did get back to sleep, even though I

cried myself dry. Every time I tried to blank my mind, new ideas would come in, or I would see that little Izzy in my head, doing her stupid back flip, which I never could have done. I tried to face the truth, but I couldn't face it, it just made me cry. I knew how disappointed my parents would be in me, if they knew.

But my whole life had been ruined. What was I supposed to do, laugh and clap my hands? Why did they expect me to be perfect? And why were they all tucked up in their own beds, leaving me alone without anyone caring how unhappy and lonely I was.

I knew what they'd say. They'd say there were people with much worse troubles. I didn't care about that, and I knew how mean and selfish that was, but I really didn't care. But I didn't like being so mean and selfish—I was supposed to be nice, that's what I was, a nice girl.

Not any more, that wasn't what I was. Now I was a cripple.

If only, I thought, I'd been killed when the car struck the tree. Hearing myself think that, I understood how depressed I was, and I wept for myself.

Morning showed gray outside the window. It was Saturday, but that didn't make any difference. When I thought that, I reminded myself of two differences. First, that on Saturday and Sunday, the black nurse and Mrs. Hughes-Pincke wouldn't come by. Second, I remembered that there was no school and so I would probably see my friends, and I didn't want them to see me like this.

6

I think it was that Saturday that my mother came in early, and we washed my hair. I stood in the walker with my head in the sink, trying not to bang myself up on the projecting faucet. She poured glassfuls of water over my head, first to wet it, then to rinse the shampoo out. It was tiring and awkward, standing there trying to hold my weight against the walker and clutching the slippery sides of the small sink, my eyes squinched shut. It took three rinses to satisfy my mother. Then she wrapped a towel around my head and started rubbing my hair dry, because she had forgotten my blow dryer.

"Can't I get back into bed?" I finally asked her. She had forgotten all about me and was just concentrating on the job. I was practically shaking from standing so long.

When I was back in bed and rubbing at my hair myself, I found that my hands and arms felt shaky too. Because—what was I going to do, how was I going to do all the necessary things, with only one leg. Like brushing my teeth, even something as minor as that.

My mother had to go, to take Francie to her gymnastic class. My father had a golf game. I kept the radio on, to the sound of the top forty, but I wasn't listening to the music. I was listening to the noise of people in the hallways and wondering when my friends would start arriving. I wasn't sure I wanted to see them, and in fact, I was listening in dread, so I'd have the right expression on my face when they did come in. I was ready to pretend I didn't see the way they stared.

I was also ready for something to happen, even just our usual conversations about hairdo's or earrings, teachers or TV shows. I didn't want them to come until after my hair dried, because I look like an otter when my hair lies flat and wet. I toweled my head and waited, wondering if we'd have enough to talk about, trying to think of things to ask about to keep the conversation going.

My hair was almost dry when Joel stepped into the room through the open door. I waited for Jack, but he wasn't there. Joel stayed at the door, for what felt like a long time, not moving out or in, not saying anything.

My brothers not only got my father's pure blond hair, but they also got my mother's light brown eyes and dark lashes. Joel's six feet tall and muscular. He keeps himself in shape. He doesn't look exactly like Jack—Jack's an inch shorter and several pounds lighter. Joel's nose is short and straight; Jack's is thicker. Jack's teeth have a dark metallic row of fillings but Joel's are perfect. Joel is the cutest, but Jack has the best smile, and he's got a smoldering kind of personality. Joel's more easygoing, Jack's the better athlete, Joel does better in school.

"Where's Jack?" I asked, when it didn't look like Joel would ever say anything.

Joel grinned. "Hey, Iz, you look great." He came over, pulled the straight-backed chair around and sat with his arms folded across its back, his big legs in pale jeans jutting out. He kept on smiling. "You always were a pretty kid, though."

I knew that I must look pretty terrible. If he'd said, the

way he often did, "I don't know how a good-looking guy like me got such a dog for a sister," I'd have known I looked all right. His flattery made me self-conscious.

"Yeah, but where is he?" I asked.

"Aren't you glad to see me?"

I didn't know if I was or not. It was like, when you've had your hair restyled and everybody you see notices that first. Everybody new I saw had the same shock, and I had to pretend I didn't notice. "Sure," I said, pretending. I took a breath. "How's school?"

"What do you think?"

I shook my head. I had no idea.

"It's OK. Biology's harder than I thought, but math is a breeze. How's yours?"

"Fine," I said. I wasn't used to seeing Joel without Jack, and I wondered why Jack hadn't come too. Jack always picked me for his partner in games of Monopoly or Clue, while Joel played with Francie; he'd call us the Stupids. "It's the Stupids against the Smarts," he'd say. And Jack would answer, "Izzy's not stupid."

"Are you home for the weekend?" I asked him. "Mom didn't say anything."

"They don't know I'm here. I thought I'd drop in for lunch, catch the old man after his golf—give them all a big treat. I borrowed a car," he explained. "It's a Dart—do you know about the old slant-six engine?"

I didn't, so he told me about it, how efficient and sturdy it was, how if I looked in the classifieds I'd almost never see a Dart, and that was because they ran and ran. Joel talked away, making jokes occasionally, about the Dart; I sat up in bed with the right expressions on my face and wondered why everything felt wrong.

I liked Joel, I really did, I liked his easy-going company and the way he could make me laugh. I didn't think he was as much less of an athlete than Jack as he always said he was. Certainly he was a smart athlete, he was an intelligent athlete—you could see that when you watched him move around the football field or the lacrosse field or the tennis court. I always had a good time with Joel. But I was having a terrible time keeping my face in the right expression for him.

Joel talked and talked, as if he was trying to fill up the air in the room with words. It didn't matter what the words were, as long as he filled the air with them. And me—I was sitting up in the bed pretending that his words were bright balloons, and I was a little kid running around laughing to catch them, pretending that it was fun to try to fill up the air with them.

But I was faking it. Inside, I was cold and gray. Joel's words—whatever it was he was saying—didn't even come close to touching me, not even their color touched the surface of my eyeballs.

It was so solitary there inside myself. I just wanted someone to reach in there and connect, just for a minute, just so I would know it could be done.

Joel wasn't planning on staying long, I could tell by the way he'd look at his watch as if he had a class to make. I could tell by the way he kept the subject on front-end suspensions that he was talking from about one-third of his attention, and the rest was busy doing something else. Just the way I was listening with about one-third of my attention, and the rest was busy. The more he talked, and the more he kept his words out between us, the more I got frightened and the more it bothered me to have him sitting there, not trying to really connect.

Finally, because it was either that or burst into tears, I interrupted him. "Why didn't Jack come?"

Joel's voice stopped dead.

"Joel?" I reminded him that I was there and had asked a question.

He shrugged, and grinned. He looked me straight in the eyes and said, "There's this girl . . ."

I knew he was lying, because that's exactly what I do when I lie. You look someone straight in the eye so they'll believe you're telling the truth. I knew that, but I didn't know what his lie was supposed to hide. He was hiding things from me, and I wondered if something terrible had happened to Jack.

Whatever it was, it was so bad that Joel wasn't going to tell me. That meant it was pretty bad. I no longer wanted to know. He was getting up, telling me he had to get going, to see the parents and get back to school in time.

"In time for what?" I asked.

"Just a party," he said, looking all around my room, "but I've been looking forward to it."

"I'll tell you who *I* think has a girl," I said. That made him look worried, and he was trying hard to keep his face cheerful. "Say hi to Jack for me, will you?"

He took his bright balloon words with him, and the room was empty. Empty, that is, except for me where I sat alone in it.

That was when I began to realize how much everything had changed. I realized then that my friends weren't going to come to keep me company, because on the weekends, on Saturday morning, we made our plans, depending on who had what shopping to do, or if any of us had a date or a party, or whatever was going on. They were probably going to be doing something anyway, in the afternoon. They probably would rather do that than come to the hospital, anyway. Probably it made them sick to look at me.

Probably nothing had happened to Jack, too; probably he just didn't want to look at me.

I'd never minded being alone, or feeling alone—like, especially, if I was out in the country somewhere, I liked to get away alone and concentrate on everything there was to see and hear. But before, I'd always been alone just until whatever was going to happen next. There was always something coming along to happen next, so I could enjoy being alone until then. Now, I was alone until—nothing was going to happen next.

As if I was being punished, as if it was my fault. As if I wanted to be crippled.

The long minutes of the afternoon dragged by. I had the TV on, for the noise and something to look at. In a way, I didn't really believe the phone wouldn't ring, or the noises in the hall wouldn't turn into someone coming to see me. In a way, I was hoping I wouldn't have to sit alone in my room all day. So, in a way, I was expecting something, as the minutes went by, one after the other after another.

I began to think about them, about Suzy and Lisa and Lauren. They ought to come and see me, they ought to know I'd like company. I'd have gone to see them, I knew that. My mother would have made me, even if I hadn't thought of it myself.

But I didn't want anybody coming to see me if they didn't want to. And nobody wanted to, it looked like. I thought I'd like to tell them a thing or two. Tears began to trickle down my face, because. . . . They didn't have to treat me this badly, and they really shouldn't do it now. Not now. Not when everything had changed.

I had half a mind to call Suzy up and tell her . . . how much she'd hurt my feelings. She should at least be feeling bad about it. I dried my eyes, scrubbing at them with a tissue, thinking about what a rotten best friend Suzy made. She could at least call.

My mother came into the room after a while and said it was time to get me into the wheelchair for a ride, because Francie was downstairs and wanted to see me. Was I too tired? she asked me. Was I warm enough in the bed jacket, which looked very nice, didn't it?

Downstairs, Francie sat with my father on one of the big sofas near the main entrance. She was clutching Pierre in her arms. My father's arm was around her. Francie just stared for a long time. I didn't know what to say, so I sort of

looked back at her and then at old green Pierre, clutched at
her chest. I looked at the goofy green face and the place
where Francie had loved off one of his eyes.

After a while, my father asked her, "Aren't you going to
say hello?"

"Hi, Izzy."

I knew how she felt, the way you feel when everybody
around you is sad and serious. Like when somebody else's
dog has died, and you're trying to think of something to say.

They didn't stay long. My mother wheeled me back into
the big elevator, where a couple of visitors kind of looked at
me, then looked away. When we were back in my room,
and I was back up on the bed, I finally asked my mother.
"Can I go home? Mom?" At home, at least, I would know
everybody there, and now everybody had seen me there
wouldn't be that first time.

"I don't think so. Saul hasn't said anything about that."

I just wanted to be in my own bed, in my own room. I
wasn't going to ask for a lot of attention, or anything, or
special care.

"I know it feels long, but it hasn't actually been that
long, Angel, and your body has had—a pretty bad shock."

She didn't even want to say yes. She didn't want me to
come home. She had that distracted look on her face that
meant she wasn't telling me something but she was thinking
about it. I'd seen it before, like when she would ask me to
babysit for Francie because she and Dad simply needed an
evening out on their own, just the two of them having
dinner and going to a movie, and then Francie came in to
say she needed help with her spelling words or her math
problems. Before she could answer Francie, my mother
would stand there with a distracted look on her face while
she juggled out how many reasons there were for them to
stay home and help Francie, and how many to go out and
pay attention to themselves.

For Francie they usually stayed home, I thought.

"Saul would have to give permission. He'll tell us when it's the right time," my mother said. She pulled my blanket up. I shoved it down. "You're going to have to be patient, Lamb."

They didn't want me at home. She didn't.

"I'm tired," I said.

"You look tired," she agreed, brushing my hair off my forehead.

I didn't want her to do that. I pushed the button to flatten out my bed. There I was, and this horrible thing had happened to me, and she was thinking that it was inconvenient to have me home.

I didn't want to think about that, because I could sort of understand how they'd feel about having a crippled kid, all the problems and all. I shut my eyes. I heard her leave the room.

As soon as she'd gone, I raised the bed again and turned on the TV. My mother didn't come back and see what I had done. Probably, I thought, because she'd been in a big hurry to get back down to join Dad and Francie and get back home to whatever was so important there.

Dr. Epstein came in for the daily examination. This time he kept me flat on my back for longer than usual because he was changing the bandage. I didn't mind, I just lay there as silent as always. When he raised the back of the bed and I hunched myself into a comfortable sitting position, he asked me, "How are you doing?"

"Fine," I said.

"How do you like Helen?" He must have seen that I didn't know who he was talking about. "Hughes-Pincke," he added.

"Oh, she's fine."

"PT going all right?" he asked. "Physical therapy," he said.

"Oh. Yes. Fine."

I thought it was time he left. It was Saturday, after all,

and he should be home with his family. He picked up my hand and looked at my fingernails, as if he was studying them. This, I knew, was a way of looking for anemia. Lauren's mildly anemic, which is how I learned that. I waited.

"Are you losing weight?" he asked me.

I didn't know.

"OK, Izzy, I'll see you tomorrow. You're doing well, you know."

"Then can I go home soon?"

"Not right away," he said, stopping partway out of my room, turning around to give my question his full attention. "Not for at least a week more, and probably closer to two weeks." That wasn't what I wanted to hear. "You're young and you're healthy, but it still takes time, even for people who are young and healthy. To heal."

I just nodded my head and bit at the inside of my cheeks.

The afternoon dragged by. I had a snack of peanut butter, crackers and an apple, but it wasn't crunchy peanut butter so I didn't eat it, and the apple wasn't at all crisp. Dinner came in, but I wasn't hungry. I ate the mashed potatoes, because the gravy was OK, but left the two thin slices of meat and the limp salad and the lumpy pudding and the peas. I never eat peas.

I thought, as the TV played over my head, that if only Suzy would come by, just to say hello, just for a minute, or call up, just to say hello—but it was too much trouble for her. For them. For any of them. They had more interesting things to do.

I thought that, somehow, I'd just disappeared from their lives, like sliding down into water and the water closes over your head as if you've never been there.

I told myself that probably Suzy had something she had to do, or maybe she thought I was too sick or something. I told myself that I ought to make an effort. So I picked up the phone and dialed Suzy's number. Ms. Wilkes answered. I asked for Suzy.

"She's out, I thought she'd have told you. They said—they had some shopping to do and they were going to stop by and see you. I guess they didn't?"

"I guess they didn't have time."

"But I've been meaning to talk to you," Ms. Wilkes's voice went on, warm and gushy, "just to say how terribly sorry I am. Oh, we all are. We all just feel so bad for you, it seems so cruel and unnecessary and—it's a terrible thing," she said.

I didn't know what to say.

"When I think that it was just a week ago. Just last week—we've been so worried and unhappy. But you mustn't mind about Lauren, dear; it just takes some people like that. Some people are like that and I'm afraid Lauren is one of them."

Like what, I wondered. What had Lauren been saying?

"And I tried to tell her, as a mother, the way I feel, because she doesn't have a *real* mother, just that stepmother and her own mother out living it up, thinking only of herself. I tried to tell her that it's so terrible, and you young people are so careless, as if nothing could hurt you, that if we can take it as a warning, or a lesson, and learn from it. Try to salvage *some* good from this tragic thing. Then maybe something good can come out of this terrible thing that's happened to you. But you know Suzy, she never listens to anyone. I just hope—"

I never found out what she hoped. I had this picture of the little Izzy inside my head, standing there waving her detached leg at a crowd of people, like a safety monitor waving her stop sign.

"Tell Suzy I called, would you please?" I interrupted Ms. Wilkes.

"I certainly will. I'll tell her more than that, because I told them how lonely it can get in the hospital, and they promised me they'd go see you. In fact, I'm pretty angry at Suzy. She let me think she'd seen you. That counts as a lie, in my book."

I rang off. Ms. Wilkes didn't know how many little lies Suzy told her, just to keep her from creeping into Suzy's life and taking it over. Suzy's friends knew. It was friends who really knew all about you, what you were really thinking about, what you really wanted. I felt that way about my friends, anyway; that they were the ones who knew me.

Listening to Ms. Wilkes really got me down, I thought. What was I supposed to do with all her pity and her learning lessons. I thought I might call Lisa, and we could talk about it and laugh about how bad what she said was—but I didn't dare. Lisa would have been there too, shopping and not coming to see me.

You'd have thought that I'd have been all cried out, but I wasn't. You'd have thought I'd have been able not to just sit there, with the light out, thinking about how I wished—

Wishing I'd never said I'd go to the party with Marco, wishing that people could, like some other creatures can, grow back lost limbs, wondering if, if I wished hard enough if maybe I could, thinking how I'd feel if I woke up in the morning to find that this whole thing was a dream. Sometimes dreams seemed so real you had to believe them. Or if I could wake up and find my leg back. I knew how that would feel, and I knew what I'd think and how surprised my parents would be, because if that happened, I'd just put on a bathrobe and walk home and I'd come to the door and ring the doorbell, and they'd open it and there I'd be, standing on my own two legs.

But the next morning, when I woke up, nothing had changed. I never knew until then, I never even suspected because I always just sort of figured people weren't trying hard enough to cheer up, how it felt to be depressed.

I'd been miserable. I'd been blue. But depressed, no, I hadn't been that. I never knew how it felt to sigh out a breath so sad you could almost see tears in it. I never knew the way tears would ooze and ooze out of your eyes. I never knew the way something could hang like a gray cloud over all of your mind and you could never get away from it, never forget it.

My parents both came and played three-handed rummy and talked about one thing and another. But their voices never got through the cloud. They didn't suspect anything, though, except that I was tired, which I kept telling them. I wasn't about to do any weeping and wailing in front of anyone. If I found myself doing that, I thought, I'd be nothing but ashamed, nothing but a puddle of shame. It was bad enough being crippled.

Lisa and Suzy did come in the midafternoon, and my parents looked relieved to see them. "We'll leave you alone to tell girlish secrets," my mother said. "See you tomorrow, Lamb."

I sat up in bed and tried not to look the way I felt. There was a gray heaviness lying on my shoulders and swelling up like a balloon under my heart. I guessed, although I didn't ask about it, that somebody had given them an earful.

The first thing I heard was a lot of excuses about yesterday, and then a lot of not-telling what had gone on yesterday evening, whatever that was supposed to keep me from knowing. Finally, not because I was interested, but just because it would get them talking and keep them from staring at me, I asked about what was happening at school. They started slow, but they got warmed up pretty soon and told stories across my bed, talking to one another. Suzy had taken the only chair so Lisa—after looking once at the foot of the bed—wandered around, sometimes leaning against the foot of the bed. I concentrated on looking normal.

After about half an hour—but it felt like about three hours—Suzy looked at her watch and said in a great fake voice that she didn't know it had gotten so late. I caught

Lisa looking at my face, and her eyes looked as if she had a lot of things to say, but wasn't going to.

"Yeah, it is late," I said, agreeing with Suzy that it was time to go.

"It's impossible during the week," she said to me, but not meeting my eyes. "I mean, I'm so busy—but next weekend; for sure. Do you want me to bring you anything?"

I shook my head, knowing that my voice would shake if I tried to use it.

"When are you going home?" Lisa asked.

I shrugged, to say I didn't know.

"I bet you're looking forward to that," Lisa said.

I pushed the ends of my mouth out into a smile to show that, yes, I was.

Finally they left. I unclenched my teeth, unclenched the muscles around my eyes, which had been holding the tears back, and the miniature Izzy in my head just stood there, hanging onto a walker, all drooped over it. They'd been forced to come. They hadn't even ever asked about what had happened to me. "How are you?" they asked and I said, "Fine," and they took that for the truth.

Gray water rose up over the miniature Izzy's bent head.

7

It finally struck me, as the next week went slowly by, Monday morning to afternoon to evening, Tuesday to Wednesday, that everybody asked the same question. "How are you?"

I said the same answer, "Fine."

There wasn't, of course, very much of an everybody. My mother came every day, whenever in her day she had a free hour or two. She's always busy, always doing something. I didn't know what was keeping her so busy, which project or which committee, but I knew I could count on seeing her every day, in the afternoon or evening. My father came to have lunch with me. He'd buy it at a deli—a big sandwich and a pickle, a carry-out container of iced tea—and I'd watch him eat. He'd knock on the door, even though it was open. I'd say come in and he'd sit down and unpack his lunch onto his lap. Hospital lunches were served early, so I'd always finished with whatever I was having. I'd watch him eat and then we'd talk about different things. "How are you?" he'd ask, as he sat down.

"Fine," I'd say.

Lisa called a couple of evenings and we'd talk for a few

minutes, general gossip and what was going to be on TV. She was the only one who called. Most of the time, the phone sat black and silent and sulky on the table. Suzy didn't call me and I didn't try calling her again. I knew what was going on. Mrs. Wilkes had made me her "Cause of the Week" to nag Suzy about; and Suzy was rebelling, as she always did. So it was only Lisa who'd be on the other end when the phone rang. "How are you?" she'd asked.

"Fine," I'd say.

The flowers around my room died off and got thrown out. My grandmother Ingram sent a second bunch of flowers, a spring bouquet with tulips and roses, which must have cost her a small fortune. My grandmother Lingard sent me a linzertorte, cut into squares and packed into a cookie tin. Dr. Epstein couldn't keep his hands off that one. He came to my room in the early mornings, before he went to his office. "How are you today?" he asked.

"Fine."

Mrs. Hughes-Pincke sat down with me for half an hour a day, eleven to eleven-thirty, leaving just as the lunch cart started coming down the hall. "Good morning, Isobel," she'd say. "How are you today?"

"Fine," I'd tell her.

She'd ask me questions. When she got close to how I was feeling about things, I'd say "Fine," or "I don't know," and she'd start up on something else. I didn't mind telling her facts. But when she asked things like, "This boy, Marco, is he a boy you've dated often?" I knew she was fishing around and I didn't say much.

"No."

"Is he someone special?"

"No," and I'd let her know in my voice that I wasn't interested at all in the subject.

Nobody, I realized, was talking about what had happened, as if everyone was pretending everything was normal and all right. So was I, but not for the same reason.

Nobody wanted to hear my troubles. "Fine" was what they wanted to hear.

I didn't think about much of anything because I watched a lot of TV. I didn't think about school, and everyone, although when Lisa called I'd ask, "How's school?" I'd ask about it and then I'd tune out her answer. It didn't interest me what was going on, not really. What interested me was what people were thinking about me, having lost a leg and all, being crippled. I wanted to know what I could expect. Nobody was talking to me about that, not at all. I figured that was because they knew it would get me down. What they didn't know was how far down I was already.

Besides, I didn't need to know what people were thinking. I could guess.

"How are you?" they asked.

"Fine," I answered, not exactly lying, but—lying through my teeth.

Only the black nurse didn't ask. She didn't care. She didn't like me much, and I didn't like her much either. I didn't know anything about her, not even her name. She looked about thirty-five; she didn't wear any rings. Every day she would come into my room and massage me for a while, then take me for a walk in the wheelchair. Never did she ask me how I felt.

One day, it was the middle of the week, maybe Wednesday or Thursday—I wasn't sure because I never was sure what day it was until I got the evening TV programs. It was the middle of the week, I knew. She didn't wheel me down to the sun room and back for our daily outing that day. Instead, she wheeled me to the elevator and pushed a button for a higher floor.

I didn't want to ask her any questions, but I did, without turning around to look at her. "Where am I going?"

"To the PT room," she answered. I had no idea what the PT room was, but I didn't ask her about that because I figured she already knew I didn't know.

PHYSICAL THERAPY it said on the door. PT. I didn't want to go in.

But of course I had to go in. My nurse put me on a rubber pathway with a big metal fence, the kind you see on March of Dimes advertisements. I didn't look at anybody else in the room. I just hauled myself down the walk, turned myself around, and hauled myself back. She never told me how many times I had to do it, so I just kept hauling along. I could hear voices in the big room. My nurse didn't say anything. When she'd had enough, she put me back into the wheelchair and took me down to my room. She helped me onto the bed and left.

As soon as she was gone, I got back off of the bed and used the walker to go to the bathroom. I stood splashing cold water on my face until I knew I was all right.

When I came out, Mrs. Hughes-Pincke was there, sitting in the chair, waiting. She didn't get up to help me or anything, just sat and stared at me while I worked the walker around and finally got myself up onto the bed.

"Good morning, Isobel," she said. "How are you?"

"Fine," I told her.

"But Isobel, you don't seem to be eating very much," she said.

I didn't know what to say. I hadn't thought about that. I looked at her, seeing mostly stomach.

"I'm not awfully hungry," I told her.

She couldn't argue with that. "The food here isn't that bad, is it? For a hospital? You aren't dieting, are you?"

"I never needed to go on a diet, or anything. I never worried about my figure."

"Really?" Her face woke up. I looked to the open doorway again. "Most girls do. Why didn't you?"

I shrugged. "I guess I was too busy."

"Doing what?"

"Things. You know. School and cheerleading and all."

She didn't ask the natural next question, "What are you

going to do now?" I was just as glad she didn't, but I knew that, because she didn't ask, it was in her mind. I didn't let it get into my mind, though.

"How big is the cheerleading squad?" she asked instead. Mrs. Hughes-Pincke knew how to ask questions I could answer. She was curious, I guess, about the life of a typical high school sophomore.

"The whole squad is twenty-four, but there are only twelve of us that actually do the cheerleading. Were you ever a cheerleader?" I asked her.

She smiled and shook her head, and her smile stayed on her face the way a happy memory stays in your mind. "I went to a girls' school, a boarding school actually. We played sports, but—cheerleading was too . . . too high school for us. One didn't carry pompoms," she said, mocking herself.

We talked about whether there was something sexist about cheerleading, and I could see what she meant. Then I asked her what it was like, going to a boarding school. "I made some awfully good friends there." That smile washed over her whole face again. I wondered what she looked like when she wasn't swollen up with pregnancy. "You get to know people awfully well when you live with them. And some of the girls I went to school with—well, they make good friends. I guess there'll be somebody moving up to take your place on the cheerleading squad."

She was going to ask me how I felt about that, about losing my place. So I said, "I think I know who. There's a ninth grader, Georgina Lowe. Georgie, she's pretty good. She's the one I'd put in." I wondered who had been put into my place. Lisa hadn't told me and I hadn't asked.

"What does that mean, being good at cheerleading?"

"Georgie's got really good coordination, she . . . her sense of rhythm is terrific. She's pretty and kind of enthusiastic. Even when practice is hard, even though she knows she'll have to wait a year or two to be on the squad,

she always works as hard as she can. She always comes to
the games and tells us what we looked like. She's outgoing
and nice, and she's got a good figure— She always looks
like she's having fun, I guess that's probably really
important."

"Is she a friend of yours?"

"She's only fourteen."

"You're not much older."

"Yeah, but— Except for the cheerleading squad, we
don't have anything in common."

"Then friends are people you have things in common
with?"

"Sure, because you can feel comfortable with them."

There was a little silence.

"Then you don't think that opposites attract."

"That's what they say about love," I reminded her.

There was another little silence.

"So you don't think of me as a friend," she said.

"You're a grown-up."

"Ah." She smiled. I could see why that amused her.
"And I'm married."

"And pregnant," I added, without thinking, just as if she
was a friend.

"What about your friends, do you have a lot in
common?"

"It's not as if we're all the same. But even though we're
different, we think about things, we have the same
standards. And things."

Even as I said that I could see that it wasn't true. But I
didn't mention that to Mrs. Hughes-Pincke. "We've been
friends for years. We're really comfortable together," I
said.

"Well, I'll see you tomorrow," Mrs. Hughes-Pincke
said. She hoisted herself up out of the chair, with a little *ouff*
sound. "Do you want me to leave the door open?"

"Please," I said, waving back at her from the bed, then

turning on the TV. It was a game show, with housewife-type contestants and an occasional man. I sat watching it, working up my dislike of it; because the gray, cold feelings that waited for me at night had started to reach out around my heart, and I could keep them away by disliking the TV show. With the door open, I wouldn't embarrass myself by crying. Because Lisa, who was the only one to talk to me, when she talked to me she wasn't talking to me the way we used to. Of course, I reminded myself as the lunch tray was set down in front of me, Lisa was the most grown up of us, so of course she would talk to me as a grown-up.

A lady won two thousand, four hundred and fifty-seven dollars and decided not to come back the next day to try to win more. She and her husband, she said, had dreamed for years of going to Hawaii, and now they could. She didn't want to risk losing the money. She didn't want to be greedy. She had prayed that they would be able to go, and now they could and that was enough for her. The quizmaster, who had a few minutes to spare, I guess, tried to tease her into coming back and trying for more.

My father had a business lunch and my mother had to take Francie to the dentist, so she wouldn't come by until later in the afternoon. I settled back to an afternoon of the soaps. I kept myself occupied during the commercials by counting out how many more days it was until I could go home, how many Mondays and Tuesdays, and how many hours, and then I took a sheet of paper and started figuring out how many minutes.

If I started down the slide, as the minutes of the afternoon ticked by, I caught myself up by listening to the noises from the TV and switching the channel, or setting out a game of clock solitaire. Clock solitaire takes a long time to play out, especially if you have to set it out on a bed.

I was sitting up in my pink quilted bed jacket, with the cards spread in a circle on the bed and the "Roadrunner Show" on TV, when Rosamunde Webber came into my room. She stopped just inside the door and just stared at me, for about half a minute.

I just stared right back, with the squeaky cartoon voices in the air.

Rosamunde looked like always, in a big blue wind-breaker with PAL on it, in denim overalls that did nothing for her figure, her brown hair thick and curly in two ponytails at the sides of her head, her face all wrinkled up around her beady eyes, the way it got when she was thinking hard. She had her hands jammed into the pockets of the windbreaker.

"You look terrible," Rosamunde said, without moving. We all agreed that her voice was the only attractive thing about her. She has a low voice that sounds grainy, as if she were always just a little bit hoarse. "You weren't taking drugs or anything, were you?"

"No." I was shocked.

"I didn't think so, but anything's possible. Are you going to ask me in?"

"Sure," I said. I turned off the TV and opened my mouth to tell her to come in and sit down.

But she hadn't waited to be asked. She slouched down in the visitor's chair. "You do you know. Look terrible. You look like death warmed over. Are you all right?" she demanded.

I didn't know what to say.

"No, that was really stupid, even for me. What is it, is the food that bad? I've never been in a hospital—what a *place*. All the way up here I was half-convinced somebody, like some nurse or a passing doctor, was going to look at me and grab me to tell me I have some fatal disease. Don't you feel that way? Hospitals scare me, I'll tell you." She stood up and moved to the window, hoisting herself up to sit on the sill. "Doesn't it scare you?" she demanded.

I shook my head, no. "Anyway," I said, getting my manners back, "how are you?"

"Well," she said, her face wrinkled again and her eyes staring at me, "I've got this ache in my little finger joint on my left hand, which might be juvenile arthritis, and I think I'm going to have to get reading glasses, or something, because of headaches, either that or I'm developing sinus problems, I haven't decided which."

"Oh," I said, trying not to show that wasn't what I meant, and she'd taken my question seriously.

"Joke," Rosamunde said. "It was a joke."

That made me feel pretty stupid. "Oh," I said again.

"You really do look terrible. Are you eating?"

The staring was getting through to me. "Of course," I said. I was going to say something about hospital food but she didn't give me time.

"I've always heard that the food's bad in hospitals."

"It's not great."

"Not great? C'mon, Izzy, you can have a negative thought."

I resented that. "It's not that bad, not at all, considering. It's just bland."

"Bland? Like what? Like those steamed hamburgers you get at Thruway cafeterias?"

"Not that bad. It's—institutional cooking."

"I guess then rice would be OK."

She was right. "Yeah, the rice is usually pretty good."

We had run out of things to say. She swung her legs back and forth, then sort of looked at herself in her faded overalls and slipped down from the windowsill. She wandered around the room. I sat in the bed and watched her, wondering why she had come, wondering how long she was going to stay.

"Is that your cat?" she pointed.

"Lisa gave it to me."

"Cute," Rosamunde said, in her low voice. "Very cute."

I heard her sarcasm, but I didn't answer it.

"So, what do you do all day?" She was down at the end of the bed.

"Watch TV."

"How can you stand it?"

I shrugged. I knew what she was thinking, about how that was like the kind of person nobody wanted to be, who just sat and watched TV all day. Eating candy and chips and watching TV.

"It would drive me nuts," Rosamunde said. She opened the door into the bathroom. "Hey, that's not bad, a private suite, not bad at all. I guess, though, you won't have to worry about paying for college, will you? That's pretty funny, if Marco Griggers—who is one of the world's prime jackasses—pays to send you to college." She went on and on, standing by the open bathroom door and watching me. "You should have seen him last week. I thought he was going to wet his pants he was so scared, like a cross between a jackass and a rabbit. He kept cornering Suzy and asking her questions. Are you going to bring charges?"

"Charges?"

"You aren't that dumb, Izzy."

I wasn't but her voice when she said it sounded like if I wasn't that dumb I was pretty close.

"Marco says he can't remember anything, but he's a liar. I guess he was drinking, I hear those parties get a little wild sometimes, or maybe smoking dope or something. That's what I think," she said.

She waited, but I didn't say anything. I was ready for her to leave.

Rosamunde began fiddling with the walker. She moved to stand inside it, and then leaned her weight on it and took a few steps. She went toward the door, and I hoped she would go out it, but she didn't. She turned around, playing with the walker, talking.

"The old club loyalty, is that it? Gees, this thing makes me feel decrepit, really decrepit. Does it do that to you?"

"Oh," I said, as if that was just the beginning of a sentence.

"It's clumsy," Rosamunde said. "I didn't think you'd lie about it. But then, who knows, maybe it's just because I know he's such a twit, the way he spent the first week twitching, and now he's hinting that since his reflexes are good, his trained reflexes, he doesn't think it could have been him driving. Maybe I should be feeling sorry for him instead. Do you think?"

I didn't think anything, except that I really wished she'd go away. I couldn't think of what I could safely say before she would start in again.

Rosamunde turned the walker so that she faced me. She raised her right leg, bending her calf up behind it from the knee. "*You* don't feel sorry for him, do you? Nobody can be that nice, not even you. Suzy does—but Suzy does all her thinking with her glands."

"Suzy's smart," I reminded Rosamunde.

"You're kidding." She looked honestly amazed.

"You know she is. She always gets top grades." I thought, with relief, of what I could say to get her to leave: "You're just jealous."

"Jealous of Suzy?" She stood there, short and clumsy-looking in her baggy pants that covered thick legs, her hair dull and its style unflattering. "Why would I be jealous of Suzy?"

"Because she's smart and she looks good and she's popular," I snapped. I figured, that would get rid of her.

Rosamunde stood there on one leg, like an overweight crane, and thought. Her eyes kind of glazed over, the way they sometimes did in class. "I hope not," she finally said. "I'd like to think better of myself."

I groaned inside my head.

With her leg still folded behind her, Rosamunde tried to take a step. She shoved the walker a couple of inches in front of her, then sort of hopped up to it. The walker rocked under her weight. She stumbled up against it, her leg went back onto the floor, and she leaned on the top railing, as if against a fence, to ask me, "How do you do it? And how do those old people do it? I mean, they're pretty weak. I guess you just get used to it, but I'm so uncoordinated, I bet I never would. Do you think?"

I didn't have time to say anything.

"I thought—when the news first broke—that it wasn't so bad. Losing a leg. As a handicap, I mean. I guess I didn't know anything about it," she said.

I didn't say a word. I knew, if I opened my mouth, no words would come out, or the ones that came would be so rude I'd be ashamed of myself for saying them. My teeth were squeezed together.

She pushed the walker away from her. "I've been even stupider than usual, haven't I?" But she didn't give me any chance to answer that. "I wondered, you know—if—well, if you had the guts for—you know, this—but I just didn't have any idea what it was like."

I made my mouth into a polite smile. "Listen, Rosamunde, it was really nice of you to come and see me, but I'm awfully tired—"

"I'm going," she said. "I've got to go and meet my father. He's my ride home; he's getting off at four."

I nodded, not wanting to delay her by a single word.

Rosamunde hesitated in the doorway, as if there was something more she wanted to say, but she didn't do any more than look at me, where I sat in the hospital bed. I kept on smiling and she moved out of sight, her shoulders hunched up under the oversized windbreaker.

For a long time I just sat there without moving, letting the solitude of the room wrap around me and soothe me. Weird, it was definitely weird, she was really weird. What was Rosamunde Webber doing coming to see me in the hospital anyway? I was almost amused by the visit, now that it was over. I hoped Lisa would call that night, so we could talk to one another about the weirdness of it.

I remembered how Rosamunde had looked, standing in the walker and trying to move. I wondered how I looked, standing in it, with half a leg hanging down. And I wanted—with a longing that rose up from my heart and ran all around my body with the bloodstreams, a longing so strong that there was no room for anything else, any other thought, any other feeling—I wanted to go home. I wanted to be home. I wanted to go home and be home and to have all of this over with, I wanted things back to normal. I had taken all I could take, I thought, and I wanted to get out of the hospital and go home, so it would be finished.

At that point my mother came in. She didn't look at me, more than to bend over and kiss my forehead, to brush my hair off it. "You need a haircut, Angel," she said, "but I've just seen the— There was a girl, probably a couple of years older than you and— Oh, not at all pretty, and not well-dressed—in front of the elevators, when I got out. And she was crying. Right out in public, almost sobbing. She looked awful. I wonder what happened?"

I shook my head. I didn't know.

"I felt so sorry for her, but I don't know her. I thought I might ask her, or say something—what the twins would call a full blast of maternal feelings." She smiled. "Oh, Izzy, we are so lucky to have each other. She looked—like she had no one in the world. Like all the troubles in the world were on her shoulders. And her hair in ridiculous childish ponytails and somebody else's windbreaker—as if nobody cared how she looked, anyway?"

Rosamunde? But that didn't make any sense.

"How do you feel?" my mother asked, sitting down in the chair. "I wish you'd try that needlepoint kit. I worry about you getting bored."

"I'm fine," I said, trying to make sense out of what she had told me, and the last fifteen minutes. It wasn't as if we

were friends, Rosamunde and I, and she certainly hadn't
looked upset when she left the room. I thought about asking
my mother about it, but then I thought that I didn't want to
hear what she thought until I knew what I thought. If I
didn't know what I thought first, I'd probably just take her
ideas for my own.

"How's Francie?" I asked, which is always a good
diversionary tactic.

"Oh, Francie." My mother smiled, half amused and half
worried. "She misses you terribly, I know, but her ways of
showing it . . ."

She went on about Francie, and I half listened to her,
while the other half of my mind was seeing pictures: of
Rosamunde restlessly pacing this room, then in the walker,
then standing crying in the hospital corridor. All the time,
behind those pictures, like an overvoice, I heard
Rosamunde relentlessly talking at me, about Marco and
Suzy and being crippled.

The phone broke into my mother's conversation and my
thoughts. I picked it up without thinking, thinking if it was
Lisa I'd arrange to call her back, although I was no longer
sure that I would tell her about my weird visitor.

"Izzy? I'm downstairs and—I feel so stupid calling; it's a
pay phone—but I wanted to tell you I know—"

"Who is this?"

"Rosamunde. I'm sorry, I should have said. But I have to
say this fast, before I get my foot in my mouth again. I think
I shouldn't have come and I'm really sorry if I upset you."

"I'm not upset," I protested. At least, I wasn't in the way
she meant.

"Listen to me," she said. "Can't you listen?"

"OK."

"I had it all figured out, see, what I was going to say
when I came in and what we'd talk about and all. But it
didn't work out that way, and I should have known that,
because that's what mostly happens to me. It's the kind of

stupid thing I do." Then she waited for me to answer. I
didn't know what I was supposed to say.

"Anyway," I said finally, "what were you planning to
say?"

"It was just a stupid joke."

"Yeah, but what was it?"

"I was just going to ask, 'What's a nice girl like you
doing in a place like this?' "

I was utterly surprised. Utterly surprised. How could she
have thought of that too?

"I told you it was stupid. Then I lied about my father,
he's not coming until five, and I just wanted to tell you I
don't think I should have come."

"Why did you anyway?" I asked. It was easier to talk to
a telephone than to Rosamunde.

"Oh—they were talking like it was so terrible."

I knew who she meant by they. Her voice took on a
special tone, as if my friends weren't even worth naming.

"And they were so stupid—I don't care what you say,
they are not nice people and they are stupid—and I thought
I'd help you put things into perspective. You know? Do my
comic routine, and cheer you up because—they were saying
how they just couldn't bear seeing you, it was too painful
for them—"

She must have heard my silence.

"See? I never can say it right. And I'm not much better
than they are, am I? I am a little better, no matter what
you're thinking—"

At that I smiled, because she wasn't going to give them
an inch, however much she might be sincerely sorry for
what she named her stupidity.

"—because, of course, when I saw you and you
looked—"

"Terrible was your word," I reminded her, thinking of
what she would have seen: the girl in the bed and the flat
blanket where the leg was not.

"Yeah, really down and trying to look cheerful. Well, anyway. That's what I wanted to say and I feel better."

"I'm glad to hear that," I said, sarcastic.

"OK, OK. But should I come back again, do you think?"

"Why?" I asked.

"Well, then maybe I won't. I probably shouldn't."

"Wait," I said. "I didn't mean *that*," I said. "Really," I said.

"The trouble with you, Isobel Lingard," her throaty voice said, "is that you're so nice, I can't even tell when you're being nice and when you mean what you're saying."

She hung up before I could answer.

"Who was that?" my mother asked.

"Just someone from school."

"What did he want?"

"*She*."

"All right, what did *she* want?"

I shook my head, because my throat was suddenly tight. My mother was thinking along the same lines, I could tell: The boys seemed to have completely disappeared, the ones who used to call up and hang around, or ask me out. Everything was not going to be what I wanted, ever again.

"We are not going to let this ruin your life," my mother said, angry.

8

I could understand it. I mean, I wouldn't have wanted to be friends with a cripple either. I had passed Jeannette Wheatley in the halls and pretended she wasn't there: I had felt my eyes being drawn to the right side of her face, where the skin was thick and lumpy, with white scars and unnaturally smooth hot-pink flesh, where the drawn muscles pulled so that her mouth was always smiling on the right side and her right eyelid slanted down over half of her eye. I had felt how my eyes were always drawn to stare at her deformity and how I made it seem as if I didn't see anything wrong by letting my glance kind of skate over her face and away. I had never spoken a word to her. Because she was so horrible to look at.

That was the normal reaction. I could understand it, even though—thinking about it—I didn't think I had acted very nice. I didn't even know, for example, whether or not she had a good figure. I didn't even know what color her hair was, although I knew how she wore it. She wore it Veronica Lake style, a long curtain of hair falling over the right side of her face. I knew that only because I had noticed how she tried to hide her scars, and how she couldn't. I hadn't even really looked at her, even though I'd stared at her. As if her troubles were contagious. As if something would show up on my skin if I said hello.

I wondered if I was being punished, somehow, for thinking I was nice while I wasn't, not really. I remembered the kind of talking Lisa and I did about Suzy, when she wasn't there. We talked as if we were concerned with her well-being, but really we were talking about whether she was promiscuous, and how far we were sure she had gone with some boy or another, and how far we thought maybe she might have gone. I never said anything about it and neither did Lisa or Lauren, but I always found talking about what Suzy got up to something of a turn-on, like reading the juicy parts of a book.

Which wasn't a nice thing at all, for a friend.

I slipped down into the gray watery feeling and could not rise up. I was tired, too tired to do much, and the daily PT sessions wore me down even more, the black nurse with her eyes always on me, never saying anything as I tried to drag myself along the rubber pathway, hauling my left leg along, up twelve feet, turn, back twelve feet, every step dragging, every minute dragging, until she said I could stop. The only thing I did that I liked was I never asked her if I could stop, no matter how my shoulders ached. After that first day, I didn't ask her for anything.

Until that Friday, at the end of the second week in the hospital. I don't know what was so wrong about that day, why it should have been especially hard for me to get through the PT session. It wasn't as if I had my period or anything, or anything new and bad had happened. The only thing that had happened that week at all was that Rosamunde Webber had come to see me, and that wasn't exactly bad even if it wasn't exactly good. Otherwise, the week had been the wet, gray world that was all I had left now, and a list of the things that hadn't happened, like who hadn't called. I was even, that morning, sort of looking forward to the next couple of days. At least, I wouldn't have to have PT. I wouldn't have to see the black beady eyes looking at me, bored with me. At least I wouldn't have to pretend to be brave for a couple of days.

It was like a vacation coming up, but somehow, that day, I knew I couldn't. Not any more. I just couldn't. So I said, about ten trips down the line, "Please, could I stop?"

She looked at her wristwatch and shook her head.

"But I'm tired."

She shook her head.

I knew how helpless I was. I couldn't even get back to my room on my own. Her eyes were watching me as I draped myself over the railings of the walkway, just to have a little rest. Her little eyes didn't like me a bit, and they were glad I was unhappy. She was glad I was crippled, I thought, because I was a privileged person, a white girl from a well-to-do background.

I didn't look at her, didn't say anything else, just did what she told me and then rode back to my room, as silent as she was. I just wanted to be alone in my room. I just wanted her to be gone.

She hefted me into bed and pulled up my covers, as if I couldn't do that for myself. She didn't look at me and I didn't look at her. But I felt her leave the room and felt the door close. I didn't see it because I had doubled up over my stomach and tears were streaming down my face, and I felt like I couldn't breathe.

I didn't make any noise, and I guess that is why Mrs. Hughes-Pincke was so surprised to see me. Because usually I was sitting up in bed with a smile on my face.

At least she didn't ask me how I was feeling. Instead, she opened a drawer of the night table and took out a box of tissues. She put the rolling table over my lap and put the tissues on that. I hauled one out and blew my nose. Mrs. Hughes-Pincke sat down in her chair.

But I couldn't stop myself. Things were piling up, over

me, swallowing me up. I wanted it to be my mother there,
who would wrap her arms around me if she saw me like
this, who would care about me. I wanted to be home, home
in my own bed, in my own room, with my own family
around me. And I wanted none of this ever to have
happened.

It wasn't fair, it just wasn't fair at all. It was Marco who
should have been crippled because it was his fault.

All Mrs. Hughes-Pincke did was sit in the chair and look
at me. I knew she was looking at me, I could feel it.

Finally, I could stop. Then I was embarrassed. I took a
long time blowing my nose and wiping my eyes. I took a
long time gathering up the wet tissues, dropping them into
the wastebasket and feeling—I was squirming inside, and I
wanted her to go away so badly I actually said it aloud.

"Could you please go away?" My voice was tiny and
high and thick with mucus. Hearing myself started me off
again. She didn't get up, she wouldn't even go away, and it
wasn't polite to sit and stare at someone as if someone were
a TV show not a person with feelings.

"There's nothing to be ashamed of, Isobel," she finally
said. I didn't look at her. My hands fiddled with the box of
tissues, turning it around and around, laying it on its side.
"Crying is like—a pressure valve on a radiator. You've got
to let off pressure sometimes."

I shook my head. She didn't understand. How could she
understand? She had both of her legs and a husband and she
was going to have a baby.

"And it's not as if you don't have something to cry
about," she said.

I didn't look at her. It was like PT—sooner or later my
time would be up and she'd go away. It wasn't as if she even
cared personally about me.

"You've got to let off pressure, just like a radiator."

If I were a radiator, I thought, I'd be thrown out, because
I was broken.

"But what happened?" Mrs. Hughes-Pincke asked, her voice cool. "I mean, today, especially, what happened."

"I was just tired," I said, "and I wanted to stop the walking because it doesn't do any good with the cast, and all. It's not making me any better, I'm not getting any better at it." I stopped speaking then, because my voice was getting high and thick again. "And she wouldn't let me."

"Who?"

"The nurse."

"What's her name?"

"I don't know. Because she doesn't like me."

"Oh, I doubt that," Mrs. Hughes-Pincke said.

I shrugged.

"There'll be some reason, Isobel. She's a professional. You're not eating enough to keep your strength up, you know." Mrs. Hughes-Pincke was assuming what adults always do, that it was the kid's fault somehow. "Crying is healthy, Isobel," she said, holding my eyes with hers. "People who don't sometimes just—blow up. Like radiators."

"I'm not a radiator," I pointed out.

"No. I know. I'm just trying to tell you that what you're feeling is absolutely normal."

I looked out the window. Because I wasn't normal anymore.

"Isobel, believe me, I know how hard this is on you. You're so young—I'd be surprised if anything really bad has happened to you before. It's no consolation to hear about worse things, is it?"

"No," I said. At least she understood that.

"Nobody ever knows, until they've been through something, how they'll do," Mrs. Hughes-Pincke said, but not really talking to me.

"It's not fair," I wailed.

"Agreed, it's not fair at all," Mrs. Hughes-Pincke answered. I wiped at my eyes. At least I wasn't feeling so embarrassed about crying any more. She was going to have to watch me cry if she didn't have the manners to give me privacy. She sat very still, but not relaxed. She had one hand resting on her belly, as if she could touch the baby inside. "Isobel, have you looked at your amputated leg yet?"

I shook my head.

"You should. I guess you'll be starting swimming when the cast comes off, so you'll have to. Dr. Carstairs did beautiful work. It's smooth, the flaps of flesh, and the seam is buried under. You've got your knee."

"So what?" It was my leg I wanted.

"Then when you have your prosthetic leg, you'll walk more normally. That's so what."

"On a wooden leg?" She could tell I was being sarcastic.

"Plastic, actually. And yes. Just think about it. If you didn't have a knee, think how you'd walk."

"From the hip, I guess," I said, feeling it. The little Izzy inside my head walked down where I could see her, her whole body swiveling as she dragged her stiff plastic leg. She couldn't bend over either, with her knee gone.

"With your knee intact you'll have some trouble with balance, but—"

The little Izzy went haltingly along. Step with the left leg. Hesitate. Pull up right thigh. Put down plastic foot—a foot like a fake doll's foot—that pale flesh color dolls have that doesn't look a bit real and that waxy smoothness. I emptied my head.

"—with practice, you'll be surprised."

I didn't say anything. She waited. "OK," I said, agreeing with whatever she wanted me to agree with.

"Our time's up," she said. "It's more than up. But don't be too hard on yourself, Isobel. Would you like me to come tomorrow?"

"Tomorrow's Saturday," I reminded her.

"If you'd like me to, I could come in. You have a seven-day-a-week disability. I don't see why I need my weekends off."

I'd never thought about it that way. I didn't want to think about it that way. "No, thanks," I said. "But thanks."

"If you feel like—like exploding, though, the nurses outside know where to find me."

If I felt like exploding, I thought, I'd rather be left alone to do it. But I nodded politely.

I felt the same kind of politeness on my face when I asked Dr. Epstein if I could watch when he changed the bandages on my leg that afternoon. He hesitated. "Well, if you want to. It's not pretty," he said.

"But Mrs. Hughes-Pincke said—"

Dr. Epstein sat down on my bed. "Dr. Carstairs did a beautiful job, don't you worry about that. But your flesh has had a severe shock. You know about shock? It's not just mental. It'll take a while to heal, your flesh will. And—I'm not sure it's a good time; you're so pale already and you're not eating well. You look like Dora—I keep thinking that."

"Who's Dora?" I asked him, because I didn't want to think about what he'd been saying.

"In Dickens, *David Copperfield*. It's mostly because your eyes look so big. You always did that, you know, especially when you were little and you had a fever. We could always tell, your parents and I, because you got this big-eyed look to you. I guess, though, if you want to watch—"

I nodded, because . . . because I thought I ought to.

Dr. Epstein just got to work, then. He didn't say anything to me, and he didn't look at me to see how I was reacting. He just took off the adhesive and lifted off the stained bandages. My knee and part of the way up my thigh was red and swollen and stained yellow. I couldn't see the underside, but I could see—when he lifted my leg to wrap fresh bandages underneath and then set it down—that my leg stopped. Cut off. I closed my eyes then and put my head back against the pillow. Inside my head that stupid little Izzy in her leotard still did back flips, but it was hard and heavy going for her and I felt like reaching my hand into my imagination and knocking her over.

I felt Dr. Epstein pull up the blanket, and then his hand on my shoulder, big and strong and squeezing just a little. But he didn't say anything except, "I'll see you tomorrow."

After supper, my parents both came. Francie was spending the night with a friend, so they spent the whole visiting time with me. We played gin rummy. That helped the time pass. My father had a member-guest golf tournament that weekend, and he'd invited some clients to play in it with him, so he wasn't going to be around. I told him I hoped he'd do well and he said he hoped he'd play well enough to keep the account, because a lot of men seemed to feel that anybody who couldn't play golf wasn't capable of managing money. My mother said she'd be back in the morning, and she thought she ought to bring some flowers, because the room was looking pretty bare. I told her I didn't know, that it seemed wasteful because the flowers just got thrown out. "I know what you mean," she said.

I slept, too tired even to wake up and be depressed. Saturday dragged by, after my mother had taken me out for a wheelchair ride and then washed my hair. Then she tried saying something cheerful. "It's been two weeks, there's only four more to go before the cast comes off."

"When can I go home?" I asked.

"Saul says maybe the end of next week."

"This coming next week or next week next week?"

"Oh, this one. Would you like that?"

"Yes," I said.

"You're being so good about it, Lamb."

"Thanks," I said. But I wished I didn't have to wait through all those days.

"Think about what you'd like to have for your welcome home dinner," her voice said.

The afternoon and evening went on by. I listened to the radio some. I took out the needlepoint kit and read the directions. There was nothing else to do so I started on it. I watched some TV. Afternoon snack came. Supper came. Late snack came. In the hall outside my room I could hear people moving and talking, all day long and all evening long. Then the hospital settled into sleep.

I woke up early Sunday, before the sky was even light beyond the window. I went to the bathroom and then climbed back into bed, looking down the long, empty day. Trying to cheer myself up, I put on the pink bedjacket. I sat up waiting in my bed for breakfast to come and go, for the day to come and go. I might go home at the end of the week, I reminded myself.

Early in the morning, an orderly brought in some flowers. As soon as I saw the big pot of chrysanthemums I knew they were from my mother. He put it in the middle of the windowsill, where the blooms shone white against the flat gray sky. I wondered what the temperature was, outside, for my father's golf game. They had said they would try to stop by after the awards dinner. I didn't think they'd be able to, because the dinner would probably end after visiting hours were over.

When the phone rang right after lunch, I was so surprised I almost didn't answer it. I knew that my mother and Francie were watching my father play part of his final round, and I had talked to Joel in the middle of the week. It was Suzy, asking me how I felt, and I wondered if she was going to come visit. She didn't say anything about that, though, just told me her mom said to say hello, and so did Bethy, and asked me when I was going home, and then I did ask her: "Are you going to come by?"

"Oh, I'm sorry, I can't. We're going to the movies; it's all arranged."

"Sounds like fun," I said. "Who's we?"

She hesitated, and then said quickly, "Lisa and Lauren and a couple of other people." I could hear that she was lying.

"And then we're going to grab supper at McDonald's." Suzy heard what she'd said and added quickly, "If we can find anyone to bum a ride with, if anybody who goes has a car. If not maybe we'll walk around to see you. So maybe I'll see you later, OK?" She hung up, and I could almost see the relief on her face as she dropped the phone back into its cradle. Her mother would have been standing behind her, listening and checking to be sure Suzy had done what Ms. Wilkes was making her do. Probably, Ms. Wilkes had refused to give her money for the movie, or something, until she'd called me.

I started on the one o'clock show, an old Roy Rogers cowboy movie. I was sort of curious about Roy Rogers, and all I knew about him was his chain of fast food restaurants. I'd heard his voice, advertising on the radio, and I'd seen big pictures on the walls of the restaurants, with his cowboy hat and all. Roy Rogers was pretty cute, as it turns out; I could see why he had been such a big star, whenever that was. He didn't look much older in the ads I'd seen, but that was probably because of makeup, because I thought he must be pretty old by now. My mother often said that she thought movie stars were taking an awfully big part in our lives, and it was a sign of the times, a bad sign. She was thinking of Reagan, of course. My father, who's a Republican anyway, said that he thought people tended to underestimate what it took to become a movie star. I thought about that, because there was nothing else to think about, while I watched the story begin, with a little western town run by a big, bad, rich rancher. When the phone rang, I answered it without turning the sound down.

"Hey, little sister," Jack's voice said.

"Jack? Wait, let me turn off the TV."

"What are you watching?"

"Nothing, now. How are you?" It was good to hear his voice.

"I'm OK. I haven't flunked out yet."

"Dad'll be pleased."

"Yeah."

There was a brief silence.

"Where are you?" I asked.

"Where am I? At school. I'm in a pretty dingy pay phone, but some of the phone numbers on the wall sound interesting."

"Yeah?" He sounded like himself, to me.

"But I thought I'd call you up first."

"Before the interesting calls?" I joked.

There was another silence. I wished he was there where I could see him. I couldn't tell if he really was all right. It wasn't like Jack to let silences happen.

"Are you all right, Jack?"

"I told you, fine. I'm fine." But his voice was gloomy.

At that moment, Rosamunde Webber appeared in my doorway, dragging a shopping cart with a big carton on it. She sort of looked at me, just enough to make eye contact, then she pulled her carrier on into the room.

"I'm just fine, nothing wrong with *me*," Jack said.

"Are you drunk?"

"No. Sober. Listen, Izzy, I guess I shouldn't have called."

I tried to think across the silence. I knew what was wrong with him, but I couldn't think of anything to say because what was wrong with Jack was what was wrong with me.

"I guess you agree about that." He sounded angry now. "I *told* Joel."

I grabbed at that topic of conversation. "Where is he?"

"In the library, getting smarter, getting better grades. As if—" He stopped. I could hear words choking up against his throat and I didn't know what to say, but I knew I had to say something. My mouth flapped a little, and I could feel words choking up against my throat.

Rosamunde stood watching. It couldn't have lasted as long as it felt like it was lasting.

"I told him," Jack finally started, "I told him, you know me, that we're alike and you—" He stopped again. I just clutched the phone against my ear, trying to think of something to say to him.

Rosamunde grabbed the phone away from me. "Who is this?" she demanded.

"What are you doing? That's my phone." How, I wondered, could anyone be so rude?

"Jack? Jack who? Jack-ass if you ask me," she said into the phone. "Calling Izzy up and I don't know what you were saying, but whatever it was it wasn't any too smart, but she's too nice to say—" Then Rosamunde stopped speaking. I could hear Jack's angry voice, and it almost made me giggle to see the surprise on Rosamunde's face.

"Oh," she said, when he'd finished. For just that one word, she seemed about to apologize. "Yeah, I remember you. . . . No, not unless you promise not to talk about whatever you were talking about. . . . It couldn't have been nothing," she insisted. Jack's voice got louder. "Then you'd better hang up, hadn't you."

Rosamunde looked at me and made swirling motions with her forefinger at her right temple.

"Make a list, ten topics of conversation. Then call. No, I won't give you Izzy back. You can go somewhere and cool off and call later. . . . Yes, I'll be gone by then. . . . Who am I?" She grinned at me. "I'm nobody, who are you? Are you nobody too?"

I almost laughed. I'd heard that poem in school more than once. I guessed Jack must have, too, and I knew how he felt about poetry. Rosamunde held the phone away from her ear.

"He hung up," she said.

I was mixed between being angry at her for grabbing the

phone and amused at the way she talked Jack down and grateful to her for getting me out of a situation I couldn't seem to handle.

"That's my brother," I told her.

"Then he should know better."

"Honestly," I started. She was standing there, lumpy in her overalls and her PAL windbreaker that was sizes too big and her thick hair just sloppy and loose, with a hairband not doing any good. Strands of hair were almost sticking into her mouth.

"Well, he should," she insisted. Then she seemed to run out of steam. "Oh, God, I'm sorry, I really did butt in. I did it again, didn't I? No, don't tell me."

"OK, I won't," I told her.

"But you looked like you were about to cry," she said, apologizing in her deep voice. "And you never do, and—I thought it might be some crank caller, or something—"

I wondered how she could think I never cried. "Just my brother. Although he was acting sort of strange."

"Sort of? He sounded certifiable. He sounded like he was about to rip the whole phone off the wall."

"That's what Jack does. When he's angry. When he's really upset he gets angry. It's the first time I've talked to him," I told her.

"Oh," she said. "Oh. He must be really upset. He was yelling."

"Yelling's better than when he doesn't say anything, because when he doesn't say anything you don't know what he'll do. He wasn't saying anything, then, when you—"

"Weird," she said, thinking.

"He had a friend who died of cancer, the twins both did, and Joel was scared and sad, but Jack—Jack took a bat and broke every single one of the models he'd ever made. It was the day of the funeral, and they didn't go—I remember— but they knew. They must have been eight or nine. Jack

spent all afternoon smashing the things. Even my father said
we'd better leave him be."

Rosamunde stood there, her eyes kind of glazed.

"I guess maybe I better do something to apologize, like
write a note?"

"No. You can't do that. He'd be furious. He doesn't like
anyone to know he has—feelings."

"Boy, does he sound like a terrific guy," she said,
sarcastic. Before I could tell her what I thought of that, she
went on. "But he does have my sympathy. I hope maybe he
does take the phone off the wall. Then he can call you back
when he's calmed down and doesn't make you look like—
somebody's sticking needles under your nails. Listen, do
you want me to go? I know, I've sort of pushed in, and you
might rather have me go away. So I'll go now, I think, but
I'll leave you the carton. There's some stuff—I better take
the carrier with me, I borrowed it from our neighbor and
she's not too keen about lending stuff to teenagers. I'm
sorry, Izzy. I guess I'm always apologizing. But I'll go now
and—see you sometime, OK?"

g

Rosamunde meant what she was saying. She had turned her back to me and was lifting the carton off of the carrier. She didn't say she was going just so I'd ask her please to stay. I guessed that was part of her problem, what made her uncomfortable to be with; she didn't talk like other people. She just said what she meant.

"Most of this is just on loan. I don't know if that's rude to say, but it's true, so you'll have to give it back." She put the carton on the floor and then looked at it. She looked at me. "I should put it on your table, do you think? Because you can't reach it and—can you get out of bed? You can't, can you? You'd fall over or something." Then she turned pink. "That was a stupid thing to say."

"Why don't you stay anyway?" I said. Actually, I mumbled it, because I knew it was what I should say, and I sort of wanted her to stay, but I also wanted her to go.

"No, listen, it's OK, I understand," she said. "I mean, I know I always say these stupid things, but I'm pretty smart." She sort of smiled and jammed her hands into the pockets of her windbreaker. "I can understand that you want me to go, and you're too nice to say so, but it's OK, really, it doesn't really bother me—"

"I wouldn't mind," I interrupted her, because she was rattling on like Suzy. "It can't hurt, can it?"

"Yes," she answered. "Yes, it could. That's what worries me, about hurting your feelings, or something. Inadvertently."

I didn't know what to answer.

"And besides—" She hesitated.

"I'd like you to," I said. "At least, I think I would, if you want the exact truth. If you want the exact truth, it gets pretty depressing, sometimes."

"Really? Boy, I'm glad to hear that." Rosamunde took off her jacket and draped it on the visitor's chair. She folded up the carrier and rested it against the wall. "I don't know why she's so fussy about that, it couldn't have cost her more than a dollar-fifty at a yard sale, the way it's rusted up. Because I was afraid you were some sort of supergirl, you know? Or, maybe, you were being brave and everything, and you'd probably go crazy if you were making those impossible demands on yourself. Or, I guess you could be too stupid to figure out how bad it is."

I just sat there in the hospital bed. You didn't *say* things like that. Rosamunde looked at my face and then put her hand up over her eyes. I guessed she knew all right that you didn't say things like that, only she never knew it until after she'd said them.

On the other hand, I guessed what she said was true.

"You know," I admitted, "I think it's a little bit of all three of those."

Rosamunde uncovered her eyes. "I knew I wasn't wrong. About you." Her low voice rang, almost like music. "I wasn't sure, but I knew it. OK, here we go. Presents—well, some of them are presents but remember—"

"I know, some of them are on loan."

"Do you mind that? I can't just go out and—buy things."

I shook my head, because I didn't mind.

"You need a haircut, Izzy."

"So do you," I answered quickly.

"Yeah, but I always do, and you always look well kept. Or made up, or something."

"My doctor told me I looked like somebody in a book," I told her shoulders. She was ripping tape off the top of the carton and not watching me.

"Yeah? Who?"

"Someone named Dora, in—"

"*David Copperfield*." Rosamunde looked up. She was crouching behind the box. All I could see in it was piles of crumpled newspaper. "Have you read it?"

"No."

"She dies," Rosamunde said.

"That's good news."

"He didn't mean that." I watched her big hands, with chewed nails, tossing out newspaper balls. Her hair wasn't a bad color, but it was a terrible texture, wiry-curly, and too thick. She pulled out a piece of cloth, bright reds and blues and yellows. When she unfolded it, I could see greens, too, in the batik. Rosamunde had brought a roll of masking tape, and she used that to hang the cloth on the wall beside the window. "It's not elegant, but it'll hold, I think."

"What is it?" I asked.

"My mother made it for me, when I was small. When she thought batik was her medium, but it isn't. I kind of like it though, don't you?"

It was a long piece of cloth. All up it, hidden underwater and behind flowers and on trees and in the sky, were animals—zoo animals, elephants and monkeys, brightly colored fish and brown turtles, parrots, tigers, giraffes. "It's neat," I said. It was perfect for a little kid, to look at and look at and find all the animals.

"I always thought so. I thought it would cheer up your room some. Then I brought you this—"

She held up a ceramic vase, made of rough clay glazed to earthy tones.

"But you don't have any flowers to put in it. Has the enthusiasm dwindled?" She moved the chrysanthemums aside and put the tall vase in its place. "My mother made that, too. She's a potter, as it turns out."

"Oh," I said. It wasn't my kind of pottery, because my style is the smooth curved kind, with designs painted on it, like the Chinese vases or the Danish ones.

"If you don't like it, I could take it back. She was nervous about letting me bring it down anyway, so that would be OK. She wants to give it to the Treasure Trove for Christmas sales."

"Does she sell things at the Treasure Trove?"

"Mugs and vases mostly, sometimes a platter. They like her stuff."

"My mother shops there," I said, looking at the vase with a more interested eye.

"All the best people do. A lot of them buy my mom's stuff."

"Aren't you proud of her?"

Rosamunde crouched back by the box before she answered me. "Sometimes I am. But sometimes I'm jealous, too, because I don't have any talents like that; and sometimes, when I can see she'd like to have a creative daughter, I just feel guilty. You know? I brought these, too, I didn't know which you liked."

These were games in boxes, Clue and Othello, Parchesi, Yahtzee. "No Monopoly?" I asked, as she piled them up on top of my table.

"No, you'd just get depressed; I'm really good at Monopoly. I wish we had Trivial Pursuit, but we're waiting to see if Santa can afford it. It sounds like our kind of game."

"How many of you are there?"

"Six. I'm the oldest, and I've got three younger sisters and two little brothers."

"Twins?"

"No. Why should they be twins? Oh, I get it, because of yours. Do you have anyone younger?"

"Francie. She's ten."

"It's a drag being oldest. All the responsibilities and no pay. Then—" She lifted out a small cooler, the kind that will keep just a six-pack of beer cold, and two shoe boxes. "Can you get those games out of the way?" I moved them onto the bed. "The eats." Rosamunde passed all three up to me and a roll of paper towels. "Don't open them yet. I've just got these left."

One after another, she pulled out library books. Two of them were big collections of cartoons. "I didn't know what you liked, so I tried one of everything. If you don't like horror, you ought to skip this one."

"I will," I promised her, looking at the black cover, with a pair of evil green eyes on it and drops of blood. She stacked half a dozen books up on my night table.

"Funny, it always seems like so much more when you're putting things together, you know? It never seems like as much when you're finished—sort of like Christmas."

I looked around my room, which no longer looked neat and clean. It looked almost messy, and certainly lived in. It didn't really look like me, anymore; but I liked the way it looked, just because it was different from the dull way it had been looking.

"This is great," I said.

"I don't know about that," Rosamunde said. "Can I sit on the bed, is that OK?"

"Sure."

She sat down awkwardly, half-sideways.

"I can't move the cast much," I apologized.

"No problem. Do you feel like you still have the other

leg? I read, somewhere, that amputees can still feel—they thing they can feel stuff. Do you?"

She was just curious, I reminded myself. I shook my head. Rosamunde was busy opening the cooler and taking the tops off the boxes. She lifted fat little pastry squares out of the cooler.

"They're hot. Fresh from the oven. Piroshkis, I love them."

"Did you make them?"

"I'm a pretty good cook, especially baking. I wasn't sure how this thing would work, for keeping things hot, but it does OK, doesn't it?"

Then she opened the shoe boxes. "And for dessert, apple turnovers with individually wrapped chunks of cheese. Do you like cheddar?"

"I don't know. What color is it?"

"Orange, Izzy, cheddar is orange and good cheddar is aged, and it's clear you don't know anything about food."

I finished chewing and swallowed the first pastry, the pillow-shaped piroshki. "I know that these are good."

"That's just the beginning." She bit into one and chewed happily. "I almost never make them, so I always forget— How is your appetite, anyway?"

"For these it seems to be OK. Or maybe I'm finally hungry."

"I should have brought some fresh fruit."

"You should have brought something to drink." I heard what I'd said. I sounded ungrateful. "I'm sorry."

"Why? I thought it was a joke. I'll think about it for next time."

"Can you do this *again*?"

"Only on weekends. I've got a regular babysitting job. But—you haven't begun to know the breadth of my repertoire."

"I'll get fat."

"You could use a little fat."

"The trouble is," I told her, "that that's all it is, fat. I'm losing my muscle tone."

"It's only been two weeks," she protested. "And we're young; it can't go that fast. Besides, aren't you doing some kind of physical therapy? That should do something. As long as you're eating."

"The food's pretty dull."

"So I guess you're not too hungry?"

"Not most of the time. I am now," I said. I took a second little pillow, ate it, and took a third. I looked at the vase sitting on the windowsill, with the sky behind it. It didn't suit the curtains, but "It looks good with the sky, your mother's vase."

"I'll tell her. Would you like to play a game of something? I looked at *TV Guide* and there's nothing on this afternoon."

We cleared off the table and I pulled myself up straighter in the bed, to give Rosamunde more room. We played Othello and talked. She told me what she knew about what was going on at school. "But I don't know much about your crowd, just what I overhear. And by observation. Like Lauren seems depressed about something—"

"Probably because she can't go to her mother's for Christmas."

"And she wanted to?"

"Yes."

"Why doesn't she? I guess they're divorced?"

"For years. Because her mother's too busy. She and her second husband run a resort hotel on one of the Sea Islands, and Christmas is their busy season."

"So what? They must have room enough, and Lauren could help out, couldn't she? It sounds suspicious, doesn't it? I don't blame Lauren—nobody likes being rejected."

"It isn't that, it's because there's a boy she met last year."

"That's what she says," Rosamunde said. "Do you believe her?"

I had never though not to believe her. Now I wondered. "I can't imagine how it would feel, having divorced parents," I admitted.

"Me either. Whatever else, my parents seem determined to stay married."

She told me who had broken up with who, and who had started going together. "They say that Deborah has finally decided to like Tony Marcel. Anyway, he's the only one she's going out with, and they always eat together, but that could be because of the newspaper."

"I can't imagine what she wants if Tony doesn't have it."

"I guess. He's OK. But Deborah—she's got success written all over her and she's probably smart enough to know that—she'll never be really serious about him. Not the way he is about her."

"Why not?"

"Oh, you know. He's king of the roost here, in high school, but he's not original or tough enough. He'll be a nice, ordinary man. Which isn't bad, but Deborah—"

"She not *that* good looking."

"There's a lot more to it than looks, Izzy."

I asked about Latin Club and she told me they were going ahead, now that everybody had settled down again. "Settled down?" I asked.

"That first meeting after Marco slammed you into a tree—well, they were pretty shook up."

I knew who she meant by they.

"They kind of—came in like tragic queens—or like close relations of the corpse? All pale and subdued and tragic whisperings, little dabbings at the eyes. Besides, everybody was—shocked. Anyway. So Mr. DePonte cancelled the meeting. I think"—and she looked up from the Othello disks she was turning over on the board—"they were disappointed. I think they expected some personal attention, sympathy and all that. But Mr. DePonte keeps things impersonal."

So that was what Suzy had been lying about, when I asked her. It didn't seem to be worth telling a lie about.

After we got tired of Othello, we started on Yahtzee. My afternoon snack came, and we shared the fruit drink. By then, we were getting sort of slap-happy, so we started betting on the games. Two turnovers against one piroshki. Plantations and daughters. A weekend with Michael Jackson against a date with Prince Andrew. When Rosamunde started rolling Yahtzees, one after the other, about every third time it was her turn, we both got the giggles. It was almost as if she was playing with loaded dice—she'd roll out the five dice and three or four would be the same. Then, she'd take those that didn't match and roll again. About a third of the time, by the time she'd taken her third roll she had all five the same. "Let's play for money," she said, about halfway through the game.

"Are you kidding?"

"I've never had such luck in anything in my whole life. It's wasted on me here. Why couldn't it happen sometime important?"

"Like when?" I grumped.

"On the SAT's, that would be a good time."

I rolled for a full house and had to scratch, since I didn't get it, didn't even get close to it. Rosamunde rolled for fours, the only number she had left. After her first roll, four four's showed.

I started to laugh.

"It's making me nervous," she said. "Things going right. You know what it means, don't you?"

I shook my head.

"It means the gods are setting you up for something really bad."

She rolled and the die came up a four. "Oh no," she groaned, laughing away.

"It's impossible. I've gone for weeks never getting a single Yahtzee. I think I'll quit. I give you this game."

"Oh no, you don't," Rosamunde said. "If the gods are going to get me later, I want full pleasure now. Every last drop. Squeeze it out, Izzy."

By this time we were both doubled over with laughing and general silliness. It wasn't actually that funny, not really; but it felt really funny at the time.

I swiped at the table with my hand, like a good tennis backstroke. The dice flew all over the room, even into the bathroom, landing with little clattering sounds. That struck us as really really funny.

When I raised my head, my parents were standing in the doorway, in formal dress. As soon as I caught my breath I greeted them. "You look terrific," I said. My father was tall and solemn in his black tuxedo with a black cummerbund and plain shirt front; my father would never wear anything but the most conservative dress shirts. My mother wore a long, frothy blue gown and her lamb's-wool jacket. But my mother had tears running out of her eyes. But she was smiling.

"Are you all right?" I asked her.

Rosamunde had gotten off the bed and was standing by the window.

"She's fine," my father said. He put his arm around her shoulder. I opened the drawer and passed her a box of tissues. "We just heard all the noise in here—"

"It sounded like a first grade classroom party," my mother said. She wiped at her eyes. "It looks like a first grade classroom party too."

"Rosamunde Webber, this is my mother, Mrs. Lingard." I introduced them. My mother put out her gloved hand to say hello, it's a pleasure to meet you, whatever has been going on in here. The room was pretty messy, with the shoeboxes dropped onto the floor and the wastebasket overflowing with Yahtzee score sheets and paper towels.

"And my father."

Rosamunde stepped around the carton of crumpled newspaper to shake my father's hand.

"You've come to have supper with Izzy," she said, taking in their formal wear. My father, whose sense of humor isn't as quick as my mother's, sort of stared at her without anything to say.

My mother didn't say anything either, though.

"Bad joke," Rosamunde said to me.

"They're going to a formal dinner," I explained. "But Mom, your eyes are a mess. Are you all right?"

I didn't really have to ask, even though I never thought I'd ever see her crying in front of a stranger, in a strange public place, not home. Her eyes were shining.

"I'm fine, really, Angel. I am. Where's the makeup I brought you—I'd better do a repair job."

"We just came to say hello, I didn't have to play this afternoon so we got dressed a little early," my father explained. "We'll try to come back later, but we wanted to—say hello."

"That means you didn't make the finals, doesn't it?"

Rosamunde was standing lumpishly quiet.

"He was playing in the member-guest tournament," I told her.

"Ah," she said.

"There's a dinner dance, the last night of the tournament."

"Ah," she said.

"I'm sorry you didn't make the final round," I said to my father.

"It doesn't matter," my father said. "I think I got a couple of new contracts out of it, which is what it's all about, after all. Isn't it?" He smiled at Rosamunde.

"I guess, if you don't win, that better be what it's all about," she answered. Then she grimaced and half looked at me and looked quickly away. My father just looked as if he didn't know what to say.

My mother came out, dropped two dice on the table top. "In the sink," she said.

"Izzy was losing," Rosamunde explained. My mother raised her eyebrows at me. "Badly," Rosamunde said. "You should bring her some fresh fruit."

"That's a good idea." My mother accepted the suggestion. "Would you like that?"

"I think so. I'm getting tired of stewed prunes."

That made her smile and having something definite to do always pleased her. "That's a handsome vase," she said.

"Rosamunde's mother made it."

"It looks like some work I've seen in the Treasure Trove."

"That's my mom's stuff. I keep telling her she should find someplace else to sell her work, because—everything else in there is so cute, you know? I guess she thinks she looks good by contrast. Or," Rosamunde told my mother, "something." Rosamunde didn't know how to talk to people, I thought. My parents, who were ready to like anybody we brought around, were getting uncomfortable. I was relieved when my mother kissed me and told Rosamunde it was a pleasure to meet her, and she hoped to see more of her. When she turned around to wave from the doorway I could see in her expression that she had put two and two together and gotten four. She had remembered seeing Rosamunde by the elevators.

"I have to go pretty soon myself. My father's picking me up at seven. I guess I'd better neaten things up here a little, too, or they'll evict you. But Izzy—that was like being visited by Charles and Di."

"Who, my parents?"

"You know what I mean. Does your mother cry a lot?"

"No, never."

"Mine does."

"Why?"

"She's artistic. They look OK, your parents. Very well bred. Like you."

"What's the matter?"

"Nothing. I shouldn't have said that, about coming to eat with you. Or bringing fruit, as if I was criticizing her. Or the Treasure Trove either. Should I have?" She had loaded the empty carton on the carrier and she put on her PAL jacket. She looked sort of deflated.

"What's the matter with you, Rosamunde?"

She shook her head. She smiled a big, fake smile. "I told you, nothing. I was just wondering again. Really wondering, because I hadn't put it into the big picture, with your parents and your whole life and all."

"Wondering what?"

"Oh—what a nice girl like you is doing in a place like this."

And she left.

It wasn't ten minutes later that the phone rang. I had been tidying up the pile of books and anything else I could reach. I had been sort of looking at the zoo hanging on the wall, seeing how many animals I could find. "Hello?" I said into the receiver.

"Izzy, it's me. I'm downstairs. But I didn't mean to be—I mean, did you know that nice has more than the one meaning, more than the way we use it now?"

"Rosamunde."

"Yeah. It used to mean, like, fine, delicate, precise, like a nice distinction, or a nice point. My dad's here. I'll see you. Next weekend? I've got to work all week."

"I might be home by then," I said.

"Really? Well, then . . ."

She sounded like she wouldn't want to come see me at home. As if, if I were at home, there wouldn't be any reason to come see me.

"You'll have to get these books and things," I reminded her.

"I guess so. Well, maybe I'll see you then." It was sort of a question.

"OK," I sort of answered, confused because I'd enjoyed the afternoon and I'd thought she had too, but now suddenly it was a question.

"I meant that about nice," she said. "I'm coming, right now," she said away from the phone.

I had had dinner and was looking through one of the cartoon books when the phone rang again. I thought it might be Jack. I hoped it would be.

"Izzy?"

"Oh, Rosamunde. No," I corrected my tone of voice quickly. "I've been sort of expecting Jack to call."

"He should. Probably he will. I wanted to say, I should warn you, I always have second thoughts about things. I always get halfway away and have second thoughts. In case you hadn't begun to suspect," and she laughed.

"I was beginning to."

"My mother says people think I'm crazy."

"Well," I said, not disagreeing.

"Anyway, I'll see you next weekend. For sure. If that's OK?"

"It is. And thanks, for the food and the books and games and—everything. I really appreciate it."

That time, I got the last word.

When the phone rang again, before I had even decided what I wanted to watch, I was all ready to complain. Up to a point, it was funny, this calling back. But this was going too far.

"Izzy? Who *was* that person?" Jack demanded.

"Hey, Jack. Hi."

"Did you hear the way she talked to me?"

"I was right here."

"Who is she?"

"Her name's Rosamunde Webber, she's a tenth grader.

They moved to Newton last year, just before the beginning
of school. I know her from school."

"Rosamunde? I never met her I guess."

I could figure out what he was thinking. "She's not your
type, Jack."

"What do you mean, not my type? I go out with lots of
different girls."

"I mean she's not good-looking: she has fuzzy hair, a big
nose and a bad figure, I think. She doesn't dress to show off
much of her figure. She's intelligent, too."

"And aggressive, I guess," his voice said. "She sounds
more like Joel's type."

"Sort of."

"Did you ever notice how Joel's type always lasts longer
than mine?"

"Yes. Yes, I have noticed that." Sometimes, Jack just
made me smile. "How are the girls up there?"

This was a topic he had a lot to say on. We must have
talked for an hour, my brother Jack and I, about one thing
and another. One of the last things we talked about was how
angry he was, about me. I tried to tell him that it wouldn't
do any good to be angry.

"You know, Izzy, sometimes you're too nice for your
own good," he said.

I knew what he meant to say, but I didn't want to talk
about it to him on the phone. "Nice means fine," I told
him. "Like, a nice distinction."

"Don't go getting smart on me, little sister, will you?"

"No danger."

"And being angry won't get your leg back, I know that,"
he said. "That's why Joel wouldn't let me come down with
him, you know."

"I didn't know. But I think I'm glad he has good sense."

"Yeah, me too, I guess. But if I'd been home, this never
would have happened. I'd never have let you go out with
him. I'd like to kill that Marco."

"What a good idea. You can kill him and you'll be in jail and I'll come visiting day with a file in a cake. Like some Thirties movie. That's a terrific idea, Jack. Good thinking."
He sputtered at me, from the other end of the phone.

10

Monday morning Dr. Epstein told me I could probably go home on Friday.

"When on Friday?"

"Afternoon. I want you to have the PT and to talk with Helen Hughes-Pincke, any last questions you might have for her."

I wasn't going to quarrel with him about anything. If I could go home on Friday, I could last through the week.

"You'll have to come back for regular PT sessions for a long time," he said.

"Does Mom know?"

"She knows. She's made all the plans. You can't go back to school until the cast comes off."

I nodded. That was three or four weeks away. I was only thinking as far as Friday. *The first thing I'll do*, I thought, *is. . . .* I wondered what I wanted most to do first.

When I looked at the breakfast tray, I knew. The first thing I'd do would be to order in a pizza. With double cheese and sausage, green peppers and mushrooms.

Then I had a practical thought: *There'll have to be someone else, to answer the door and all*. But that was OK.

If I could only be home, I wouldn't mind being a little dependent on my family.

All through the massage and the PT session, I kept reminding myself that when it was over there would only be four more sessions, and I got through all right, without feeling too depressed. Mrs. Hughes-Pincke asked me how I was feeling and how PT was, but she didn't wait for my answer because her eye was caught by the wall hanging. I told her about it, and she stood in front of it, saying what a great thing that was for a child's room. She wondered where she could get one. I told her I would ask, but I warned her that Mrs. Webber had become a potter, so she might not be doing batiks any more. Then Mrs. Hughes-Pincke sat down for our talk. She asked me about Rosamunde, remembering that I'd never mentioned her before. I found myself answering her questions, trying to explain the non-friendship we had, talking about Lisa and Suzy to show her what the difficulties were. "What about that other good friend, you mentioned earlier—Lauren?"

"Oh. I don't think—" I started to say, but I could feel my throat closing up and I didn't want to talk about Lauren. "Why are you always asking me about my friends, anyway?"

"You can tell a lot about a person by her friends," she answered. "Don't you know that?"

"I never thought about it."

"And when something like this happens," she said, "sometimes your friendships change, because there are a lot of changes, and that can be unsettling."

"I'm going home on Friday," I told her.

"I know. You're glad?"

"Yes."

"You look pretty cheerful today. It won't be easy though, Isobel; have you thought about that?"

"Not really, I guess. But I will."

I won't be able to get upstairs to my room, I thought,

thinking of what the hard things would be, after Mrs.
Hughes-Pincke had left and before my lunch arrived. *Not
with this cast on, too*. I considered the ground floor of our
house, with my parents' bedroom and bath at one end, and
the kitchen and family room at the other, with the living
room, hallway, den and dining room in between. The den
was where the TV was, and there was a phone in there; it
was close enough to the kitchen and had the powder room
nearby. *I'd sleep in the den for a while*, I decided.

At lunchtime I was peeling apart a ham sandwich when
my mother came in, her arms full of bags. She set a basket
of fruit down on the night table, apples and bananas,
oranges, green grapes and purple grapes, and three brown
hairy things.

"Oh good," I said. "Thanks a lot, Mom." I dropped the
slice of ham back onto the plate. I reached over to take a
banana. I was hungry enough, and bananas are the most
filling fruit. I picked up one of the brown things. "What's
this?"

"A kiwi. Don't eat that banana yet."

My mother had brought me a lunch of my own: a thick
roast beef sandwich made with butter and mayonnaise on a
kaiser roll; a huge dill pickle. I salted and peppered the
sandwich. She sat down to eat the container of tossed salad
she'd gotten for herself.

"This was really nice of you," I said at the same time
that she said, "You *are* hungry, aren't you."

That was what she'd said last night, late, after the dinner
dance, as we all shared the last of Rosamunde's apple
turnovers. I didn't answer, just ate away, nodding my head.

"What's a kiwi? It sounds foreign, like a foreign bird."

"I'm sure it is." My mother ate neatly, a napkin over the
skirt of her tweed suit, a light blue jabot-blouse neatly tied,
her hair shining and in place, her face made up for daytime.
For daytime wear she has low-heeled shoes. She looked
altogether British that day, I thought. She showed me how

to peel a kiwi and then slice off bites of the bright green
fruit. She left a penknife with me, to use on the rest. "Every
lady should have a penknife."

"Sure, Mom."

"She certainly can cook," my mother said, "your friend
Rosamunde. She quite surprised us. I hope we weren't
rude."

"I don't think so." I remembered what Rosamunde had
said about Charles and Di, which made me smile again. "I
don't think she thought so. She thought she might have been
rude, I think."

"Well, my guess is she's not an easy child, she's not at all
like Lisa and the rest. Is she? Probably she feels uncomfortable because of the way she looks."

"Oh, I don't think so."

"With that nose, and hair? And her figure?

"She's never said anything about it," I pointed out.

"She wouldn't, would she."

My mother had to go to a meeting of the committee for
the hospital Christmas ball, a big fund-raiser. But she said
she'd bring me lunch tomorrow, that she and my father
would be having lunch with me all week. "I've never been
in the hospital for so long. I hadn't realized how unappetiz-
ing the food would be."

"It doesn't matter."

"Well yes, it does, if that's why you've looked so
peaked. I'm grateful to your friend for bringing it to our
attention."

"Don't you like her?"

"I don't know her at all, do I?" my mother answered,
which was her way of avoiding the question.

She had some time before her meeting, because most of
the ladies ate lunch later than the hospital served it, so she
started me on the needlepoint kit she had brought. She had
gotten it at the Treasure Trove and they had imported it from
Denmark. The design was a basket full of flowers, done in

shades of red, yellows, blues and browns. It had a green leafy border and a white background. It was all the basic tent stitch, my mother said, showing me how to lock a piece of yarn under the first few stitches, advising me to start with the design and then work the background last, so the finished piece would hold its shape better. "I thought we might have it made up into a pillow, when you're done. I thought it would look nice in your room."

"I can come home Friday," I told her.

"Saul told us."

"After lunch."

"We'll be here. Your father is taking the afternoon off. Do you know what you'd like for dinner?"

"Pizza," I told her.

I'd better have a walker at home, I thought, *at least until the cast comes off. I'll have to use their bathroom for baths, and I'll just be careful to hang my left leg out over the tub.*

I worked away on the needlepoint, which was kind of soothing and gave me something to do with my hands while the TV was on. Joel and Jack called the next night, both sounding a little frantic with papers and midterms. My parents brought me deli sandwiches for lunch and kept the fruit basket filled. The people who came regularly to my room worked on the basket of fruit. That is, Dr. Epstein and Mrs. Hughes-Pincke did, and my parents. The PT nurse just grunted when I asked if she'd like some.

Except for the dark of nights, if I woke up, which I usually did, I felt all right. If I woke up then, and I usually did, I would get frightened and depressed—as if I couldn't keep my mind from going down that slide thinking of all the things that I managed not to think about during the days. I didn't turn on the light, because the night nurse might notice it and come in to find out what was wrong.

On Wednesday afternoon, just as the cartoons were beginning, Rosamunde knocked at the door. She had her PAL jacket on, with a thick sweater underneath. She had a

woman with her, a short dumpy woman in layers of
roughwoven clothing, her long nubbly skirt a mix of grays
and browns and hanging down over her boots. Her face was
plump and her thick hair was pulled back at the nape of her
neck into a long braid. She wore no makeup, not even
lipstick. "This is my mother," Rosamunde said.

"How do you do, Mrs. Webber," I said.

She smiled at me, a good smile that made me want to
smile back. Her eyes went to the batik and to the vase. I
liked the way the most interesting thing in the room for her
was her own work. Much more interesting than me, for
example.

"So you're Izzy," Mrs. Webber said. She didn't know
what to say. "Rosamunde's told us about you."

I didn't know what to say to that. I looked at Rosamunde,
who was standing between us. I looked back at Mrs.
Webber.

"Nothing too bad, I hope," I said, the way you always
do when somebody says they've heard about you.

Mrs. Webber didn't have any reply to that. She just stood
there, wrapped around in heavy homespun shawls.

"Rosamunde tells me you're an artist."

"A craftsperson," she corrected. "Not an artist."

I'd said the wrong thing. "Oh," I said.

"We got you something," Rosamunde said. "Well, Mom
did. Give it over, Mom."

Mrs. Webber passed me a brown paper bag. "I see you
already know how to stitch." She picked up the canvas I'd
been working on. I'd finished a couple of flowers and a few
long leaves.

"This is my first. My mother gave it to me, to have
something to do."

"Ummn," she said. She studied the canvas. "You've got
nice even stitches. She's got a smoother temperament than
you," Mrs. Webber said to Rosamunde.

"Doesn't everybody?" Rosamunde asked, and her mother laughed.

"I don't know about this," Mrs. Webber said, indicating the bag I held in my hands. She had packed in a blank needlepoint canvas, its sides bound off, and a pad of graph paper and two sharpened pencils.

"It's Mom's version of a kit," Rosamunde said.

"I can design it myself?" I asked.

"It's more fun that way—challenging. At least, I've always thought so." Mrs. Webber was thinking she'd done the wrong thing. I was thinking I'd said the wrong thing.

"That's very thoughtful of you," I told her. "And you put in a needle too."

"Mom, don't you have errands? I'll be downstairs in an hour, I promise," Rosamunde said, while I was trying to think up something to talk about, and Mrs. Webber was studying the way her vase looked in my window.

"Yes, yes, I do. It was a pleasure to meet you, Izzy." Mrs. Webber smiled again, and once again I wanted to smile back. However uncomfortable she might be, it felt OK; there was something in her smile and in her expression on her face that let me know that—however words might stumble and however hard it is to meet somebody's mother, especially if you're in a hospital bed—she planned to like me.

"I'm sorry," Rosamunde said, right away. "But she insisted. I told her you'd just make her nervous."

I thought I knew what she meant, because crippled people do make other people nervous. *At home, I'll have to have a blanket to cover up my legs*, I thought. "I can understand that," I told Rosamunde.

"Can you? She's such a reverse snob—I kept trying to tell her, to warn her, to remember that you're just a person like everyone else, but she gets all defensive about—oh, you know—and then she sort of puts on her artist act, the artists-are-better-than-ordinary-mortals one."

"She has a terrific smile," I told Rosamunde firmly.

Rosamunde relaxed. For a minute, she looked a little sheepish. "Yeah, OK. Parents," she concluded.

"Can I ask you a personal question?" I asked.

"Depends on how personal."

"Are you self-conscious, do you think?"

"What made you think of that?"

"My mother said she thought you were and I said I didn't think so."

"It's interesting." Her face got thoughtful-looking. "What made your mother say that?"

"Don't say it that way."

"OK, I won't."

I giggled. "Oh—" I realized I might offend her by telling her.

"You're in too deep to get out, Izzy."

"Why are you here, anyway? I thought you babysat in the afternoons."

"Dental appointment, and Mom had some errands. Some stuff to deliver to the Treasure Trove. Don't change the subject." But Rosamunde was grinning. "She didn't happen to mention my—attire, did she?"

I couldn't help laughing.

Rosamunde sat down in the chair, her legs looking thick in the overalls and her ankles thick in heavy socks. "Or maybe," she continued, "it was just my looks." She'd stopped smiling. "You know—there are things about the way you look . . . that would be the thing about being black—people see it right away, black skin."

"Hunh?" She was going too fast for me.

"No." She leaned forward, intense. "It means you have to face up to peoples' preconceptions right away. Don't you see? If you're black, well, the first thing people see is your skin color. You can't hide it. If you see what I mean."

"I see what you mean," I said. I saw exactly what she meant. Because people were going to look at me and think *amputee*.

Rosamunde's expression changed, from thinking to embarrassed. I didn't know what to say, because I was trying not to think about what I'd just figured out. For once she didn't know what to say.

"Izzy, I'm sorry, I didn't mean—"

"It's OK," I said quickly. "My psychological nurse wants to buy your batik," I said.

We talked about safe things, until Rosamunde got up to go. Then she asked me, as she was snapping her jacket, which wasn't necessary because it wasn't even cool in the hospital, "What did happen, with Marco."

"Why do you want to know?"

She shrugged.

"I can't remember," I said.

Rosamunde looked down at me. "You're lying."

I didn't know what to say.

"That's OK, I mean, you can trust me with the truth if you want to, but you don't have to. Do you want me to tell my father you still can't remember?"

"Why should you do that?"

"He's a policeman. They were going to come back, when you were stronger, to get a report from you."

"I didn't know your father was a policeman."

"He'd know you're lying. Your eyes get—they kind of give you away. But I'll tell him so you won't have to lie, and I won't be lying. I can say you said you couldn't tell them anything more than you already have."

That was so precisely and exactly true, I felt like thanking Rosamunde. She had given me something to say that wasn't a lie. I didn't like lying, and she was right—I wasn't any good at it.

"If you would—I'd be so—"

"No problem."

"That's what PAL stands for, isn't it? Police Athletic League."

"You could say that. I like to think it stands for pal, you know, good buddy and all."

Thursday night I called Lisa and Suzy, to tell them I was going home. They sounded pleased. They both said they'd see me, and that pleased *me*. I didn't like the way me being in the hopital had broken us up. *I'll have to ask Mom to keep in a good supply of drinks*, I thought, *and chips, and popcorn. For when there's company, since I won't be able to go out for a while.*

And I did finally ask the black nurse her name, because of what Rosamunde said. I had to work up my courage, because she didn't talk to me and I didn't talk to her. But when I was saying goodbye, I asked her: "I never knew what your name is."

"Adelia," she said. At least, I had surprised her into really looking at me, as she pulled the sheet back up over my lap. "It's not like you're through with me," she said. "We've got weeks of work ahead."

"Oh," I said.

"Adelia Jones," she said.

"I guess I'll be seeing you, Miss Jones," I said.

"Mrs."

But she didn't wear a wedding ring. I wondered why she didn't. I wondered what would happen so that a woman wouldn't wear a wedding ring but would still call herself Mrs. I looked at her, strong and square, her dark skin showing chocolate brown in contrast to the fresh white uniform, and I tried to see past the color of her skin to who she really was. But I couldn't.

Friday afternoon, waiting for my parents, I almost couldn't stand it. My mother had emptied the room the night before so all we had to take with us was an overnight bag. The bag was by the door. I was dressed in a skirt and blouse and sweater, dressed for the first time in weeks. I had moved myself to the chair and sat waiting.

The room was empty, like a bare cupboard. The bed was empty by not yet stripped. I looked at the bed.

I'll have to practice on stairs, I thought. *Once the cast comes off and I can go back to my own room, it'll be hard work getting up the stairs.*

I was finished with the hospital. I had served through, like an indentured servant, or someone just about to get out of jail. Every minute I waited felt a week long.

There won't be much privacy, downstairs, I reminded myself and then I realized, *I'll need a place to do my homework.* I was going to have an awful lot of school work to catch up on.

After the cast came off, Dr. Epstein had told me, they would give me crutches.

I heard voices in the hall and my heart beat a little faster, but it wasn't my parents. "As soon after lunch as we can," my mother had promised me. I made myself sit patiently, although the nerves just under the skin of my hands made my fingers want to jump. The time in the hospital was already slipping away from me, and I was glad to have it do that. I just wanted to get out. I just wanted to be home. I just wanted—things to feel all around me the way they would feel as soon as I was home again.

I should have known better. I should have learned by then, but I hadn't. I shouldn't have expected anything. If I had to expect something, I should have been more realistic about my expectations. But I was like a little kid, about to turn a year older, waking up on her birthday morning and thinking the whole world was going to be different, better. The miniature Izzy inside my head was standing there, holding onto a big red balloon that floated above her head. She let the balloon go, to see it fly up and away; but she hadn't realized that in order to let it go she was going to have to lose it too.

They wheeled me down to the elevator and then through the lobby; my father shifted me to the front seat of our station wagon; we drove away from the hospital and through town, then out of town and into the hilly countryside.

The area where we live is called Westwood, because the original estate belonged to a family named West. All the houses were built at about the same time, in the late forties. Our house faces the road squarely. It has a first floor longer than the second, and it is only one room thick, so that every room looks out on trees and grass. The driveway goes by the front door before turning behind to the white clapboard garage that matches the house exactly, even to slate tiles on the roof and the gunpowder gray shutters on the windows. My father pulled up in front. My mother opened the door for us, while he helped me up the steps with his arm around my ribcage, lifting me. "Ready? Up now. Ready? Up again."

I stood within the circle of his arm as my mother closed the front door behind us. The soft green carpet under my feet; the long beige curtains on the windows with the trim my mother and I had searched for weeks; the wallpaper, its ivory background traced over with soft green fern fronds, the polished wood of the bannister, which matched the wood of the entryway table, where a bowl of cut flowers sat—I was home.

I breathed in the quiet, the colors, the smell of wax and flowers. I relaxed, all down along my bones and in my head and heart. Leaning against my father's tall, strong body, I smiled to myself.

My mother left us and came back carrying a walker. The four tubed legs of the thing were tipped with white rubber. "We got you this and we've rented a wheelchair, but that's in the kitchen. I think it'll take some practice.

I looked at the gleaming metal and the curved bars that made railings, joining the four legs. My smile slipped away.

"And wait until you see what we've done—"

"What your mother's done," my father corrected.

The walker waited, like half a cage.

Clumsily, I unzipped my jacket and worked my arms out of it, while my father held me steady. Then I pulled the walker toward me until I stood inside it.

My father was staring at me. I had no idea what he was thinking.

"Shall we?" my mother asked. I didn't know how I was going to manage the stairs.

But she led me down the hall and into their bedroom. I followed her, slowly and clumsily.

She had turned their bedroom into a girl's room. New curtains hung on the windows and the same print made a quilt to cover their big bed. New bookcases were in the room, filled with my books and stuffed animals. My own pictures hung on the walls. All of their personal items were gone. In the bathroom, my towels hung on the racks and it was my bathrobe that hung behind the door. My mother's desk had been cleaned off and my own desk lamp was on it. I knew that if I opened the drawers I would see stacks of lined paper, ball point pens and sharpened pencils.

"But what about you?" I asked my mother.

"We've moved upstairs."

"But my room's too small for you."

"Well, I'm using the boys' room for work, all my sewing stuff's in there, and we have all three closets for our clothes, which is more than enough."

"What about Christmas?"

"We'll worry about that when it comes along."

"Or Thanksgiving."

"We'll get through that, somehow. Do you like it?"

I didn't know what to say. I didn't like it, no, because it wasn't what I had imagined. But my imaginings had been unrealistic. I thought it was terrific, the trouble she had gone to, the details she had thought of. "I'd sort of thought I'd move into the den, for a while. This is—much nicer."

"We thought—it's going to be hard enough, this at least could be made easier," my father said.

I knew that. And I knew also that this was as hard on them as it was on me. I suspected then that they had known how I would feel, about coming home, and how I would be disappointed. Because I was disappointed, and it wasn't anything to do with home and I knew that, but I was still feeling disappointed with home.

"Do you like the room?"

"Yes," I told her, because I did. "In fact, I think I might like a nap. I don't know why, but I'm kind of tired."

"Of course, you are," my mother said, whizzing into action. "I wouldn't even bother getting undressed, just lie here on top of the quilt; here are the pillows. Hendrik, let's leave Izzy to have a nap. Francie's going to insist on seeing you the minute she gets home," my mother warned me. "I'll make sure you're awake, shall I?"

"Thanks. And I really am glad to be home."

"I know, Lamb," she said. "I know how you feel."

Maybe she did, I thought, lying on the bed, staring at the window of the strange new room.

11

We waited for Francie in the kitchen. I sat in the wheelchair, which was narrow and lightweight; a heavy plaid blanket covered my legs. I had a cup of hot chocolate, made from scratch. My parents drank tea.

"You should take more afternoons off," my mother said to my father.

"It's certainly a different world, the afternoon not in an office." He smiled at us across the round wooden table. "I'm not sure I have enough to do at home to take the afternoons off."

"We'd find things," my mother promised him. She was thinking of all the long-range projects they occasionally tried to get around to, the building of a workroom in the cellar and shelves for books in the attic, the vegetable garden they talked about every spring but never put in.

"How does it feel to be home, Angel?" she asked me.

"Pretty good. But a little strange."

"Strange?" my father asked.

"I never realized how big the rooms in this house are. Then, you've changed some things. Like—" I looked around the kitchen, across the sand-colored no-wax floor and beyond the white formica counters to the door into the dining room. "Like that door." They had taken down the heavy swinging door, even removing the fat hinges it hung from. The door frame had been filled in and repainted, so it looked as if there never had been a door there.

"We thought, until you get steadier on your feet, it would be too much of an obstacle," my father explained.

"I know that, but it's different. Who built that shelf by the tub in your bathroom?".

"Mr. Katz. You know that, he does all our plumbing."

"I didn't know he could do work like that."

The shelf was made from tiles and looked like part of the original wall. There was no way to make the long metal bar that had been put in so that I could haul myself out of the tub look like anyone's idea of a design feature, but the shelf actually looked nice. Lined up on it were my favorite shampoo and conditioner, the glycerine soap that's better for my skin, and a jar of bath beads.

"Mr. Katz enjoyed the work," my mother said. "I'm surprised we hadn't thought of it years ago, aren't you, Hendrik? It's so convenient, everything right there at hand and deep enough so things won't fall off."

Every room I looked at had changes in it, like the carpeted ramp going down the two shallow steps into the living room, or the sixth chair for the table we sat at, which had been whisked away out of sight somewhere to leave a space for the wheelchair. "You've been busy."

"Mostly your mother," my father said.

"Oh, well, you knew there had to be good reason to keep me from spending all day with you, Lamb. Do you mind the changes?"

"No," I said. But yes, I did mind; I minded things being different when I wanted them to be exactly the same; I minded the guilty feeling I was having, for having caused all the changes. "What have you done with this chair?"

"It's in the attic," my father said, "just until you get the cast off. That bedroom," he told me, "is only yours temporarily too, so enjoy the luxury while you've got it."

For some reason, I was glad to hear him say that.

"It's so good to have you home," my mother said. But it was my father's hand she reached for across the table. She looked at my face. "You've done your eyes again. I almost forgot what you look like, with your eyes done. And lipstick too; that looks nice, Izzy."

"But my eyes don't?" I challenged her.

"It's funny, I never noticed it at the time, but I guess I got used to seeing your eyes without any makeup."

"I have light lashes," I reminded her.

"Ummnn," she said. I had her full attention now. "You know, I noticed, when you weren't wearing anything on your lashes, that they're rather lovely, your lashes. Because of the way the tips are gold."

"You have to be about an inch away to even see them."

"Ummnn," she said. "I was thinking—"

"Uh-oh," I said to my father.

"That there are some girls—women—who sort of—put it all out on display."

"The trashy example," I said to my father.

"I'm not sure," he said. "It could be the woman-of-mystery example."

"If you two would listen, instead of telling me what I'm going to say, which I'm not going to say anyway," my mother interrupted. "What I was thinking was, there are some girls, or women, who the more you look at them, the more you see of how attractive they are. As if you were discovering it instead of being told it. Which makes it, somehow—oh, I don't know," she said, over our laughter.

Francie ran into the room. A cold draft blew in with her and she slammed the door shut. She rushed toward me and then stopped dead in her tracks, staring. For a second, I didn't know why she was staring. For a second, I had forgotten.

"Hi," Francie said. She stood there, in jeans and a vest. "You got home all right."

"What does it look like?" I asked her, staring back.

Francie is tall and skinny, with long legs. She wears her hair in one long braid down her back, except when she's doing gymnastics when she pins the braid at the back of her neck. She went to hang up her vest. The shirt she wore that day had "In training for '92" on it.

My mother heated up the hot chocolate, to pour a mug for Francie and to refill mine. Francie made herself a jam sandwich with mayonnaise, her usual snack, and sat down. "I don't have any homework this weekend."

It seemed like a long time since I had seen Francie, a long time since she had sat at the table with me. Her face is round, with rounded cheeks, and her eyes are round and deeply lidded, with dark eyelashes thick around them. She talked on about the news of the day, how she had done on the spelling test and the math quiz, how strict the teacher was with her especially. Francie's nose doesn't belong on a child's face. It's too bony, it has too much character for a kid. My mother always said that Francie was going to be better looking, the older she got.

"Wanna see what I can do now, Izzy?" Before I could answer, Francie hopped up from the table.

"Not in here, Love," my mother said, as usual, and as usual Francie just ignored her. Francie took a running start and then did a cartwheel that turned into a somersault. Her skinny legs moved over her head with clockwork precision, and her whole long body tucked up into the somersault fluidly, without hesitation. She ended up on her feet, her arms stretched behind her.

"Very nice dear," my mother said.

I thought they should enforce what they said to her. She knew she wasn't supposed to practice in the kitchen, she knew because they had told her and asked her, time after time. She sat down again, waiting for me to speak my turn.

"Very nice," I echoed my mother.

"Since it's a special occasion, can we watch cartoons? Since Izzy's home."

"You're suggesting that a good way of celebrating is to watch cartoons?" I didn't try to hide my sarcasm.

"Just because you don't like them," she muttered into her mug. "Besides, I already said we should have a party and invite my friends and your friends and their friends, but they said we ought to let you get used to things for a while. They said you'd be self-conscious. Are you?"

"Yes," I said. The little Izzy inside my head hauled off and punched Francie in the mouth.

"Everything's changed upstairs," Francie said, sipping at her cocoa. "Mommy's sewing machine is in the twins' room and she's jammed the beds together against the wall, and I have to wait for Daddy to get out of the bathroom, every morning, every single morning."

"You're closer to us when you have bad dreams," my father reminded her.

"And they catch me if I'm reading late," she continued her catalogue of woes.

"I think Francie should be allowed to watch cartoons," I said. "Since it's a special occasion." I didn't want to listen to her complaints about everything that had gotten worse because of me.

"So do I," my father said. "You go ahead, Francie."

She jumped up from the table, her face perfectly happy. "Gee, thanks, Izzy. This is great. I'm really glad you're home," she added, hurrying out to the den. She turned around to ask me, "Do you want to watch with me?" but didn't wait for my answer.

That night we had pizza in the kitchen. My father and Francie drove out to pick it up. My mother set the table and made a tossed salad, even though she knew no one would eat it. She set out glasses. "Root beer or milk?" she asked me and I told her root beer, as usual. She and my father had

some of the Swedish beer she gave him a case of for each
Christmas and birthday.

As usual, there was too much pizza, two medium-sized
pies. Both had double cheese and thin crusts. One was
plain, the way my father likes it; the other had crumbled
sausage and slices of green peppers and mushrooms and
onions, the way I like it. For a minute, I didn't even take a
piece for myself, I just breathed in everything—the tomato
cheese smell of pizza, the bright kitchen with darkness
outside, my parents and Francie serving themselves with
little bits of conversation, "Thanks," "Elbows dear," "If
someone would pass me the salt," "Don't forget salad,
anyone." I breathed it all in, and the little Izzy inside my
head did her back flip. Then I helped myself to the biggest
slice.

If there is anything like the first bite of pizza, crisp crust
and gooey cheeses with tomato underneath, I don't know
what it is. Strands of cheese hung down over my chin. I
pushed them in my mouth with my fingers and chewed.

"Boy, does that taste good." I reached out to take another
piece.

"Don't forget salad," my mother said. I ignored her.

"Are we going to have that party?" Francie asked.

"I don't know," my mother said. "Izzy, we didn't know,
would you like to have a party? To get everyone together
again?"

"No," I said. "Thanks, but no. I don't think so."

"You'll have to see them all sometime," my mother
started.

My father stopped her. "If you ask her and she says no,
Jane, that seems pretty clear."

"If Izzy doesn't want it, can I have it? My friends want to
see her too."

I could just imagine that.

"You'll want a quiet weekend," my mother told me.

"During the week, you'll have therapy every morning. How tiring is it?"

"Not too bad."

Francie wanted to know all about it, what I did, but I didn't want to talk about it. "Every day?" I asked.

My mother nodded.

"Why every day?"

"It's what Saul said. Once you get back to school you won't be able to go in as often. Which reminds me, we have to do something about your assignments, so you won't be too far behind."

"If you call the school they'll get all that ready for you at the office. So I won't be doing home teaching?"

"You won't be home long enough for that," my father said.

"I didn't know," I said. "How long—?"

"Once you get onto crutches, and when you feel well enough, Saul said you can go back," my mother said. "He knows what a social bird you are, he's known you all your life—which reminds me . . ." She shifted the subject, ". . . do I expect lots of people around this weekend?"

"I don't know."

"Anyone besides the usual? Should I lay in extra sodas and chips?"

But I really didn't know. The only one I knew might be coming by was Rosamunde. "I called Suzy, to tell her," I told my mother. I felt like I was trying to deceive her, because she didn't know that things had gotten queer between me and my friends. "But I don't think. . . . All I really want is just to be home," I said, so she wouldn't get worried.

"You won't get bored?"

"I have three weeks of school to catch up on. I doubt I'll be bored. Besides, Rosamunde might be coming by, because I've got some library books she took out on her card, and things."

"Who's Rosamunde? That's a funny name," Francie said. She had to repeat her question because she had asked with her mouth full. "Is she somebody from the hospital? Did you make a lot of friends in the hospital? You should teach me how to make friends, you really should."

"I'm not sure that can be taught," my mother said gently. "Besides, you have friends."

"But she never even tried to teach me," Francie continued.

"For heaven's sake, Francie," I said, since neither of my parents seemed about to say anything. "Don't be such a baby."

"Izzy, can't you talk nicely to your sister?" my mother asked gently.

I filled my mouth with pizza so I wouldn't have to answer. It was no use talking nicely to Francie. She had her own ideas about things, and she only listened when you agreed with her. She had always been jealous of me, I knew that. Little sisters are always jealous of older sisters, who have more privileges; and she was jealous because I was prettier and easier to get along with. I couldn't figure Francie out, and I didn't really want to. Why Francie should have been jealous of me then, I didn't know, but it was there in her face across the table. I should be jealous of her, I thought, remembering her long legs as they swung in perfect control over her head, jealous of her perfect body and her coordination.

And you are, I said to myself.

But I had never been jealous of Francie before. In fact, I'd always been glad I was myself, not her. I was glad I didn't have her problems, her moods and her intensity. That night, however, I almost wished I had those qualities, and the self-centeredness too. It would have made it easier on me. I wished I could get away with the kind of behavior she got away with, just because my parents said she had a lot of rough corners to knock off.

I liked it better when Francie was jealous of me and I could agree with her that she had reason to be jealous.

"Izzy?" my mother said. "I asked you a question. Didn't you hear me?" I hadn't. "You must be tired. Why don't you take a long hot bath and get yourself into bed. Would you like any help?"

"Maybe I will," I said, suddenly discouraged. "Anyway, I'd better unpack."

"I'll do that," my mother said. "While Dad and Francie do the dishes. But you have to have some salad."

"I'd like to watch a little TV. I'm stuffed, Mom."

"I get to choose TV between eight and nine," Francie said. My father glared at her. "Unless there's something you especially want to see," she told me.

It was almost pitiful, how much it mattered to her. "No," I said, "there isn't."

In the den, Francie sprawled out on the sofa and I maneuvered the wheelchair into place. On the screen, somebody advertised their soda with people on the beach playing volleyball. Francie said, her eyes on the screen, "I'm really sorry Izzy—about what happened to you."

I knew that at that moment she really meant it. "It's not your fault, Francie," I said.

"If it was my fault—I'd die. I'd kill myself."

"No, you wouldn't," I answered. "You know, you are pretty emotional, Francie. Did you ever think that people don't always like all that drama? That maybe people like things to be a little more relaxed?"

"You think you're so perfect. You just think you're the perfect one."

I had the needlepoint kit on my lap, so I picked up the canvas and went back to making stitches and stopped trying to talk to Francie.

I did take a bath. I had wanted to take a long, steaming bath, but it was so uncomfortable with the cast hanging out over the side of the tub, and the other leg just—there under the water—and my mother waiting in the bedroom just in case, that I washed myself quickly and hauled myself out. My mother made a point of not helping me. I could feel her worrying as I moved around the room. It was good to be in a big room, I thought, but it made for long distances between the bathroom and the bureau, between the bureau and the bed. The room had been built for people who could walk.

I don't know why I was so depressed that night. Maybe my mother was right about my being tired. Maybe just because it had been so uncomfortable and awkward to take a bath that I couldn't get relaxed. And then, my mother hadn't even put a box of tissues beside the bed, so I had to get up and go into the bathroom for toilet paper, to blow my nose on, to wipe my eyes with. I couldn't turn on the lights, because then they'd know I was awake. I couldn't ask her to give me a box of tissues, because then she'd know I needed them. She'd just have to think that for some reason I was using an awful lot of toilet paper, I thought, taking a handful back to the dark bed with me. Because I couldn't even go out and get a box of tissues for myself, privately.

Nobody woke me up the next morning, but I still got up early, just as the sun was starting to lighten the curtains. I got myself washed and dressed—another skirt, and an oxford shirt because it was pretty warm with that blanket over my legs. I noticed, when I opened the closet to pick a skirt, that my mother had removed all my right shoes. I hadn't seen that before, and I thought for a minute I'd have to go back to bed. Then I thought about how it didn't matter what color shirt I wore, whether it matched the skirt or not, since the blanket covered the skirt. I picked a white shirt anyway and settled myself in the wheelchair.

Getting out of the room was tricky. I had to wheel up sideways and lean over to twist the handle so I could pull the door a couple of inches open. Then I had to back around, without touching the door because it would swing shut again, which happened a couple of times. Once I had backed away, I had to lean forward to pull the door entirely open so I could leave. It took me a while to learn how to back up to a closed door.

By the time I got to the kitchen, I was starving. Everybody was there. My father had showered and dressed. He was going to spend the morning at the office, then play golf in the afternoon. My mother and Francie were in their robes. A place had been set for me at the table, with a glass of tomato juice waiting, so I rolled right up and drank it down. My mother started to get up, leaving her breakfast half eaten. My father told her he'd scramble me eggs, "and how about some bacon? We've got it made."

I thought I might tell them about the trouble I had getting through the door, because I thought it was sort of funny, and curious, the kind of thing you'd never think of; but then I thought it might make them feel that they'd forgotten something they shouldn't have forgotten.

"We're talking about getting a VCR," my father said.

"We could rent movies, and the library has some too, if you have a VCR," Francie explained.

"Why?" I asked.

"It's good home entertainment," my mother said.

"It's not like watching television," Francie explained earnestly. "Because it's movies, not TV shows, so it's not junk."

My father turned around from the stove and raised his eyebrows at me. I smiled.

"We could make our own tapes, too," my mother said. "We could tape you playing a round of golf, Hendrik."

"That would be exciting." He poured eggs into the frying pan.

"Or me, you could tape me at meets," Francie cried, jumping up from the table in her excitement. She hadn't even gotten it that my parents were making a joke.

"Isn't it expensive?" I asked. "We already have cable, why do we need movies too?"

"I thought—it might be fun. We could make a bowl of popcorn and watch movies," my mother said. "Like old Fred Astaire movies, or the ones we wanted to see but never got to . . . doesn't it sound like fun to you, Izzy?"

"Say yes, Izzy. Please," Francie begged. "If *you* say yes, they'll do it."

I knew what she meant, and I guessed she was right, from the way my parents exchanged a look after that remark. But I couldn't think of any objections, and I knew I couldn't object only on the grounds that I knew they were doing it because I was crippled now. And I wouldn't be doing much of anything else with my time. "Sounds OK to me," I said.

"I'm going to be downtown Monday morning, so I'll price them—while I'm getting your things at school," my mother said. She and Francie rinsed their dishes and went to get dressed for gymnastics.

My father waited for me to finish so he could get my dishes into the dishwasher before he left for work. "It's the price I have to pay for taking yesterday afternoon off," he said, bending down to kiss me as he left. "But don't tell your mother, she'll feel guilty. Or something." He turned back at the door to look at me, where I still sat at the table. "Besides, I don't think I could have gotten anything done anyway. It's good to have you back, Izzy. I'm awfully proud of you, do you know that?" He stood there, tall and dependable, and glad to see me—proud of me, he said. It made me feel good.

12

I sat there for a minute, thinking that I had to go to the bathroom but not wanting to move just yet, because it felt pretty good to be sitting in my own kitchen, with a full stomach and the memory of my father's words. Then my father came back in, followed by Suzy and Lisa. Their faces got serious as soon as they saw me.

"How are you feeling?" Lisa asked.

"Fine," I said. I was surprised, at first, then glad. "Hey, take your coats off, sit down. Get yourselves something to drink—Suzy knows where everything is. What's up?" I asked them. "What's on?"

"Nothing special," Lisa said.

"We'll be like three old ladies, won't we," Suzy said. "We can sit and talk, over a cup of tea." She made her voice high and creaky: "I don't know what the world's coming to." I started to laugh, but stopped because it made me have to go to the bathroom more.

Suzy wore a heavy white letter sweater, which she didn't take off to make the tea. She just rolled the long sleeves back.

My mother and Francie came hurrying through the room.

"It's good to see you girls," my mother said. "And you could help me out—Lisa? Could you ask the office to get Izzy's assignments and books? I'll be in around eleven on Monday." She didn't ask Suzy, because Suzy is liable to say she'll do something and then, if something more interesting comes up, she won't do what she said.

"I'd be happy to, Mrs. Lingard," Lisa said.

"Thanks a lot." My mother bent over to kiss the top of my head. "I'll be back in a little while. Is there anything you need?" Her hand rested on my shoulder for a minute, as I shook my head no. She wasn't about to hug me with my friends there, because she knew it would embarrass me, but she wanted to tell me she was glad that they had come over, because I was glad.

We three sat around the table. I dumped sugar into my tea and didn't look at them, to give them time to look at me. "Anyway, how are you?" I asked. "What's on?"

"Nothing much," Suzy told me. "You look different."

"I think I lost some weight."

"Some people have all the luck," she grumbled. "But it's not that, it's something else."

I didn't know what to answer because the obvious answer—I am different—was so obvious it couldn't be that she was talking about. Lisa asked if I was glad to be home.

"You can imagine. At the hospital they wake you up at six."

"But that's awful," Lisa sympathized. "Why did they do that?"

"Routine," Suzy told her. "In a hospital, everything's run by routine. It's your eyes, Izzy, they look different."

"Oh, I'm not wearing mascara."

"Why not?" Suzy wanted to know.

I didn't want to talk about myself. "Is there going to be a lot of homework to catch up on?"

"It hasn't been too bad, no worse than usual," Suzy told me. "We started *Romeo and Juliet*, we're already in the

Second Act, and we've done some translations in Latin. I don't know about your biology class, we've had—what's it been, two weeks?"

"Three," Lisa said.

"Two lab reports and a chapter test. There were only three grades above a ninety. I got a ninety-one."

"Good for you," I said. "Who got the other two? What were they?" We were drinking tea and talking without really looking at one another, which felt just right to me, because it was the way things usually went with us. We'd sit around and say whatever crossed our minds. I knew that I couldn't do that any more, but I wanted them to feel that they could.

"Rosamunde Webber got one, and Billy Sachs got the other. I don't know what they were. I mean, what does it matter? If Billy got a less than perfect paper he'd probably hang himself anyway. He hasn't got anything else to do except work for perfect grades. Rosamunde too; she only got a ninety-eight, big tragedy."

"Where's Lauren?" I asked, although I'd made up my mind not to.

"Who knows?" Suzy said.

"We're meeting her later, for lunch. I need some stockings and Suzy wants to look at formals." Lisa wanted to divert me from the topic of Lauren. I didn't want to be diverted, because I wanted to be able to say that I knew something was wrong. But I didn't quite dare insist on talking about her and I didn't know how to say outright that I knew what was going on, that they weren't fooling me, that they didn't have to try to fool me. I figured that they probably wanted to think that they were.

"Why formals?" I asked.

"For the Christmas dance," Suzy said eagerly. Then she stopped herself. "In case, you know."

I didn't know why she was being so secretive. If she was going to wear somebody's letter sweater, did she expect me not to figure out that she was dating an upperclassman? And—since we'd talked about it for years, complaining that only upperclassmen could go to the Christmas dance—did she think I couldn't put two and two together? I was feeling a little uncomfortable, only partly because my bladder was pressing against my stomach. I didn't like to think that my friends thought they couldn't talk about boys with me anymore. Since I knew that a lot of what we talked about and thought about was boys. So I did ask that question directly: "Whose sweater is that?"

Suzy hesitated. "Oh—I'm not sure. I picked it up at the party last night because I only wore a blazer. Don't ask me why, except my mother started giving me grief about only wearing a blazer. She should have known better."

"And you forgot to return it?" I asked.

"Sort of. You know how these things happen."

She knew that I knew exactly how they happened. No boy would forget his letter sweater. No girl would just take it home accidentally, since the wearing of a letter sweater was the way you said you were a couple.

But I didn't want to let this one go by, because I knew— although I hadn't thought of it until just then—that if we had too many things we couldn't talk about, we'd never manage to stay friends. They were deciding what those things were, as if I was too stupid to notice: me being crippled, Lauren, boys—that was the list so far.

"You know," I said, "you can talk about boys with me."

Lisa waited to hear what Suzy would say, since Suzy is the smartest.

"No, really," I said. I knew what they were thinking, that since I wouldn't be having boyfriends anymore, it would be unkind. That was a word Lisa would use, unkind. I could almost hear her voice saying that to Suzy, before they came over. Suzy would agree, partly because Lisa knew best, but mostly because she liked making things complicated. She would like the idea of having a list of forbidden topics and working the conversation around them. Coming as close as she could. She'd rather do that than find out what really did bother me.

What bothered me was figuring that out, that and having to go to the bathroom. I thought about just wheeling myself out of the room, but I couldn't. I couldn't break the illusions that we were all just like normal, which was possibly true as long as I didn't roll away from the table. Sitting around the table you barely noticed that I was in a wheelchair. You couldn't see that I was, so we were just like before—as long as I didn't move.

"Look at the time! We're going to be late, we're not going to get everything done, because we have our bikes—" Suzy explained, as if I couldn't see that there was something else they had decided not to tell me.

"We've got lots of time," Lisa said. "Besides, it doesn't matter if we're a little late."

"Lisa," Suzy's voice was heavy with secrets.

Lisa gave in. "You make a list of what boys you want to talk about," she said to me, "and we'll give you all the gossip."

"Good." I smiled a bright smile, knowing that I would never do that. One of the ones I wanted to ask about was the one whose sweater Suzy was wearing, but I guessed I could figure out who that was without asking. Marco.

I had a not-at-all-nice thought: They deserved each other. That thought made my smile genuine.

As soon as the door closed behind them, I whipped out of the kitchen and down the hall to the bathroom. One thing about the hospital, I thought, you didn't have to go a mile to get to a bathroom.

My mother was surprised to find me alone. "What time will they be back? Do you want to ask them for dinner? I could do something like hamburgers and fries."

"I don't think they are. Coming back. Don't say it, Mom, OK? I know what you're thinking."

"All right, Izzy, I won't. Is there anything you'd like to do today?"

There wasn't anything.

"I'd never realized before how much Suzy influences people," I said.

"She's got a pretty strong personality," my mother answered.

"All right," I told her. "I guess you're right. I guess I do want to hear what you're thinking."

"I don't even know what I'm thinking. Except, how much nicer you are than any of your friends. Let's go get your room straightened up, shall we?"

While Francie was out of the house, I practiced some with the walker, up and down the hallway. I spent the afternoon in the den, with whoever was around. I got myself onto the sofa and covered up my legs with the blanket. I watched TV, did needlepoint, and talked on the phone to a few people who had heard I was home again. That wasn't too bad. They would just say welcome home, when are you coming back to school? I felt a little better about things, with the phone not dead silent. Dr. Epstein dropped in to look at me and have a drink with my parents and say that it looked like I was surviving my first day out in the cold, cruel world. My mother made steak for dinner, and Francie started in complaining about how everything was done special for me. They pointed out that she had steak on her plate, too, which left her with nothing to say, but didn't stop her from thinking. I didn't know why she was acting that way.

It wasn't until I was alone in my room again that I started to think over the day. All around me everything was quiet, and dark. I could hear an occasional car, or a dog barking. I wondered who was in the car, and where they'd been, and how I was going to stand it. I thought about all the boys I had danced with, and how nice kissing felt, and I knew all of that would never happen again, but I wished it would. I wished . . .

I hobbled with the walker into the bathroom to get another handful of toilet paper. I almost missed the hospital, where they knew, at least, what I would need to have near me. Where you could always hear quiet noises of the nurses at work, all night long, where everybody had something wrong with them. Not just me. I almost wanted to go back to the hospital, which struck me as a little bit crazy. I wondered if I was going to go a little bit crazy with all the pretending I was going to have to do. I considered for a minute asking my mother to have that party. We'd invite everybody I knew and get it all over with at once. I could just see it: me in my wheelchair, in the hallway maybe, and all around me people moving and talking, dancing, staring.

The twins called in the morning to say they were glad I was home. A couple of girls from school called to say hello. One of them was a cheerleader and she told me Georgie Lowe was taking my place. I sent Georgie a message to say good luck. I finished my needlepoint and my mother said she'd get me another, to keep my hands busy. She added that to her Monday list. Francie and my father raked leaves while I stayed in the kichen with my mother, who was marinating chicken to broil. "I'm feeding you up," she told me. "Just like a good mother should."

It was a nothing afternoon, I thought, bored but not badly bored, because it did feel good to be home. My mother talked on the phone and I played games of solitaire. It was odd not to have things to be doing, to be just sitting there on the edges, because I didn't know how to be a person on the edges. But I didn't want to go to my room, because I didn't want to be alone in there. However peculiar it felt, being out with everyone and not knowing what to say or do, at least I wasn't likely to think about things I didn't want to think about.

Francie and I were watching a space movie in the late

afternoon when Rosamunde arrived. She wore her PAL windbreaker, with a long scarf hanging around her neck and a heavy sweater underneath. Her cheeks were bright pink, as if she'd been outside for a long time. "Did you ride a bike over, or what?" I asked. "Sit down."

Rosamunde shook her head. I was embarrassed then, because I realized that I had assumed she was going to stay and visit, but in fact she had just come by to pick up the things she'd loaned me for the hospital.

"I'm sorry," I said. She didn't even undo her jacket, just stood there in the doorway with the noise of the TV making it hard to talk. I couldn't get over to turn it down and Francie never thought of doing things like that. "I'll get your stuff," I told Rosamunde.

Pretending it didn't matter to me to be in the wheelchair, I maneuvered my way out of the den and into the hallway. Rosamunde stood back to give me room. I know it was unreasonable for me to feel ashamed, but I did, because I was in the wheelchair, and clumsy, because I hadn't seen that she only wanted to collect her things and then get out of the house. I wasn't used to being clumsy. I wasn't used to not knowing what people were expecting. I'd thought she wanted to be friends, but I should have realized that if you don't come over until late Sunday afternoon, you aren't planning to visit long. I didn't want Rosamunde to see that I had expected her to stay, because that would make her feel sorry for me, and it might make her stay, which she didn't want to.

It was confusing, and I knew I couldn't just ask her outright. I'd never realized how hard it is to talk to people when everybody you talk to has something they want to hide from you.

"You better come with me," I said over my shoulder. "It'll be easier than me trying to load the stuff. My mom's got it all in a box for you."

I was tired out, anyway. The little Izzy inside my head

was draped over the bars of her walker, exhausted. I rolled into my room through the open door and parked myself beside the walker. There was no sense in trying to ignore it.

It isn't my fault, I thought, but nobody seemed to be thinking about that. They seemed to be thinking that I was getting what I wanted, sitting there in a wheelchair. With a walker. And crippled. It made me angry how stupid they were but I couldn't show my anger because then—then I would have really changed.

"It's in the closet." Rosamunde was kind of lurking like a lump. She slid the closet door open and looked in, to find the box. I watched the square back and the baggy overalls. Her shoulders started shaking and she just stood there with her shoulders shaking. She didn't get the carton or anything. After a couple of minutes of that, she started laughing out loud and turned around. Her eyes looked like they wanted to apologize for the rest of her face.

"I'm sorry—it's sick, really sick—I shouldn't be laughing, Izzy—" She sort of gasped words out. Her voice didn't sound as low and musical as usual, when she was laughing like that.

I wiped all expression from my face.

"It's just—look at them. It's so bad, it's funny," Rosamunde choked out.

I looked at the line of shoes. They were all left feet. I didn't see anything funny about it: one sneaker, one loafer, one red flat, one blue flat, one slipper, one sandal—all lined up in a row on the floor of the closet, with no spaces between for a match to the pair. There *was* something funny about it, it was like a "What's Wrong with This Picture?" I didn't want to, but I started to smile.

"It is sick," I agreed.

"Horrible." Rosamunde got her giggles under control.

"I'd never noticed." I started to really smile.

"It's like a cartoon, isn't it? Your mother must have done that—"

"Being thoughtful," I pointed out.

"But she wouldn't have thrown the mates away, would she?"

"I don't know. I never asked. Why shouldn't she get rid of them?"

"You'll get a wooden leg or something, won't you? Plastic probably. Do they come with shoes painted on, like doll's shoes?"

"My dolls' shoes always came off."

"Yeah, well, on cheaper dolls they paint the shoes on. But you'll need the mates, I'd think."

"Anyway, there's the box," I said.

Rosamunde pulled it out and then slid the closet door shut. "I didn't mean to laugh. Are you angry? I'd be angry."

I shook my head.

"Do you want me to go now?"

"I thought you wanted to."

"No, I could stay for a while, if you'd like. I'd like to. I've been so busy—I had a couple of babysitting jobs, and on Saturday mornings we always clean the house. I'd like to relax over here for a while."

"Take off your jacket then," I suggested.

She dropped it on the bed and sat beside it, looking around. "Did you like the books?"

"I didn't read them."

"Oh."

"I never did read much."

"I guess I can see that." She kept looking around. "Some people do and some don't. I sort of thought you didn't."

"I'll probably take it up, reading. Now."

"Anyway, is this your room?"

"Actually it's my parents', but I can't get upstairs."

Rosamunde got up and wandered around. "It's nice."

"Mom made some changes for me."

She went down to open the bathroom door. "You've got your own bathroom. It's almost worth it. We've got all of us using one bathroom at my house. This is very luxurious. I always wondered—I mean, here you are, the nice girl at home, in her natural habitat."

I wondered if she was trying to start a quarrel.

"What about school?" She returned to the big bed and sat crosslegged on it. "When are you coming back? How about making up the work you've missed? You want me to get your assignments?"

"Lisa's going to do that. My mother's picking them up tomorrow, but thanks anyway."

"If you get stuck, I could help," Rosamunde offered.

"Thank you."

"Because it's going to be bad enough, going back, I bet. You don't want to be behind or anything, on top of that."

"Yeah, I'm not looking forward to my return. But—I can ask you, is Suzy going with Marco these days?"

"That she is. Can you beat it? Did you know she was that dumb?"

"I thought so."

"I guess he's got his car all fixed so he has a lot to offer a girl."

"She was trying to keep it a secret from me."

"That sounds like her."

"As if she thought—I'm not looking for any revenge," I told Rosamunde. "It's not as if I think nobody ought to talk to him ever again or anything."

"But you have to admit it's tempting," she answered, her voice rich with laughter.

"Well . . ." I admitted.

"What I really can't figure out is—it's not as if he's learned his lesson, or anything. Unless he's just boasting, to keep up his reputation as a drinking man, or showing everybody that he doesn't feel guilty by not changing the way he acts. Unless he's lying, he's still driving around

more drunk than he should be. And someone who can't
even learn from experience—even *I* would have thought
Suzy would have better sense."

"You're kidding." She had shocked me. "Are you sure
about him?"

"Sure as I can be without going out with him myself.
Which I have no desire to do. Yeah, I'm pretty sure."

"I can't believe it." But I found I could; it was the kind
of person Marco was. I'd known that all along. He never
even had the nerve, or the manners, to call me up, after. Not
even to say he was sorry, if he was; some people thought if
they said they were sorry then they lost face, or something.
That sounded like Marco, too. "I was such a jerk to go out
with him."

"You were unlucky, that's all, really," Rosamunde said.

"Do you realize that the only reason I said I'd go was
because he was a senior?"

"Yeah, but we all have to do stupid things. Everybody
makes mistakes—just, most people aren't as unlucky as
you. If you see what I mean. I mean, you wouldn't have
gone out with him more than once, would you?"

I thought about that—remembering how frightened I was
as the car swerved down the dark road, how I had longed to
be safely home. "I don't think so."

"But Suzy is, going out with him. She must have an
underdeveloped sense of survival."

"She said she felt sorry for him. When I talked to her,
after."

"Marco's no fool, he knows how to get around people
like Suzy. At least everybody else is an awful lot more
careful about driving under the influence—under the influence of anything. But that's too grim to talk about." She got
up. "Except, of course, we've been thinking about it a lot,
most of us. Even those of us who have no social life.
Besides, I have to meet my father. He said he'd give me a
ride. I didn't mean to come here and upset you, Izzy."

"It's OK," I said. "You didn't. Not that way, anyway. Nobody has talked to me at all about what people are thinking. So, I guess I sort of fret about it."

"Figuring that it's too horrible to be told to you?"

"Something like that."

Rosamunde put on her jacket. "Well, here's my opinion, which could be wrong. There's an awful lot of pity, lying out there, waiting to get you. I don't know—I wouldn't much like that, if it were me. And most people sort of say, 'Whew, it wasn't me,' like when somebody dies. Along with the pity. That's how they feel. Marco now—he doesn't have too many friends anymore. Everybody's sort of . . . waiting for him to kill Suzy off."

"That's terrible."

"Yeah, well, she doesn't listen to anybody. And a lot of people who were at that party feel pretty guilty about you, from what I hear."

I nodded.

"I don't know how you're going to cope with it," Rosamunde said, carefully doing the snaps on her jacket. "It'll be hard getting back to being the nice girl, when everybody feels sorry for you and guilty. I mean, that's not a very popularity-conducive role, the victim."

"Maybe I won't go back."

"I can see why." A horn sounded outside. "But there must be a way to show them—that you're still yourself. Because you are, aren't you?"

I wasn't sure. I was hoping she would have told me.

"Anyway—call me if you want any help with home-work, or anything."

The horn sounded again, and I heard my mother open the front door. My mother would not be pleased to have somebody sitting outside out house, just leaning on the horn.

"You'd better go. I'll see you. My mother doesn't like honking—I mean, she really doesn't like it."

"Yeah, well, my father's had a pretty long day. I don't blame him."

I had kind of wanted her to stay for dinner, but there hadn't been time to ask my mother. Then, also, I wasn't sure how it would be, if Rosamunde stayed for dinner with us. The way my mother asked me, "Is her father a policeman?" gave me a clue about how the dinner might have gone. "Wasn't he in a city police uniform?"

The city police are lower on the respectability scale than the state police.

"Mom," I told her, from my place back at the kitchen table, "your class prejudices are showing."

"Don't tell me you like having someone just lean on the horn, just sit there and honk his horn for you." She hacked away at tomatoes.

I knew what she meant, and I agreed with her, but, "He wasn't honking for me," is what I said.

13

By the time I got into the kitchen Monday morning, everybody had left the house. My mother had set me out a bowl of cereal and a jug of milk. She had moved the toaster to the table, with bread beside it and the butter plate. She had poured me a glass of juice.

I ate alone, the room bright with sunlight, the whole big house empty around me. After I'd finished, I tried to clean up after myself. I didn't have anything else to do. Putting things back on the counter wasn't too bad, it was just awkward. I got the milk back into the refrigerator without any trouble. But when I tried to rinse off my dishes—grabbing the sink to hoist myself up to turn the water on, the wheelchair braked under me so it wouldn't roll away backwards, holding the cereal bowl under the water but unable to stop water spraying all over, and then I had to get a paper towel and try to mop up all the wet places . . .

I'd never thought how little I'd be able to do, all the things I'd taken for granted before. I'd never thought about how much I would be handicapped, even with chores. I'd been planning to make my bed, but I didn't even leave the kitchen. I sat there in the bright silence, alone in my

wheelchair. Inside my head, the little Izzy was all folded up
on the floor. She looked like a bad imitation of the dying
swan, her leg-and-a-half stuck out and her head bowed
down. I wished they hadn't left me all alone in the house,
and I wished there weren't five whole days to get through
before the weekend, when there would be people around
again. It wasn't that I wanted to be with people, particularly,
not even my family. It was just that whenever I was alone
my mind slipped down into grayness and I couldn't stop it.

There wasn't, after all, anything else to think about.
There wasn't anything to look forward to, or anything. I
used to do a lot of daydreaming, romantic stuff about the
boys I liked, so I never used to mind being left alone. But
romance was not in my future anymore.

The little Izzy put her arms around over the back of her
head.

When it was time, my mother managed me into the car and
then put the wheelchair in the back. We drove down to the
hospital, where she unloaded me by the front door, then
parked the car in a visitor's slot. I wore a skirt and sweater,
jacket and scarf; I kept my eyes on the sidewalk, then on the
carpeting, then on the linoleum floor as we went up to the
PT room. The same black nurse was waiting for me. "Good
morning, Mrs. Jones," I said to her. "Have you met my
mother?"

They shook hands, and my mother went off to get my
assignments, while I got put onto the walking ramp. Up and
down, I went up and down. Then my mother came back to
pick me up. "Thank you, Mrs. Jones," I said. Mrs. Jones
didn't answer.

After my mother had unloaded me, she emptied the car.
She had books and assignments, everything from my
locker. She had a new needlepoint kit, color-coordinated
with the one I'd finished. After lunch, I set myself up at the
desk in my room to start catching up.

Biology and Math were easy, and for World History I had to read the chapters and write answers to the questions. But the English—I couldn't understand Shakespeare's words, and the *Romeo and Juliet* paraphrase assignments were nothing I'd done before. So I wrote out a plot summary that took me three pages, front and back. Latin was translation and memorizing vocabulary and the subjunctive. I made vocabulary cards.

I worked about half an hour on each course and made a good start at everything. The assignments were all typed out by the principal's secretary. Each class had its own typed sheet, so it was easy to keep track. My mother had the tests to give me when I thought I was ready.

That afternoon and evening, I tried to call Suzy, but she wasn't home. I left a message with Ms. Wilkes that I had some questions about homework.

Tuesday was about the same, and I was really out of patience with Suzy by the time I went to bed that night. I was embarrassed to call her house anymore, like I was begging her to call me up. I knew Lisa couldn't help me with the homework and I wasn't calling up to try to get Suzy to talk to me. I had a reason for calling. All Wednesday afternoon I waited, but Suzy never called back. My mother asked if I'd like her to try to help, but I already was taking up so much of her time, I felt guilty enough without having her spend hours on my homework. Besides, I was doing all right with three of the courses, so it wasn't desperate.

It was just that I didn't understand why Suzy couldn't at least call me back to say she didn't have time to help. Only I did understand, because Suzy wouldn't want to say that, and she wouldn't want to say, yes, she would help; so she would just pretend she didn't have any calls to make. When Ms. Wilkes reminded her, she'd probably lie. Once she had lied, she couldn't possibly pick up the phone and call me.

I was tired of Suzy and her problems and her lies and her friendship that wasn't worth having. I quit, I said to myself.

I knew she had troubles of her own, but I was sick of being nice about it. I thought, Wednesday night, that I'd better call Lisa, even though I knew how hard it would be for her to try to explain to me what she had to work so hard to understand herself. Then I thought of Rosamunde.

But I didn't want to call up Rosamunde. It was like, if I did that, I would be asking her to be my friend, and she wasn't the kind of person who I had for friends. She was different from the people I had for friends, different from me, too. Except I knew I liked talking to her. She had a lot to say. And I knew that when she came to see me I had a better time than when my friends came to see me.

I didn't understand my reluctance to call her. I guessed, because I'd never had to ask anyone like Rosamunde for any kind of help before. But I still wasn't sure I was ready to take that step.

You can't take any steps, I reminded myself. Rather than think about that, I rolled myself down the hallway into the kitchen and pulled out the phone book, to see if I could find her number. I didn't even know where she lived, or anything; I didn't even know her father's name. I flipped the pages of the directory, looking for Webber, reminding myself that she had offered to help, if I wanted her to—reminding myself that Rosamunde seemed to mean what she said.

There were only two possibilities, and one of them was in a luxury condominium complex, so I decided to start with the other. "Is this the home of Rosamunde Webber?" I'd ask. I moved the wheelchair over to the wall phone, the directory open on my lap.

Then I just sat, looking up at the phone. I could sort of jump up to get it off the hook, but I didn't know how I'd be able to dial the number. I started to memorize the number, thinking that I could hang onto the phone—and hope my weight didn't pull it off the wall—while I dialed. If I had the number memorized. I didn't want to ask someone to dial the phone for me; I didn't want to be that helpless; I didn't want to need their help for such a small thing.

Frankly, it was pretty depressing, sitting there, thinking all of that, feeling angry and helpless and confused, and I couldn't keep the numbers straight, and I wasn't sure I even wanted to make the phone call. After all, they wouldn't flunk me or anything. People didn't do that to cripples. Mr. DePonte wouldn't do that, would he? And I didn't want to go back to school anyway, did I? And have everyone staring at me.

I tried to concentrate on the number. Francie was in the den with the TV on, so I couldn't use that phone without driving her out and hearing what she had to say about that. It wasn't hard to memorize a phone number. I didn't know why I was having so much trouble doing a simple thing I'd done dozens of times before.

When the phone rang over my head, I leaped up and grabbed it, then fell back into the chair which was moving away behind me.

"Hello," I said.

"Izzy? What's the matter? You sound out of breath."

"Rosamunde?" I didn't have to ask, though; nobody else had a voice like hers. "I was just going to call you."

"It's OK," she said, kind of slowly. "It doesn't matter to me."

"No, I was, but I don't know where you live, and then— we have a wall phone, so I was trying to memorize the number—"

"I said it's OK."

"But it's true. I don't tell lies."

I could hear her breathing and thinking. "No, you don't, do you? What did you want?"

"Help. With English and Latin. Could you, do you think?"

"Hey, I'd be glad to." The voice did sound glad. It sounded like she was smiling. "But it'll have to be after supper, and my dad's on night shift. Could one of your parents drive? The weekend is easier. I've only got a Sunday babysitting job this weekend. How desperate are you?"

"Pretty desperate, if you count not understanding anything I'm supposed to be doing—except the paraphrases, I've almost finished the first act, but I can't believe she really wants us to do all that work. But I don't understand what they're saying."

"Look, see if someone can do the driving tomorrow night. You'll feel better if we take a look at it, won't you?"

"Yeah, I would. I'll call you back, once I ask and all. What is your number?"

She told me. My guess had been correct. "That was the one I was going to try," I told her. "Because, I figured you didn't live in a condo."

"Why do you sound surprised? You're not stupid, you know."

"Ha," I said. Then I remembered, "What were you calling about?"

"I just thought I'd read something to you I thought you'd like."

"OK. Read it."

"Now?"

"Why not?"

"Well, it sounds pretty silly, now that I think about it. I just thought you might be interested."

I waited.

"But now that I look at it, I don't really think—"

"Just read it."

"Well, maybe . . . Do you remember Dora?"

I thought. Dora? Dora who? I didn't know any Doras— then I did remember that Dr. Epstein said I looked like Dora in a book. "The one who died," I remembered.

"This is before, it's when she first meets David Copperfield, or when he first meets her. Listen: 'I don't remember who was there, except Dora. I have not the least idea what we had for dinner, besides Dora. My impression is, that I dined off Dora entirely, and sent away half a dozen plates untouched. I sat next to her. I talked to her. She had the most delightful little voice, the gayest little laugh, the pleasantest and most fascinating little ways, that ever led a lost youth into hopeless slavery. She was rather diminutive altogether.' I told you it was a stupid idea,'' Rosamunde's voice said quickly in its normal tone.

"No, it's good. It was funny. You read well, don't you. Did *that* remind you of *me*?"

"Not exactly, I just always liked that scene. You reminded me of Dora later. When she's dying. She's sort of a twit, but essentially a really nice person."

"Thanks a lot," I said.

"You know what I mean," Rosamunde protested.

"No, I don't, not exactly. But I liked that, I liked the way it sounded. I don't think I've ever liked a famous writer before. I mean, other than Judy Blume."

"There's famous and famous," Rosamunde said.

"Look, I'm going to find my mother, and I'll call you back. Are you sure you've got time tomorrow?"

Rosamunde was sure.

My mother wasn't so sure. "I didn't know you two were friends," she said; but she was willing to do the driving, she said; it would be no trouble.

Once Rosamunde got to work with me, sitting in the kitchen again because there wasn't room for the two of us at the desk in my room, I was the one who wasn't sure. The first thing she told me was that I'd wasted my time writing endless summaries of *Romeo and Juliet*. "Your summary's supposed to be one paragraph per scene, and then you paraphrase only the lines she indicated," Rosamunde told me, skimming over the pages and pages of painstaking writing in which I'd tried to disguise the fact that I didn't know what was going on most of the time. She looked at the typed page of assignments and shook her head: "You'd think an English teacher would be able to write clear directions. I can see what happened."

I didn't care about that. "Do I have to do it all over?"

"It'll be easier this time."

"Ha."

"Do it aloud. Tell me what happens in the first scene."

"There's a fight."

"Between who?"

"I don't know, all these people, I don't know what's the matter with them. Then the Duke comes in and stops it. That doesn't have anything to do with Romeo and Juliet, so I sort of skipped it."

"Wait, wait. Izzy, think. This is Shakespeare. He's got a terrific rep, right?"

I shrugged.

"Well, he's had it for years, so it's probably deserved, so you have to assume he knows what he's doing. The first scenes in Shakespeare tell you what the themes of the play are."

"But Romeo and Juliet aren't even in it."

"Think, Izzy. What does that make you wonder about?"

"Why the scene is even in the play, since it's just a fight scene—which is pretty funny, too, since you don't even know what they're fighting about. They're only servants, aren't they? Why should they be fighting?"

"Good question," Rosamunde said.

"Don't be smug." I didn't much like feeling stupid. When I did homework with Suzy, she just told me the right answers. "Things must be pretty bad, if even the servants are fighting. But there isn't anything they're fighting for, is there? Except just to beat the other servants. It's not as if they'll win a war, or freedom, or somebody's love, or anything. That's terrible. I'd hate to live in Verona during those times; you'd never know what was going to happen when you went out the door in the morning, would you? No wonder the Duke is so angry at them. No wonder— Stop grinning at me like that. What are smiling at?"

"At you."

"You mean that's right?"

"Right, wrong, those don't matter. See, Shakespeare sort of sets out this problem, and his characters deal with the problem."

"And he's setting out the problem in the first scene." I understood.

"And you're defining the problem," Rosamunde agreed.

Working with Rosamunde was a lot more time consuming than working with Suzy, which was all right with me because I had a lot of time. It was also more fun, because she would drift off to talk about what something meant. Like, if you bit your thumb at someone in ancient Verona, what it was like today. "Giving someone the finger?" she asked me, "Do you think?"

"Except doing that is—pretty bad. Is biting thumbs so coarse?"

Rosamunde made her eyes into slits and glared at me. She lifted her thumb to her mouth and bit it. I bit my thumb back at her.

"I think it's more like thumbing your nose," I said.

All we did in the two hours was the first scene, but it was actually fun. We also drank cocoa my mother made and ate a bowl of popcorn Rosamunde said she didn't need. "Thanks," she said, putting on her PAL windbreaker while my mother—who had been drifting in and out—waited. "I had a good time." Her face was kind of lit up from all the talking she had done.

"Me too," I said.

"I've got a job tomorrow night, too, but I could come over on Saturday. We didn't even look at the Latin," she reminded me.

The next morning, maybe because I was still thinking

about the stupidity of hating somebody because of the color of the livery they wore, I found myself thinking about Mrs. Jones again, and thinking about myself, too, because I had what Rosamunde had called an external mark. I guess I was staring at Mrs. Jones while I thought about things. "What're you staring at, Miss Lingard?" she finally asked me, her eyes black and hard.

"I'm sorry, Mrs. Jones, really. I didn't mean to be rude, I didn't mean to stare. I was just thinking."

"Thinking what?" she demanded.

"Oh," I said. "I was thinking about *Romeo and Juliet*." That was as close to the truth as I could get. I started to turn around and head back up the walkway, but the smile spreading across Mrs. Jones's face stopped me. The smile moved as slowly as molasses. "Good Lord," she said, "what you girls think about."

I didn't try to explain. As I thanked her, at the end of the session, she said, "Lord, you'd better call me Adelia, since we've got months of work ahead of us."

I didn't know what to answer. My mother wouldn't approve. But my mother wasn't there with us, doing the work. Someone you work with, it's different. "If you'll call me Izzy," I answered. Adelia was, I thought, really a nice name.

"I'll see you Monday morning then, Izzy," she said. She looked a little self-conscious saying that.

"OK. And thank you . . . Adelia." I felt about ten times as self-conscious as she looked.

My mother had been making noises for days about having my hair cut, and as we drove toward home she told me she had nothing to do that afternoon, why didn't we go in and have it done.

"I'm thinking of growing it long." I stared at my hands in my lap.

"Lamb. Izzy," she said. Then she hesitated. "Izzy? I think I can guess how you feel, but—I hope, I really hope, you'll be able to tell me the truth. Because if you can't, then I can't help. That wasn't the truth, was it?"

"No. I guess I don't feel ready to go out in public."

"Because people will stare," she said.

I looked at her profile as she drove the car. We were both belted in. Nobody in my family was careless about seat belts anymore. She looked so—well-groomed and well-dressed and pretty, my mother, and a little worried, too. "Yes," I admitted.

"I can imagine," my mother said, sort of thoughtfully, her pink lips forming the words slowly. "But you're going to have to get used to it."

"I know."

"But it makes me so angry, sometimes. The way people act. Like, a lot of people asked if we were going to sue the Griggerses for damages, because we could make a lot of money."

"Yeah, Rosamunde said that."

"If we could sue them and get your leg back . . . I'd be camping out in the courtroom."

I knew that was true. I'd already known it, and I could hear it again in her voice.

"But there's nothing we can do, except—cope with it as well as we can."

"I know," I said.

"So, don't you want to get your hair cut? I was thinking, maybe something short and feathery. That's easy to take care of, and it might look terrific on you, because your face is much less round, you know."

I knew. What I didn't know was why I should bother trying to look terrific. Nobody was going to think of me as a pretty girl again. But I didn't want to tell my mother that, since she didn't seem able to accept that idea, that my whole life had changed. If she thought I was going to have a normal social life now, well, I didn't want to depress her.

"I'll tell you what," I said, "give me a couple more days to get used to the idea.

"Next week then?" She was pleased.

"Next week. I promise."

"And if anyone says or does anything, anything, to make you uncomfortable, I'll dump permanent lotion all over her head," my mother promised.

"Well, that's a relief to know."

She laughed. "Since we've got the afternoon free, do you want to stop at McDonald's for lunch and then take a drive in the country?"

She hadn't understood at all what I'd been saying to her.

"I mean, in the drive-through, Lamb."

"You know, I would like that. I feel like—I've been cooped up for ages."

"You have, silly, you have."

We ate in the car and my mother drove us out into the low hills, past working farms and posh estates. The trees had all turned to fall colors, so the entire landscape was like a quilt of colors, yellows and reds, mostly, and browns. I'd never noticed before the way the hills flowed, or the way the trees grown over them made the world look like a huge feather bed with the quilted colors laid over it.

I'd never noticed also what I saw as the car crested a hill and a valley opened out before me: The way the sky overhead completed the picture. That day, the blue sky was crossed by heavy gray clouds, which charged up toward us. There were soft, smoky grays in the clouds, which turned whiter at the edges. In the distance as if a charcoal painter had smudged in a darker line, curves of darker gray echoed the curves of the hills. I felt my eyes drinking it all in, or—more precisely—breathing it all in. Breathing was what it felt like.

The gray in the sky made the colors of the leaves glow deeper. We rounded a curve and I saw one tree, standing in the middle of a little pasture, a golden tree. Of course, it wasn't really gold, but it looked as if every leaf had been painted over with liquid gold, the way it shone. I watched that tree as we came up to it, with the gray clouds behind it; I kept my eyes on it as we drove away and left it behind. In my head, the miniature Izzy was just sitting there, knocked down by it, her eyes big with looking.

14

The next morning, Saturday, that tree was still in my head, glowing under gray clouds. "Sometimes I wish I could paint," I told my mother.

"It was weaving I wanted to do."

"Why didn't you?" I'd never even known she wanted to.

"I took a class, when I was pregnant with you. But— some people have good hands, and I don't. It was depressing."

"I'm sorry."

"So was I. I would like to have been a craftswoman."

Suzy and Lisa arrived at midmorning. I was half-expecting them. They hadn't called to say they were coming, but it seemed likely that they might, so I had washed and dressed and gone to the bathroom and all, just in case. Suzy and Lisa wore jeans and sweaters. Lisa's sweater was a pale blue Fair Isle crew neck. Suzy wore the same letter sweater, which she draped over the back of the chair, forgetting that last week she had denied owning it. Or, perhaps, thinking that I would forget her denial, or that if I remembered I wouldn't dare ask. Or hoping that I would.

I didn't ask.

We had mugs of tea and English muffins. We talked about what was going on at school, the latest issue of the newspaper, what couples had formed up or broken up, what new oddity any teachers had developed. We talked about the two boys Lisa had dates with that weekend, comparing them for looks and interest and likeability. After an hour, Suzy started looking at her watch and trying to catch Lisa's eye, while Lisa ignored her. Lisa asked me if I had enjoyed studying with Rosamunde. "Sure," I said.

"Yeah, she was boasting all around about it," Suzy said.

"Boasting?" I asked.

"She wasn't," Lisa said. "I don't know why you have it in for her."

"Saying how she'd been here at your house, as if that was some great privilege. You know how she is, Izzy, sort of a leech. I mean, she is definitely not cool at all. She's desperate to have friends and she hangs around the in-crowd—and there she was, yesterday, acting so big because *she'd* been over here, helping you with your *homework*, for God's sake."

"I didn't know you were having trouble," Lisa said.

"Acting superior," Suzy muttered.

Well, I thought, she certainly looks superior to you. The little Izzy inside my head clapped her hand over her mouth. Like Lisa, I ignored Suzy's muttering.

"With English."

"Did it help?" Lisa asked.

"Yeah, she's really smart. She'd make a good teacher."

"That's about all she'll make, with her looks."

"Do you like her?" Lisa asked.

"She's pretty funny."

"Who wants to talk about her anyway?" Suzy wondered. "Lisa, if we don't get going we'll be late. There was this boy, well, a college man actually, at the mall last week, when we were having lunch, and I told him we have lunch there every Saturday." Suzy grinned at me. "He was pretty cute, wasn't he, Lisa."

"He was. Kind of like Robert Redford."

"Sounds good," I said.

"But I still don't think he was in college," Lisa told me.

"He wasn't dressed like a high school kid," Suzy said.

I had the feeling they'd had this argument before, all week long.

"I thought he was one of the boys from Saints," Lisa told me. Saints is a local boarding school. "Suzy believed him."

"Why shouldn't I? Can you imagine how my sister will feel if I get invited for a college weekend? She'd die. She'd be so jealous, she'd turn green. He looked as old as the twins, didn't he?"

"What college did he say he went to?" I asked.

"He didn't, not exactly. You could tell," Suzy told me.

"Would someone in college go to meet girls at a mall?" I asked.

Suzy stared at me for a long time. "You're just jealous," she said, finally.

"No, I'm not," I told her, "I'm just trying to be logical." But I thought to myself, Of course I am, you jerk, what do you expect?

"Anyway, Lisa, you said you'd go back with me."

I didn't pay any attention, because I was realizing that Suzy had just said to me what you said when you wanted someone to go away, get out. I was realizing, watching them get up and put on their down vests, that of my three best friends, only one of them seemed to want to continue our friendship.

"Lisa," I said, "you know, I went for a drive yesterday—for about the first time—"

"Sounds like a good idea, getting out of the house," Lisa agreed.

"And I saw—"

"Are you coming or not," Suzy demanded. "I don't much care, except you said you would, but if you're going to we had better get going."

Lisa shrugged, following her out the door, saying she'd talk to me later or something. I thought that Lisa wouldn't have minded staying.

Rosamunde arrived on the dot of one, which was when she'd said she'd be there. I had finished my day's allotment of algebra problems and the biology reading, and she suggested that we work on Latin. We spread the books out, but Francie came in and sat down with us, asking Rosamunde questions that had nothing to do with anything. I sort of sat back, waiting for Francie to tell Rosamunde all about her great gymnastics achievements. Once Francie had made her point about how great she was, she'd go back and watch TV or something. "Do you do gymnastics?" Francie asked, with all the subtlety of a sledge hammer.

"Listen, kid," Rosamunde said. "Your sister and I have work to do. Why don't you beat it?"

"I do," Francie went on. "I'm on a team and we have meets and—"

"You're not listening to me," Rosamunde interrupted. She got up and took Francie's arm. She marched Francie to the open doorway. "Later, maybe. But now you have to scoot. We've got stuff to do."

"I'm going to tell, Izzy. It's everybody's kitchen, not just yours."

"You do that," Rosamunde answered. "Go ahead. Just don't come back."

Francie's lower lip stuck out, but she left. She didn't go upstairs to where my mother's sewing machine was purring. Instead, I heard the distant TV go on. "How'd you do that?" I asked.

"I've got a herd of little brothers and sisters," Rosamunde explained. She sat down again, hunched over the Latin textbook and her open notebook. As she started explaining about the subjunctive, I heard her digestive track rumble. I tried to concentrate on what she was telling me, but I kept being distracted. I wondered if she was sick, or something. She didn't look sick. She looked like always, sort of lumpy and badly dressed and not pretty.

"Are you sick or something?" I finally asked.

She shook her head, concentrating on what she was trying to explain about *let us* verbs.

"Hungry?" I guessed.

She shook her head.

Her stomach rumbled.

"You are too," I said. "Did you have lunch?"

Rosamunde shook her head, getting impatient with me.

"Do you want something to eat?"

"I wasn't invited for lunch, it's OK. Are we going to—"

"I can't concentrate when your stomach sounds like that," I told her. "Why don't you get yourself something to eat."

"It's not my house," Rosamunde said. "It's your house. If you want to get me something, I'd like that. But I can't just barge around and take things out."

She made me cross, although I don't know why exactly. We'd had hot dogs for lunch, with plenty of extras because my father likes hot dogs for lunch on weekends, so I made her hot dogs. It took me a long, awkward time, rolling around in the wheelchair, to get everything out of the refrigerator, to take out the frying pan from the low cupboard and put it on the stove and drop a pat of butter into it. I hauled myself up with one hand to reach down a glass, for milk. "You could *help*," I complained.

"It's good for you," Rosamunde's low voice answered me. I didn't turn around. "It's important for you to feel self-sufficient."

"What are you, a psychiatrist?"

"Are you angry at me? I didn't mean to make you angry, do you really want me to do something?"

"Well," I said, "if I wasn't—in this thing—you'd be helping, wouldn't you?" Until I'd said it, I didn't know I was thinking it. But once I'd heard myself say it, I knew it was true. "So why don't you watch the hot dogs, because I can't. Unless you like them burned."

"I'm sorry." Rosamunde got up and stood by the sputtering pan.

"Stop apologizing, OK?"

"I'm sorry," she said again. Her face looked curiously without expression, especially her eyes, which were watching the two hot dogs lying in butter as if the fate of the whole world depended on turning them at the right time.

"I guess you're right," I said. "I guess, I'm not doing enough for myself. Do you know that yesterday it was the first time I've been out of the house? Except to go to the hospital for therapy."

"But you've been home over a week."

"I guess I didn't want to."

"What did you do yesterday?"

"We just went for a drive. It wasn't any great achievement. But I saw this tree—it made me wish I could paint. It was gold, like the metal gold, you know? Like liquid gold, the way it shone."

"Does liquid gold shine?" she asked.

"Who knows? If it does, this is what it would look like. And it was so—beautiful. Under a gray sky and the grass all around it sort of deep green, the way grass gets when the sky is gray."

Rosamunde turned the hot dogs. I buttered the sides of the rolls and gave them to her to grill in the pan. Then I went to pour our milk, a little embarrassed about what I'd just said, about beauty, especially since she didn't have anything to say in response.

"I wonder," Rosamunde said at last. "Have you made up your design for that canvas yet?"

"What canvas?"

"I guess that answers my question." She chuckled, turning around to see my face go red, because I had remembered what canvas, and who had given it to me. "That's OK, I'll never tell, she'll never know. But you could try to make that into a needlepoint design, if you wanted to."

"I can't draw."

"It has nothing to do with drawing. You just x in the squares on the graph paper. Then you pick out colors. Your mother could probably help."

"But needlepoint things aren't like that, they don't look like what I'm picturing." Even while I protested, though, I wanted to try it.

"Kits are different, but you know how I feel about them. I think you ought to try it."

"Maybe I will. But how could wool get the colors right?"

"My mom'll know about that, there must be something—like silk or something—that would look the way you want it to. Once you get the design done."

"I *would* like to try," I said. Rosamunde put the hot dogs into the rolls and slathered them with mustard. She carried them to the table. I followed with the glass of milk, which I handed to her before I parked myself again. "Will you help?"

"Of course not." She swallowed. "It's no good unless it's your own design. Then it doesn't matter how good it is, because it's yours."

"It *was* beautiful," I remembered.

We got back to work, and she had me copying out conjugations because it was the best way to memorize, she said, when the back door flew open and the kitchen filled up with people and noise.

The twins had come home.

"Where's Mom?"

"What's for dinner?"

"Hey, Izzy, hey. Hey, how are you, you look great."

"You look like a human being again, not some starving refugee. You look like yourself."

"Dad's playing golf, right? Good, then he won't get a chance to ask me about grades."

"What is this, Latin? I passed that course."

And, to Rosamunde, who was sitting silent, "Who are you?"

I introduced her. "You're that one," Jack said. Rosamunde nodded, but didn't seem to have anything to say. Then she laughed. "Yeah, I'm that one."

"What'll we do, Izzy?" Joel asked. He had pulled down a box of cookies from the shelf and taken the milk out of the refrigerator. Jack was making himself a sandwich. "You want to go out for a pizza or anything? How about a game of Monopoly?"

I didn't want anything more than just to be in the same room with them for a while. They were talking back and forth and laughing; they brought sunlight into the room and they filled it with words in their rough voices. They made me feel good. I sat back smiling at them, until they slowed down a little. They had come home, I knew, to see me. They hadn't told anybody, I knew, because my mother had only defrosted one package of pork chops for supper. They had decided, even though it wasn't long at all until Thanksgiving, that they wanted to see me right away.

"What are you, a tutor or something?" Joel asked Rosamunde.

Before she could answer, Jack said, "No, she's the new friend, I told you about her. The one who yelled at me."

"I'm even more pleased to meet you," Joel smiled.

"I'm not so sure," Jack said, grinning at Rosamunde. He

looked good, I thought, leaning back with one arm draped over the chair, with the grin that suited him on his face. He knew he looked good, too, and I knew perfectly well he was waiting for Rosamunde to giggle or blush or something, the way my friends did around my brothers.

Rosamunde didn't do any of that. Instead, she looked uncomfortable and asked me if she shouldn't go, since we were through working. Jack looked surprised and Joel's eyes smiled. But I could tell that Rosamunde really was uncomfortable and sort of embarrassed, feeling out of place and in the way. "You haven't even looked at the conjugations I did," I argued. "And you said there were three points about the subjunctive and we've only covered two. And besides, if we're going to play Monopoly or something there's no reason for you to go, is there?"

"Or Clue," Jack said. "I'm unbeatable at Clue."

"Are you?" Rosamunde asked, sort of measuring him with her eyes, as if she doubted that he was as good as he said. "What about Trivial Pursuit?"

"We don't have that one yet," Joel said. "But we could get it. We should have it. Are you an expert? Your family plays every night?"

"No," Rosamunde said, "but we'll probably get it for our parents for Christmas. It's pretty expensive."

Jack was up from the table and halfway out of the room. "We can go to the mall. Let's say hi to Mom first, that'll give you girls about forty-five minutes so you better work fast. Joel, what are you waiting for?"

"She's upstairs, sewing. In your room," I called after them. I heard the two sets of feet thundering up the stairs. I didn't think my mother would be too surprised to see them. The whole atmosphere of the house changed when they were in it, as if all the air in all three stories had received an electric charge.

"Boy do they have energy," I said unnecessarily.

"Yeah. How'd you manage to keep your own personality, with them around?"

I couldn't answer, partly because it was such a new way of thinking about my brothers that surprise had me quiet.

"Makes me glad I'm the oldest."

"Do you think that's why? Because they're the oldest, not because they're boys?"

"That too," she said, "and because there are two of them I bet. Are they like you?"

"What do you mean, do you mean are they nice?"

"Don't pick on me, Izzy, you know what I mean. Are they good people, that's what I mean. Although, none of you seem to a have a realistic sense of money—those games cost thirty dollars, or thirty-five."

That wasn't much money, I thought, then I thought that it clearly was to Rosamunde, and I wanted to drop the subject. "If you want to know what they're like, stick around for the afternoon." I thought of telling her that it looked like Jack was flirting with her. Then I thought that wouldn't be a very nice thing to do to Rosamunde, because I knew Jack was a big flirt. He used to love it when Suzy and Lisa and Lauren came over, and he'd sweep through the room impressing them. I guessed Rosamunde wasn't used to having people flirt with her and I didn't want to make her self-conscious. It was hard to behave normally with someone you thought might notice you, especially if it was someone older, in college, and I didn't think Rosamunde would have a good time if she couldn't act normal. Even though her normal wasn't what everybody else's normal was.

When we sat down around the table, the new game spread out while Joel read the directions, my mother left to get a dinner. "What a pleasure," she said. "What a treat to have you here for dinner."

"She didn't feel that way last year at this time, did she?" Jack asked Joel.

"Last year, it was all complaints about how much we ate."

"Now she appreciates us," Jack said.

My mother laughed. "Absence makes the heart grow fonder," she reminded them.

"Fonder enough for lobster?" Jack asked. "A good mother wants to give her children everything."

"A good mother knows how to moderate her sentiments," my mother said.

Rosamunde said we should play in teams, so Jack claimed me for the stupids. "Wait," Rosamunde said. "I know, we'll play boys against the girls."

"That's not fair," Joel said.

"Why not?"

"Well, we're older, and—"

"Uh-oh," Rosamunde said. "Izzy, do you hear what he's implying?"

"Yes, and he's probably right."

"I don't believe that and you shouldn't either. Don't you have any faith in me? Besides, where's Francie? How can you have a family game without Francie?"

She was right, and we all three knew it. Joel went off to haul Francie in. We decided to play girls against the boys, simply because nobody could give Rosamunde a good enough reason not to. Francie wanted to play with the pink piece. "We're the girls," she said, "so we'll be pink."

"And you take blue." I tossed the blue piece at Jack.

"I want green, don't you, Jo?" But Joel didn't care.

"Blue, you've got to be blue," Francie insisted. Rosamunde and I just laughed. I sat between Francie—who kept nudging into me in her excitement to move our piece around the board—and Rosamunde. It was a good game. Joel was the best on their side, but Jack knew surprisingly accurate details about sports and science. Rosamunde would read the questions and nag them about what high school course they should know this from. Rosamunde was by far the best on our team, although Francie had a surprising knowledge of entertainment, when it came to rock stars and TV programs. I even had a moment of glory, brief, but important since it got us the brown Art-and-Literature triangle for our piece. Jack looked at my question and smirked at Joel. "This one's for Izzy, my soul mate, who hasn't read a book outside of school for years. Izzy? What's the name of David Copperfield's first wife?"

I said it quietly and confidently: "Dora." Then I broke up laughing at his expression. "Come on, give us the piece, you know that's right."

"Dora what? The rules say it's got to be what's written down."

For a minute I thought he had me, then I realized: "Dora Copperfield."

Joel drummed on the table, pleased. "She's got it, Jack."

"Spenlow," Rosamunde offered. "Dora Spenlow—if they asked for her maiden name."

Joel looked over Jack's shoulder at the answer. "It's just Dora, you creep."

Jack sputtered, grumped, and muttered, "Girls." Francie crowed aloud that we were going to win.

We didn't win, but we came close, and the only reason we didn't was because we had bad luck with the die, trying to get into the middle before the boys did.

My mother took Rosamunde home, late in the afternoon, even though the twins offered to do it. As soon as we were just ourselves together, the family started giving its opinions. "She's sure different from the rest of your crowd," Jack said.

"I like her," Francie announced. That surprised me. We were picking up the game. Francie gathered up the little triangles to put back into the plastic sack. "I do. She looks at me as if I'm really there, not like I was some—bug."

"She's not good-looking like the rest," Jack said, "but then, she's not dumb either."

"Suzy's not dumb," I said.

"C'mon, Izzy," Joel said. "There's a lot more to being smart than having the right answers in school."

"Although, I kind of like her nose," Jack said.

"Yeah, I approve of her too," Joel said to Francie.

"Now that you've settled my life," I groused.

At dinner, my mother finally said, "What a strange child. Really. Her father's a policeman."

"I told you that. What difference does it make?"

"A city policeman."

"The dregs." Jack defined it.

"But because of the school system," my mother went on. "Hendrik, would you do that? Would you take a job that was—well, you know, nowhere near your first choice of the jobs you were offered, one you probably wouldn't like—so your children could go to good schools?"

"I never had to face that decision," my father pointed out. "And I'm glad I didn't." We were all chewing on barbecued spareribs, one of our great favorites.

"My question is, what does she see in Izzy?" Jack said.

"You're kidding," my mother asked him. "I wonder what you see in her," she said to me.

"Jack means because she is pretty high-powered, intellectually," Joel said. "But Jack always underestimates Izzy's brains. We all do, because she's so easy-going—even you do, Sis," he told me. "But Jack's just . . . working to his own convenience when he does that."

"Oh yeah?" Jack said, his temper rising. "You just idealize people, Jo; you're not realistic at all. Right, Izzy?" He grinned at me.

He expected me to go along with him, as always. I didn't want to, although I didn't want to disagree either, because I had no idea. So I bit my thumb at him.

Nobody else said anything either. They all thought they had figured me out. I wondered what my father, quiet at the head of the table, was thinking. I was willing to bet he was thinking along the lines I was, that nobody should be so sure of what I was like, not anymore.

15

The next morning it stormed rain, and the wind blew around the house. My mother said she was glad after all that the twins had driven back to school after dinner, although she had tried to convince them to stay over. After breakfast, I went to my room to do the Latin exercises and try some translation. As I worked, I heard the rain sluicing down and spattering against the windows. The wind hummed fiercely around the house.

When my mother interrupted, late in the morning, to tell me I had visitors, I thought it must be Lisa and Suzy, and I hoped they wouldn't stay long. I had promised myself that when I finished a week's assignments I could try to design the needlepoint. It wouldn't hurt to try, I thought.

"A boy and a girl," my mother said. "I don't know them," she asked me.

When I rolled myself into the front hall, expecting—still trying to figure out who it might be, so not expecting anybody—and saw it was Tony Marcel, with Deborah beside him, standing in our hallway with rain dripping off his hair and his slicker . . . I wanted to turn around and wheel back into my room. And shut the door.

But the wheelchair where I sat, looking up at them, was too clumsy. I would have had to back it around and everything, like a remote control car, and that would have been even worse. So I said hello and introduced them to my mother and couldn't think of anything to say when she left us.

I had forgotten how slender Tony's neck was, how long his legs were, what a good straight nose he had. I had never noticed the green in his light brown eyes before, or the way one of his eye teeth just overlapped the front incisor. My mother had said we'd want to sit in the living room but I would have died if I'd had to roll the wheelchair down the ramp. "Let's use the den," I said. "It's warmer. On a day like today." I didn't know what to say.

"That's some storm, isn't it?" Deborah asked. She sounded pleased by the storm, as if it were a personal pleasure to her.

I agreed and led the way down the hall, into the den. I would rather have gone behind them, but they didn't know the way. At least, I didn't have to look at them watching me. I didn't know how I was going to get through whatever conversation we were going to have.

They sat on the sofa, facing the blank TV screen. The Sunday paper was piled on the coffee table and the curtains were drawn closed, against the weather. I sat, or rather, I parked my wheelchair near the doorway, where there was plenty of room. I made sure the blanket was spread out all over my lap and legs.

"They say the winds may gust up to seventy," Deborah said. "That makes it almost a gale."

"Oh dear," I said, since it was clearly time for me to say something. As soon as I said that, I felt really stupid. "How are you?" I asked them, which was equally stupid.

"We're fine," Tony said. He was sitting forward, not relaxed. He was wearing a light gray sweater and jeans. "You look—"

He couldn't finish that sentence and I felt a kind of bitter pleasure. At least, he wasn't a liar.

"Izzy," Deborah said, taking pity on Tony, "we have felt—terrible, really terrible. And we've come to apologize."

I didn't much want to talk about this. "It's OK," I said, "it wasn't your fault."

"Not precisely," Deborah agreed, "but we know Marco better than you did."

I swallowed. I watched Tony swallow. But it wouldn't do any good to have people feeling sorry for me, and guilty. I didn't want to be the object of everybody's pity. "I can see how you feel," I told them, looking especially at Deborah. "And I think—well, I think it's nice of you to come tell me that. No, I do. As long as you know I don't think it's your fault, at all, really. I mean—well, I was just unlucky, I was the unlucky one."

I said that, and I half meant it. In a way, I really believed it. In another way, for the other half, I wished—

"You are something, Izzy," Tony said then. "You know that? You are really something. I really—" He couldn't finish that sentence, either.

"A better man than I," Deborah said, smiling at me. I could feel in her smile that she had relaxed, after she had made her apology, and that she was beginning to think I might be interesting, an interesting person, and that she approved of me. I liked her thinking that about me; I liked being a person of whom Deborah thought well.

"We wondered, when you come back to school—we'd like . . ." Tony's words stumbled around; he looked from the hands spread out on his knees to me, and then back to his hands again. "Can you believe how badly I'm saying this?" he asked Deborah.

"I can believe it," she told him.

"We'd like you to try working on the paper," Tony said. "I don't know what you'd like, or be good at, writing, or the business end, or editing or what, but we all—everyone on the staff—want you to try. What do you say?"

Talk about not knowing what to think.

On the one hand, being on the paper was. . . . Well, it was a select crowd of people, about the best people in the school, who were on the paper, the ones who were smart but not weird, the most interesting people. On the other hand, I couldn't think of anything I could do on the paper, except be pretty bad at whatever job they gave me. It wasn't as if I was talented or anything. So I'd probably flub it and be an embarrassment. I knew, as well, that if—if this hadn't happened, they would never have considered me. I would still be one of the cheerleaders, which I couldn't do now, but because I couldn't do that now they were asking me. Besides, I didn't know anybody on the paper.

"I can't," I said, looking now at my own hands. I didn't want them feeling sorry for me, I didn't want people coming around out of pity because I couldn't be a cheerleader anymore. I didn't need to go out and not be able to do something else, while everybody around me let me go on trying because they felt sorry for me.

"Why not?" Tony asked. He sounded offended, as if he really cared about having me on his paper. I guessed he felt as if he had offered me a great treasure, and I had just turned it down, which hurt his feelings.

"Because," I said. "Because—well, because you feel guilty and that's why. Why you've asked."

Tony got up from the sofa and sort of paced around the small room. The room didn't give him much room for pacing, because his legs were so long.

"OK, OK," he said.

"I'm sorry," I said, trying to let him know that I didn't mean to insult him. I wished Deborah would say something. I was feeling uncomfortable, out of my depth in this conversation. It wasn't as if we knew each other well enough to talk like this.

"For God's sake, Izzy," Tony said. "Look, of course it's because we feel guilty. I mean, who wouldn't? I should have gone ahead and taken you home, I should have had the guts. And the brains too. And it's because I feel sorry for you, too, if you must have the truth."

I didn't feel any need for the truth, frankly.

"And I thought this would be easy," Tony said to Deborah. "Once I nerved myself to do it. We underestimated you, Izzy."

I didn't know what to say.

"But I really want you to try it, and I think you *ought* to, for your own sake." He stood in front of me, waiting for my answer. "If it makes any difference, I'd feel a hell of a lot better about myself if you'd agree to try it."

I tried to think, but I couldn't. I felt sorry for Tony, because he was essentially a nice person, and felt he should have prevented what happened to me. It wasn't his fault, and he knew that, but he also knew that he was connected to what had happened, and he felt responsible to do something, whatever it was in his power to do. I liked that about him.

"I don't want you to feel badly about yourself," I tried to tell him.

"So you'll say yes?" he asked me.

Deborah laughed. "You're rushing her, Tony. Give her a little time. Right, Izzy?"

I nodded my head, grateful to her. I felt like a little kid, but I didn't mind that, just as long as I could get some time to really think about it.

"But you will think seriously about it, won't you?" Tony asked.

"Are you kidding?" I asked him, looking up into his greenish eyes without even realizing what I was doing, just as if I wasn't crippled. "You know what a—compliment it is? I mean, everybody wants to be on the paper." Then I remembered and stopped looking into his face.

"Good. Good. Then we'd better go, before I say something wrong again. Deborah came along to give me moral courage." He laughed. "Now maybe I can concentrate on that history paper."

Deborah offered to wheel me back out to the door. I refused her offer, but had to let her turn me around and head me in the right direction, trying not to show anything of how that made me feel. I think she understood that, because she talked to Tony about the paper over my head as she worked the wheelchair around, but then—she remarked to me as I wheeled down the short hall, "That's harder than I thought to move."

"Well," I told her, "it's not so bad on the level, especially if there's no rug, and downhill is easy. It's only going uphill that's hard."

Tony had his slicker on and his hand on the door. "Isn't that the truth," he said to me. As if I had meant to say something profound.

"See you, Izzy," Deborah said, going back out into the rain. "Say yes, please, OK?" and she pulled the door closed behind them. I sat for a minute, absolutely still, not thinking about anything in particular. Thinking how sad everything was. Thinking that I could see why Tony was so wild about Deborah.

16

Everybody thought I was adjusting well. Dr. Epstein said so, when he came by after office hours on Monday, to look at my leg and admire the way it had healed, to look at my face. "You're adjusting very well, Izzy," he said.

"Thank you," I said.

My parents didn't say so, but I could tell from the way they looked at me that they thought so. The twins had left in such boisterous good humor that I knew they had been relieved by what they had seen in me. Francie had gotten entirely used to the idea, forgetting—the way children do—that things had ever been different and Rosamunde . . . I don't think it ever crossed her mind that I wouldn't. Adjust, that is.

I knew what they were thinking because everybody began talking about when I was going to go back to school. "The cast comes off at the end of the week," Dr. Epstein told me. "How do you feel about going back to school?"

"You'll want to have it cut and styled," my mother said, asking me when I wanted to make the appointment for my haircut, "before you go back to school."

I could see why they thought I was adjusting so well. But

I knew I wasn't. It was as if my life had cracked in half, and
the two parts of it were as different as night and day. The
day Izzy was the one everybody saw and talked to. The
night Izzy, only I knew about. She was scared; she did a lot
of weeping and whining alone in her room. She was
ashamed of herself, and she tried hard to make herself
accept what had happened, but she couldn't accept it. I
couldn't accept it. The shock had worn off, but whenever I
started to think of everything that had changed, everything I
could never have or do now, there was nothing I could do to
make myself accept it.

I wasn't sure I wanted to go back to school, anyway; in
fact, I was sure I didn't want to. When we went to have my
hair cut, I knew why.

I used to like going to have my hair cut. I liked the
mirrors in the room and all the smells of lotions and
shampoos. I liked to sit there—young and fresh and
pretty—and see what the women were having done, to
make themselves look younger and prettier. I liked the way
my mother's hairdresser teased me about boyfriends and
dances. Not anymore, though. Somebody held the door
open so my mother could wheel me in, and a few people
who had met me came around to say how sorry they were.
What was I supposed to say to that? It's all right? There
were too many people in the room, and their eyes avoided
me, and they stared.

At least, there was no waiting. My mother parked me
beside one of the big chairs a normal person would have
climbed up into, and Leigh—who always did my hair—got
right to work. I don't think I said more than three words all
the time I was there. She clipped and cut. My mother
talked, and I concentrated on keeping my face set into a
pleasant expression. I didn't care what they were doing to
my hair. I didn't care about the pockets of whispered
conversations all around me. I only cared about getting
finished with this.

Leigh sprayed and trimmed, then worked over my head with a blow drier, then trimmed a little more. She must have been half an hour solid on that haircut. When she finally gave me a hand mirror, she sounded pretty pleased with herself.

I didn't mind the hand mirror, I looked into it. My face looked pale and my eyes dark blue, and my mother was right about my eyelashes. Somehow, the short hair, feathered around my head and blown back from my face, looked especially good on my eyes. I looked, I thought, a little older. My hair even looked more blonde. "Thank you," I said over my shoulder. "It's really nice."

I guess that's five words already. I meant it, of course, because it was a good haircut. I looked pretty. I thought if I was going to have to be crippled I'd rather not look pretty. I thought, any other time she would have teased me about boyfriends loving it. I thought I wouldn't be able to stand the way all the women, who had been pretending not to notice me, now had some comment to make about how nice I looked—the other hairdressers and the women with curlers all over their heads.

"That wasn't so bad," my mother said, once we were settled in the car again. "Was it?"

"It's a really good haircut," I answered her. Because it was bad, and these were only strangers. It would be worse, I knew, if they had been people I already knew, from before.

Adelia had me working on crutches that week, getting ready. She recommended the old-fashioned kind, tall wooden crutches that fitted into my armpits, because eventually I'd have canes and things and the tall crutches would keep me walking straighter. I propped myself up on them, trying to remember how the people I'd seen with broken legs or ankles had used them. My blouse pulled up out of the waist of my skirt because of them.

"It'll be much more comfortable once that cast comes off," Adelia told me.

I nodded, concentrating on how wide to space the crutches, how to step them forward. After a couple of days, I could really sort of move around. Not fast, or anything, but I could go where I wanted, turn or go forward, and keep my balance easily. I started going down the whole length of the room, moving between the other PT patients and their nurses.

That was my mistake, because while I was looking at the floor and concentrating on balance, I walked myself right up to a full length mirror.

I couldn't stop myself from looking. There was this blonde girl with feathery hair, on crutches, with her shirt pulled up and hanging out over her plaid skirt. Her right leg hung down about two inches from the hem, and then stopped.

It was grotesque.

It wasn't so bad, actually. It wasn't anything as bad as Jeannette Wheatley's face, in terms of looking at it and wanting to never have to see it again. The skin looked sort of normal colored. There wasn't a big mass of lumpy flesh at the end of my leg. Just a stump.

The stump hung down about two inches below my skirt. It looked grotesque.

Adelia stood behind me, and I looked at the two of us in the mirror. She was much bigger than I was, taller and broader. Her ankles were thick and her calves muscular. I looked at myself again, trying to make myself see it and accept it. That was my grotesque stumpy leg there. I'd never seen it like this, the way it would look to other people. I had to accept it, I guessed, but I couldn't accept it, and I didn't want to have to.

Adelia spoke from behind me. I kept my eyes on the stump, making myself look at it. "There isn't anything you can do about it, Izzy."

I didn't need her to tell me that.

"Except maybe wear trousers. You'd pin them up in the back."

I'd never thought of that. My mother had removed all my pants from my drawers, so I thought there was some reason not to wear them. But maybe there wasn't, maybe my mother just thought pinned-up pants looked too crippled, or something.

I looked at my stump. Pants couldn't look any more crippled than that did. I saw, out of the corner of my eye, Adelia's bright white uniform and her dark skin. I thought again that she and I had the same kind of problem: Everybody who saw us knew right away what label to use. When Adelia said there wasn't anything to do about it, she knew what she was talking about.

I looked into her eyes in the mirror, but she was checking the time. I wondered, then, if she'd ever *wanted* to do anything about what she was. I did about myself, but that didn't mean she would change to white if she could. Because we had different kinds of problems, however much they were the same in one way. She'd probably say hers wasn't even a problem at all, not for her. I hoped that was what she'd say.

"Definitely pants," I told her, turning away from the mirror.

As my mother drove me home, my legs covered with a car blanket and the wheelchair folded in the rear of the station wagon, I asked her. "Why did you take away all my pants?"

She didn't answer.

"I need some pants to wear. These skirts are too short— and—and—I wish you hadn't gotten rid of my pants."

"But I didn't."

"Oh. Do we have any safety pins? To pin them up with."

"You wouldn't rather have a hem?"

"No. That would look worse."

"But we can't get pants over the cast, Izzy." My mother sounded like she was apologizing.

"Oh."

"After Friday, though. Unless—how much does it matter to you? We could certainly sacrifice a pair of jeans. We could easily slit the the leg to make room for the cast."

All along the road the dried leaves were being blown by the wind. Leaves rushed toward us, brown and yellow and red, skittering along the roadway, just being blown along.

"Yes, please," I said to my mother, suddenly exhausted. "I'm sorry."

"Oh, Love, it's OK. That wasn't even much of a show of temper. It wasn't anything like the performances you put on last year."

"I'll have to try harder," I joked back.

"You're doing just fine," my mother said, serious again. "You're doing just right. I'm so proud of the way you've adjusted."

You adjust the hem of a skirt, making it longer or shorter, so in that sense I guess I was adjusted. You adjust the temperature in a room, or an attitude, which means changing it, and in that sense too I had been adjusted. But these were all, as we said in Latin, passive verbs: I was the subject but I didn't do anything. Everything was done to me, had been done to me. I thought about that, and then, when we got home again, I took out the bag Rosamunde's mother had given me in the hospital, to think about a design for the blank canvas, to stop thinking about adjustment.

My mother was going out for lunch and then doing errands and the grocery shopping, so I had the house to myself until Francie came home. I spread out the square of canvas and looked at it: It was brown mesh, with white tape sewn all around the edges, about a yard long and a foot and a half wide. I tried to see a picture on it but I couldn't. So I took the pad of graph paper and a pencil and started sketching.

It was something to do, I thought, making a lot of little pictures all over the paper, trying to find a shape I liked. It didn't matter if I couldn't do it, because there was nobody but me in the house. It didn't even matter, I thought, looking at a sketch with a tree that looked like one of those rocket lollipops and a straight line for the grass and pillows for clouds, if I couldn't draw—which I couldn't. When I got a general design I liked, I took a fresh sheet of graph paper and tried it larger. The tree was in the middle, at stage center. Behind it, I put clouds in layers, trying to make the edges wavy so the sky wouldn't look striped.

The hardest thing, I discovered, with that sketch by my side as I tried to x in the squares, the way Rosamunde had said I should, was to get a sense of the tree. I couldn't figure out how to get the leaves in, the layers and layers, each individual leaf there but making only a part of the whole golden tree.

Just before Francie was due, I packed all the papers away into the bag and returned them to my room. When Francie came in, I was sitting in the den, reading a beginning needlepoint book. I was looking at different stitches, wondering how I might use them to get the effect I wanted.

I was having a good time. I was entirely happy right then. I remember recognizing the feeling and looking up, surprised. As soon as I had recognized it, however, I lost it. Like a little kid grabbing at a soap bubble, I thought: When you touch it, it bursts.

Francie slouched into the room and dumped her knapsack on the floor. "There's nothing to eat."

"Have some fruit. Have a jam sandwich. Have some milk. Do you have any colored pens I could use?" I asked her.

"What for?"

"Just something. Do you?"

"Yeah, I have some upstairs."

"May I borrow them?"

She shook her head.

"Why not? What's the matter with letting me just borrow your pens? I won't break them or anything."

"I don't have to," Francie said. "You can't make me."

I knew that. I tried to think of some bribe I could offer her.

Francie dropped her vest down on top of her knapsack and put her hands on her hips, glaring at me.

"Boy, what's wrong with you today?" I asked.

"Wendy's having a birthday party."

"So what?"

"She said, she wasn't going to invite me."

"Yes, she will, Francie; she always does. Don't be silly. Why did she say that, anyway?"

"Because I didn't vote for her to be the princess in our Christmas play."

I almost burst out laughing. It was just like Francie. "And you told her about it, right? Why did you tell her?"

"Because she was saying it wasn't fair and somebody must have counted the votes wrong. Because I don't think they did count the votes wrong."

"Who did you vote for?"

"Me."

"Oh." I knew I shouldn't laugh, and I didn't. "Did you win?"

Francie shook her head, emphatically. "It's going to be a slumber party. But I told her."

"Told her what?"

"Her mother will make her ask me. So that's all right."

Francie left the room and I sat there in my wheelchair wishing my mother would come home right then, so I could tell her about that conversation. She would get a kick out of that conversation.

"Anyway," I called after Francie, wheeling down the hallway to follow her into the kitchen, "can I please, please, borrow your colored pens. Just for an hour?"

"I told you, no. Ask Mommy to get you some. She gets you anything you want, anyway, now."

If I hadn't been in a wheelchair, I would have stomped out of the room. As it was, I had to back around a couple of times to reverse my direction. If they hadn't taken the door off the hinges, I could have swung it behind me so hard it would rock back and forth, *clump, clump, clump*.

I went back to my own room and took out some homework. If my parents had been home, Francie would never have said that. I scratched out the answer to a problem, waiting for the tightness in my throat to ease up. No wonder Francie didn't have any real friends.

There was a knock on the door. "Who is it?"

"It's me, Francie."

"Go away," I said.

She opened the door and came in. "What are you doing?"

"I said, go away. That means, don't come in. I meant what I said."

"Yeah, but you can't do anything about it," Francie told me.

I thought I would burst into tears of shame and frustration. I thought I was angry enough to get out of the wheelchair and hustle my sister out of the room by the scruff of her neck. I was angry enough to move normally. Inside my head, the little Izzy blew up like a red balloon. I thought I would throw the math book at Francie's head.

I did none of those things. I sat there, half turned toward her, getting control, holding control. I don't know what I looked like, but Francie got up from the bed and started backing toward the door. I paid no attention to her. It had nothing to do with Francie. It had only to do with me, with my relationship to me.

"I'm telling," Francie said. "I'm going to tell Mommy on you. You're being mean and you're jealous and I'm telling."

She didn't close the door but that didn't matter, because she wouldn't be coming back. I didn't have to worry about Francie. She was my parents' problem: handling her, teaching her how to behave like a human being.

I felt sorry for her, and I would have liked to help. I even knew what was wrong with her. Here was this older sister she envied and admired, who could do anything, as far as Francie knew, and I had turned into a cripple. For years, she had been sort of comparing herself to me, with me as the example, and however she felt about it, she still thought I was the perfect example. Then a terrible thing had happened to me. Francie had to figure out—she was smart enough, that was half her trouble—that terrible things could happen to anybody, whether you were the good sister or the bad sister, or anybody.

I knew Francie was frightened, but I couldn't do anything about that. I had myself to take care of, first. Because I was frightened too.

I was sorry to be the cause of Francie's fears, but she was also blaming me for them. As long as she did that, I knew, thinking about it, as long as she couldn't stand to feel sorry for me—which she couldn't stand, because she felt so sorry for me—I couldn't say anything to her, couldn't tell her in any way, or show in any way, that this wasn't as bad as she thought.

Unless, I thought grimly, it was just as bad as she was thinking it was. And I wasn't so sure it wasn't.

I got back to math, which was pretty soothing stuff at that point. I heard my mother drive up, but she didn't come to say hello. I guessed she was occupied in the kitchen with Francie. After a while, after a biology chapter and two scenes of *Romeo and Juliet*, I heard the TV go on. I came out at about the time my father would be home. I rolled right along into the kitchen. My mother had a roast cooking and the salad made, ready to be dressed. She was sitting at the table, going after the legs of a pair of jeans with her big sewing scissors.

"That's great," I said.

She held out packets of diaper pins. "Will these do? I didn't know if you'd want pink or blue or yellow pins, so I got all three."

"I can color coordinate," I told her. "Thanks, Mom. It won't look too awful," I tried to tell her. "I don't think."

"I don't care how it *looks*," she said, not meaning exactly what she was saying. But I knew what she meant.

"Anyway, isn't Francie watching an awful lot of TV?"

"Oh, Francie," she said, with no amusement in her voice. "Izzy, I'm sorry—if half of what she told me is accurate, she really was—"

"Francie-ish," I finished for her. "It's OK, Mom. I guess, I can live with her."

"I'm not sure I can." She got up to pour herself a glass of wine, then sat down again. "I know—in my bones—she's going to be all right; she'll make a good person when she grows up. It's just going to be so hard on the rest of us, getting her there."

So my mother was just as surprised as I was when my father came in a few minutes later and handed me a bag. "Francie said you wanted these," he said. "She said I had to get them on the way home, or everybody here would be upset."

It was a box of forty-eight colored pens, stretching out across like a freshly ironed rainbow. I looked at my mother. She didn't know anything about it. Francie came into the room, as if she was coming in about something else, and looked at the box on my lap.

"It's much better than mine."

I ignored that. "Thanks, kid," I said. "And you too, Dad. It's just what I wanted, better than I asked for. You were nice to call Dad, Francie."

She nodded her agreement with me. I took a careful look

at her, wondering just what did go on in her mind, wondering how she couldn't know that the way she was standing there so smug, expecting everybody to be thinking good thoughts about her, would make it hard for people to feel loving toward her. She really didn't know much about people, I thought, looking at her gangly body, her long arms and legs, and then her long hair, almost ashy blonde, her deep eyelids and her bony nose. I looked and looked at her, seeing her.

"What are you staring at," she finally said.

"You. You really are going to be lovely, do you know that?" It was true, and I'd never known it before, however much I'd figured my mother was probably right about Francie's looks.

"I don't care," she muttered, sulky.

"I don't care if you care or not," I snapped. "But I do like these pens."

"I knew if you told, they'd make me give you mine."

Little sisters, I thought. I wondered if a little brother would be any better.

17

On Saturday, after we had put in a couple of hours on schoolwork, I asked Rosamunde what the difference was between little sisters and little brothers. "When push comes to shove, none," she told me. "Are you going to get rid of that wheelchair now? I hope so, it's pretty depressing, sort of sitting there empty—like it was waiting. Is Francie acting up? She's not like you, you know, and never will be, if you ask me. Are you going to show me how you do on the crutches? I mean, I've been admiring the way you sit on a real chair, just like a real person," and she smiled at me. When Rosamunde really smiled, her eyes lit up and her whole face lit up too.

"Do you ever wear lipstick?" I asked her.

"What goes on in your mind, Izzy," she demanded, but still teasing me. "Whenever I think you're coming along well, you start talking about lipstick, or something."

"You're avoiding the question. I'd like to make up your face sometime. Well, I would, it would be interesting."

"It would be disappointing. Are you going to show me how you do on crutches? You're the one who's avoiding."

"No, I'm not. Why do you want to see that, anyway?"

Rosamunde had piled all of our books on the table. "To see how mobile you'll be. I've been thinking you ought to see if all of your classes—how many classes do you have on the second and third floors?"

"Just Math and Latin. Why?"

"If they could be moved to the ground floor. Your mother should ask. When are you coming back?"

"I haven't thought about it. After Thanksgiving, I guess. Maybe." I took the crutches she was holding out for me and went down the kitchen for her, turned around at the dining room doorway and came back. Turning was slow and awkward, but the rest was all right. I felt about thirty pounds lighter without the cast on my leg. It felt good to be wearing jeans again, too.

"Don't you ever put on weight?" Rosamunde complained, sitting there and watching me.

"I guess not."

"What about your wooden leg, when do you get that? What does that mean—that with a cane you'll be all right?"

"I don't know. I only look just so far ahead." I leaned on the crutches to talk with her. "All I know is next I start on a Nautilus machine, which even Adelia says is hard work, and her idea of hard work is—more than I can imagine. After that comes swimming."

"Swimming? What, to keep in shape?"

I nodded. I didn't want to think about how I would look in a bathing suit.

Rosamunde changed the subject. "Let's cook something, do you want to? Do you want to learn how to make piroshkis, or anything?"

"What?"

"OK, how about a cake."

"There are some mixes in the cupboard to the right of the stove."

"Mixes? Mixes?" Rosamunde stood up in mock horror.

"We'll make it from scratch, once we see what supplies your mother has in."

Rosamunde was opening and shutting the cupboard doors, nosing through the supplies. "We have to polish up your domestic skills, or else what will you have to offer a potential husband." She turned around to look at me while she hit that subject, so I knew it was something she'd been thinking about. "I've been wondering about that, and I bet you've been worrying too. I don't know what's going to happen, I never know what boys think, and I don't care much—"

"You will," I said, as if she was a kid Francie's age.

"Probably. But not yet, thank heaven—although it could be a defensive mechanism, you know? I worry about that. Anyway, they say the way to a man's heart is through his stomach, so I could teach you how to bake things. Although," she went on, rattling on, no longer looking at me, "I've observed that the way to a man's heart is through his eyes, if you know what I mean."

"I know what you mean." I stood watching her, embarrassed and amused.

"I'd like it if it was through his brain. I'd have a better chance. Good, your mother gets real butter, we'll make a genoise, you can beat it sitting down. You need a stool in here, you know."

"Why?"

"For you. You can lean against the counter, but you ought to get her to get a stool for you to sit on, since you're going to take up cooking."

I started to laugh. Rosamunde hesitated for a minute before joining in. "Yeah, I do sort of take over and give orders, don't I?"

We made the cake, with me sitting at the table and following directions. While it baked, I went back to my room and brought out the design I had drawn. I'd made two careful copies, one in pencil on the graph paper, one with dots of color on another sheet of graph paper, to show what the colors would be. "What do you think?" I asked, leaning my crutches against the table and sitting down beside Rosamunde.

"I don't know how you're going to carry your books, at school," Rosamunde said. The two sheets of paper that I'd carried into the kitchen in my mouth had damp tooth marks on them.

"Let's not talk about that, OK?"

Rosamunde looked at my drawings. She didn't say anything. I knew they weren't any good, but I'd thought I rather liked them. Now, I wasn't so sure.

"Well, what do you think?" I asked again. She was going to say they were pretty bad, and I guessed that wouldn't upset me or anything.

"Well. . . ."

I started to reach out for them. She put her hands on the papers.

"Wait. I'm still looking at them. You won't make my mother jealous, that's for sure."

"I know."

"It's not at all what I would have done."

"Never mind, it's just something I tried." It made me a little angry, even though I knew a lot of the anger was disappointment. I wanted the design to be good.

"It might work up all right. I can never *see* these things until they're finished. I have no imagination. My mother gave up on me long ago," Rosamunde said, studying and studying the two sheets of paper.

I didn't say anything, just kept my hand on them and, when she removed hers, pulled them in front of me.

"Hey, Izzy, you're not offended, are you? I mean, you said you didn't have any talent. You didn't expect them to be wonderful, did you?"

"No," I said. "It doesn't matter. I didn't expect—"

"That would be too much to expect," Rosamunde went

on. "I mean, you lose your leg and now at last you can be a brilliant artist. Life doesn't work like that."

"I never said that."

"You've got a good sense of design, though."

"I do?"

"Sure. You must know that. And you've got good taste, which means good color sense—like your mother. So, I think this will work up. Can I take it to my mother and ask her about wools? If you had something with a kind of sheen to it, like floss or something, for some of these leaves—"

"She'll laugh at it."

"Well, if she does, you won't be around to hear it."

I liked the way Rosamunde thought about things.

"Rosamunde," I asked her, letting her keep the two pages of drawings. "What did you mean, good people?"

"Hunh?"

"When you were asking me about the twins, remember?"

"Oh. I remember. I meant, good people. You know."

"Do you think I'm good people?"

"Make that singular," she told me. "But yes, I do. I mean, I always did. I mean, I always thought of you as kind of what people like you should be like. Best of breed," she explained.

I giggled. I couldn't help it. "Like a dog show?" I'd never thought of myself, or my friends, like that, as a breed. "I think I'm flattered."

"Maybe that's a stupid way of putting it, but it's what I always thought. I always wanted to be friends with you, you know. But—well, you didn't want to be friends with me."

"I know," I said. This was an apology I owed her. "That was pretty stupid of me."

"Agreed," Rosamunde smiled again. "So, while we're on the topic, what do *you* think of *me?*"

"You?" I didn't know what to say. "What do I think of you? Now? You mean, like, good people or what?" I was trying to figure out what to say. "I never thought much about it," I said, which wasn't exactly true. "I mean, I like you," I said. But I knew that wasn't what she was asking. So I took a breath and told her the truth. "Weird," I said. "You are definitely weird, but good weird. You're a good person to be around, you know? You sort of make me think about things and get me doing things. I was pretty stupid, I think, about people, before—"

"Well, experience broadens us—or what's the good of it, right? You know, I figured we'd get to be friends, eventually. Maybe."

"You know what my mother thinks? She thinks you ought to have your hair cut short."

Rosamunde pushed her chair away from the table. I felt her anger. I had never felt her anger before, and it was a little frightening. I wondered if I ought to apologize, but I didn't see why she should be so angry at me. What was wrong with suggesting a new hair style?

"Your mother thinks—I get pretty sick of mothers. I get pretty tired of not being left alone to be who I really am. As if that weren't good enough," Rosamunde said. She was pretending to study the way the cakes were rising in the oven, the three layers in their round pans. She punched the button that turned on the oven light, crouched down to peer in, then punched the light off. "As if all we were going to do is live exactly their lives all over again. As if we thought their lives were so perfect."

It was as if I'd tapped into some deep well of emotion. The little Izzy in my head leaned over a stone wall, peering down and down. I'd had no idea about Rosamunde.

But my mother had seen her sobbing by the elevators that first day, when she had been making jokes and acting super-practical all the time she was in my room. There was more to Rosamunde than I'd been admitting to myself. I wasn't sure how I felt about the part I hadn't admitted.

I thought if I apologized we'd get back out of deep water

and onto safe ground again. Then I thought that if we did that, I'd never really know her. If I wanted to really know her. But if I started to quarrel with her, even about the question of what my mother said about her hair, she might blow up—like Jack. Jack had that same deep well of emotions, hidden away.

"You mean you won't even think about it?" I asked Rosamunde. "But what's the worst that could happen if you tried a new haircut?"

"I could look like a real jerk," she told me, turning around and leaning back against the stove. "Me,"—she waved her hands in front of herself, sort of pointing at her overalls—"with a cute little haircut?"

The nice thing to do would be to reassure her that she would look great, I thought to myself. Then I realized that that wouldn't be very nice, since she might look just the way she was afraid she would. "I see what you mean," I said. "But I do wonder, you know. It might look sort of— really stylish."

"Or really jerky."

"Next time you're at the mall, you ought to try on a wig, a short-haired wig, but curly, so it would be something like what it would look like. Just try it on and see what you think."

Rosamunde burst out laughing. "You are so—feminine, do you know that? It's terrific. I'd never think of that—and I'd never dare do it. Unless you come with me, because I'd trust your word about how it looked. Would you do that?" She was tempted.

"I can't go to the mall."

"Why not?"

I didn't answer the truth: Because I don't want to go out and be stared at.

My mother liked the cake a lot, but she was a little concerned about Rosamunde. "I'm grateful to her, don't mistake me," she told me that evening in her I'm-about-to-give-you-a-warning-for-your-own-good voice. "But—she's not really your kind of friend, is she? She's so different, in everything, her attitudes, her background, her values. You're seeing an awful lot of her, Izzy, Lamb."

A year ago I would have told her not to pick my friends for me, and then stomped out of the room. But it's impossible to stomp with crutches, anyway. "I like her," I said.

"So do I, sort of. And I am grateful to her, because your other friends—"

"No, they haven't, have they."

"But Lisa has always struck me as such a nice girl. I guess, I'd hate to see you drop your friendship with Lisa, while you're going through this period of adjustment. That's all."

I wanted to tell her that I didn't think it was a period of adjustment, but a change. A big change. But I didn't want to upset her. It must have been hard enough on her, acting calm and collected and grown up because that was what I needed her to be. I knew sort of what she wanted for me, in my life, what she thought was important. I agreed with her, too; I wanted the same things for me. But I didn't think I could get them, not any more; certainly not in the old easy way. And I wondered, too, if there weren't other things I might want, not instead of, but along with what the old Izzy would have wanted. I couldn't tell my mother that, though, because she would think I thought what she valued wasn't important, and that wasn't true. "I don't plan to lose touch with Lisa."

"And she's a clinger, I'm afraid," my mother went on, still talking about Rosamunde. "She's the kind of person who clings to a friend. You've always had lots of friends, and she could cut you off. I feel terrible saying this," she admitted. "I feel terrible thinking it, because sometimes I feel like just—hugging Rosamunde, I feel so sorry for her and so grateful to her for . . . caring about you, all the time she spends. You know what I mean?"

"I know what you mean," I told her, which was true. "I don't mind, Mom. I like you to tell me what you think," I told her, to reassure her, if she wanted that reassurance. I reached over and covered her hand with my own, but I didn't tell her what I was thinking.

I was thinking about how I thought there were other reasons than pity for Rosamunde to be my friend, a lot of other reasons. I wondered if my mother thought pity was the only reason.

I thought about what she'd said, though, alone in my room that night, with the radio playing softly in the darkness. I lay on my back, staring at the ceiling, feeling pretty bad. "I just called," Stevie Wonder sang, "to say, I love you." I lay there listening, wishing miserably that someone would just call to say he loved me.

Of all the stupid things.

18

Thanksgiving is an odd sort of holiday at our house. It's supposed to be a big family thing, a Norman Rockwell occasion, and that's how we all think of it; but as it always works out, the family spends most of the long weekend doing separate things. Maybe that was why the glooms set in earlier that Wednesday than usual. I wasn't ready for a holiday season.

When the twins arrived on Wednesday afternoon, they made a lot of noise about how good it was to be home, but the first thing they did was start making phone calls, making plans. Francie was going to have supper and see a movie with her friend Alice. My parents had a couple of cocktail parties to go to. My mother, who had driven up to get the twins, got right to work on the laundry they brought. The house was filled with people, and then suddenly empty. I ate the supper my mother had left for me, folded the laundry, and dried out slices of bread in the oven then ripped them up into chunks for stuffing. I had told my mother I would make stuffing for the turkey. Rosamunde had assured me that homemade was miles better than any bagged kind, and a lot cheaper too, although that wouldn't, she said, make much difference to us. I ignored the crack about money and decided to try her recipe.

I was glad, even thankful, to be on crutches. First thing Monday, my mother had returned both the walker and the wheelchair, so I knew she was as happy as I was to get rid of them. On crutches, I could move from room to room without feeling like too much of a cripple. I spent some of Wednesday in the kitchen and some in front of TV with the needlepoint. Rosamunde had been as good as her word and had brought over, Monday evening, not only a short list of assignments for the week, but also a bag of wool. My mother reimbursed her, while Rosamunde explained carefully, showing my mother the sales slip, that she had gotten too much because she wasn't sure just what shades I wanted, and that as long as a skein hadn't been broken into it could be returned for cash. While I worked the needlepoint, I had the TV on, but I only had it on for the company the noise made.

I had my fingers busy, making neat stitches, and my ears busy, and I kept an eye on the clock because Francie was due back by nine-thirty. I kept my mind occupied with an inner argument about whether it would be smarter to wait until after Christmas to go back to school. I was doing all right on the assignments, had been getting B's on the graded work. So I wasn't falling behind in school, and I wasn't sure I had my strength up enough to get through a school day. Adelia had started me on a big Nautilus machine, lifting and pulling with my arms and legs. I thought I should probably continue intensive physical therapy for a few more weeks. Once I started school, I'd only go two times a week.

Francie came in, dead tired, and went up to bed. I would have liked to talk to Rosamunde, but I knew she was babysitting almost all during the holidays, except Thursday, when she would be with her family.

I was depressed, or maybe just sad. My heart felt kind of sore and swollen. I told myself—stitching, waiting for it to be time to go to bed, wondering when my parents would get in—that I would feel better in the morning. I reminded myself of the way my moods switched. That didn't make me feel any better, but it kept me from feeling much worse.

Maybe because the day was gray and drizzly and the trees were bare, or maybe because I woke up so much earlier than anyone else, maybe that was why Thanksgiving Day wasn't any easier than Thanksgiving Eve had been. I was just as glad it was gray and drizzly outside, since that matched how I felt inside. However, once everybody was up and hanging around the kitchen, either frantically busy getting the turkey stuffed and into the oven, or sitting around being bored until the next period of frantic activity began, I forgot about being gloomy.

This was, in fact, the best family time of any holiday. We all knew it, I think, but we all pretended it wasn't true, because we thought the best ought to be when we were dressed up and sitting around the table together. My mother loves that kind of family occasion. I think she likes to sit at one end of the table, looking at the food she's cooked and the children she's raising and the husband she's been married to for twenty good years. I don't blame her. But she never seems to learn that by the time dinner's on, everybody is sort of frazzled, and bored with one another. Families don't work according to holiday timetables. By the time we all sat down to these ceremonial meals, everybody was already thinking about what was coming up next. My father, who is more realistic and practical, seems to know this. He always has a couple of discussion topics he brings to the holiday table with him.

We always start Thanksgiving dinner out with a minute of silence. I looked all around, while that slow minute ticked by. Ivory and rose were the colors of the room. The silver on the table shone against the linen cloth. My parents sat at either end. Francie sat quiet beside me. My brothers, in dark suits and striped ties, sat across, looking young and handsome, looking mischievous but reliable. They sat quite solemn, both of them, and as the minute ended I nudged Francie and whispered, "Look at them, just look at them."

She knew what I meant, and smiled sideways at me. I thought, for an unexpected lifting moment, that we would eventually get to be good friends, my sister and I; then her eyes went to my father, who held the carving knife over the turkey, to measure her share of skin against everyone else's, and I thought it would be a while before that time came.

I got too much attention that dinner, for Francie's taste and for mine, too. I was wearing dark corduroy pants, which was the closest thing I owned to dressy trousers, with a blouse my mother had loaned me. They all agreed with my mother that I looked pretty, a little older, and certainly well. "But I like long hair on a girl," Jack said. "I wish somebody would cut my hair," Francie said and Joel winked at me. My mother wanted to give a party for me, maybe over Christmas, which everybody thought was a great idea. Everybody except me, that is, and Francie too, if you count her insistence on having equal time for a party of her own as disagreement. Nobody listened to my objections until I finally asked them please to lay off. Then they stared at me. "I don't even know who I'd invite," I told them.

My mother started to override that, but Joel and Jack said that maybe instead they'd give a party, over Christmas, one of those open house parties, and invite almost everybody they'd ever met especially kids from school, to catch up with what was going on. That diverted my mother, who wasn't sure she wanted to take on a party for the twins. Jack said we'd invite Rosamunde too, and I said she probably wouldn't come, and he raised his eyebrows in disbelief. I said Rosamunde and I would go to the movies, or something, or I'd find someone else to go with me. Francie said she'd go with us, if it wasn't a horror movie. My father cleared his throat. He cleared it again. We all gave my father our full attention.

"I've been thinking—your mother and I have been talking about it—how would you children like to have a swimming pool put in?"

That was odd, I thought, because we had asked him before if we could have one, and he had always said it was too expensive.

"That's expensive, isn't it, Dad?" Joel asked.

"I think we could find the money."

"With a diving board?" Francie started on a list of requests.

"Where would it go?" Jack wondered.

"We've got plenty of yard space. We'd have to fence it in, so nobody would just—wander into it," my mother told us. "But not chain link, something wooden."

"Could I invite people over whenever I wanted?" Francie asked. "Will it have a deep end?"

"I guess," Joel said thoughtfully, "it would increase the value of the property. It's probably not a bad investment."

My father agreed. "However, it would mean we wouldn't take a summer vacation. And we'd have to do the maintenance on it ourselves."

"We'd still go to the club pool, wouldn't we?" Francie asked.

"Yes," my mother said. "We can't ask Daddy to give up his golf."

"Or my tennis," Francie said.

"Besides," I said, since they seemed to be waiting for me to say something, "you can take it off taxes." I had figured out what he and my mother were doing, and I did think it was pretty nice of them, but I also felt—bitter. They would put in a pool, build a high fence all around it, and I would be able to get exercise. Swimming was good exercise. It was even going to be part of my PT program, after Christmas. With our own pool shielded from anybody looking in, they thought it wouldn't be so embarrassing for me.

"Do you like the idea, Izzy?" my father asked me.

I knew he wanted me to be excited about it. But I couldn't be, because I could just see myself in a bathing suit. However, I wanted to say something right to him, because he was doing what he always did—taking good care of us, making sure everything was the best he could provide for us. The trouble was, he couldn't possibly understand how depressing it was to even think about swimming, and summer, and how I would look in a bathing suit. I didn't know how I could swim with only one leg, anyway.

"It would certainly be convenient," I said.

He was disappointed, but the look my mother gave him warned him not to say anything. He wanted me to be really pleased, but I just couldn't be. I was grateful, and I knew I would like having our own pool to swim in privately since I had to swim.

"Thanks, Dad, both of you," I said. He couldn't know how it felt to be a fifteen-year-old girl with part of a leg amputated and my whole life changed. "I'm pretty lucky," I said to him. He liked hearing that; he thinks we ought to appreciate what we have.

"You're talking like it's going to be Izzy's pool," Francie objected. "It's mine, too; I'm in this family, too. I'll get to use it too, won't I?"

"Sure, except for whatever we decide is Izzy's special time," my father said.

He had it all worked out in his head, because he's thorough about things. I didn't want to talk about it any more. Summer was a long way off.

"But that's not fair, unless I have a special time too," Francie argued. "And if she has a special time, what if I have a friend over and we want to go swimming? What if it's a really hot day and we can't go swimming because it's Izzy's special time. What if I have a friend who can only come over at a certain time—"

"Francesca," my father warned her. Jack and Joel were

just laughing at the way Francie's mind worked. I was wishing I could leave the table, because—because my being there, in the family, was making demands, and they were acting like I wanted to make them or had no right to make them. Nobody understood, nobody could understand. I felt shoved into some special area, away from everybody else; I felt like they were trying to pretend I was still normal, ignoring the useless stump of a leg that would hang down if I stood up. I didn't know what to think—except that I wanted to get away where I wouldn't have to think about it at all.

Instead, however, I tried to quiet Francie down, before she worked herself up into a real fit and totally ruined the day. "We can negotiate," I said. "I'll let you trade TV hours or something, if you want to. If you'll give me two of your TV hours, I'll give you one of my pool hours."

"But that's not fair, that's twice—" she started. Then she said, "Are you teasing me?"

"Sort of. But we can change our schedule, if we need too."

"OK. If you promise."

"I promise," I promised. That was the end of the scene. I didn't feel any better, but everybody else did; and since I couldn't feel any better, it was good enough that they did. "How about one of those slides?" I asked my father, who was glad to have a practical question.

We went on to what kind of material we'd want the walks around the pool made of and what kind of planting up against the fence and what kind of poolside furniture. My father and Jack talked about the machinery involved in keeping the filter system working. They were both eager to learn how to run the kind of pump-house equipment a pool would require, and they had forgotten, in their eagerness for machinery, what was the first cause of all this. That is, me. I watched them talk and thought how alike they were in that.

If there was a problem, they both wanted to do something about it, build a pool or kill Marco.

I couldn't blame them for not understanding, and I didn't want to. I just realized, for about the first time in my life, I think, that there were some things, if I expected them of my father, I was bound to be disappointed.

That didn't bother me, or anything. Neither did realizing the same thing about Jack. I could count on them to take care of me, but—

It is possible to be too busy being practical. There are some problems that don't have practical solutions, or that have more kinds of solutions than just practical ones. Or that have no solutions.

Francie and I did the dishes, with her grousing that all I did was stand by the sink and rinse off while she had to do everything else, and it was hard, until I finally did blow up at her. I told her she was entirely too self-centered. She went wailing out of the room and I tried to finish the dishes by myself. I was glad when Joel came in to replace her, because rinsing a plate, then hopping along until I could put it in the dishwasher, then hopping back to get the next one—I didn't know how I was going to manage to scour the roasting pan. Joel told me that he and Jack were going to take me out for dinner the next night.

"But—" I said. I didn't want to go out. I didn't want to think about it.

"Nowhere fancy, we thought we'd drive up to the Inn at Kirk's Crossing. You don't have to wear a tie or anything."

"I never have to wear a tie."

"C'mon, Izzy. You'll be with us; it'll be all right."

"All right? Going out with you two wild men?" I knew I'd have to do it, for their sakes if not for my own.

"You want to ask a friend?"

"Lisa?"

"No, not her, she's—Rosamunde?"

"Did Jack suggest her?"

"Yes, why? Mom says she's the one you're seeing most of these days. Jack says he can put up with her, for your sake—if she'll wear a decent skirt or something."

But Rosamunde couldn't come with us, because she had a babysitting job. She wouldn't, she said, try to get a substitute. She needed the money, and besides she'd given her word. Jack got on the phone to try to argue with her, but she shut him up in about half a minute, demanding to talk to me again. "Do you mind?" she asked me. "I mean, do you want moral support? I don't have anything that would look right anyway, Izzy."

"Just the three of us then," Jack said.

"You could take me," Francie suggested.

"No, we couldn't," Joel said.

"Izzy gets everything," Francie complained. "Just because she's crippled."

There was a silence after that remark. The silence was so immediate that even Francie realized what she'd said. The twins couldn't think of anything to say. My parents filled the thick silent air with their anger and embarrassment. Everybody looked at me. Francie's eyes were wide and scared.

I was standing on my crutches, and there was no way around the situation. The little Izzy in my head was beet red. But why, I asked myself, should I feel embarrassed? Because I did, I felt like I ought to be saying I was sorry.

Nobody said anything and the silence filled up with all the things nobody was saying. Nobody said, "No she's not." Nobody could say that. Nobody said, "That doesn't make any difference," because it made all the difference in the world. Everybody just looked at me, wondering what I was going to do, everybody worrying about me.

"Well," I finally said, "every cloud has a silver lining."

That exploded them into talk. My father sent Francie to her room, until she could learn to govern herself, which Jack suggested might take several years. My mother said she hoped I wasn't going to get bitter. I said I thought it was a joke, and I did think it was pretty funny, if you thought about it. Joel told all of us to take it easy, please. Jack said he was—oh hell—going to have a brandy, and my parents didn't argue. I went to bed, leaving them alone to worry and wonder and make plans where I wouldn't have to be aware of it.

As Thanksgivings go, it was one of the worst I remember.

19

On Sunday, I was trying to tell Rosamunde about the way the vacation had gone, trying to explain to her—and to myself—what I had been thinking about. I never told her, because I never told anyone, because I tried to forget about it and I succeeded, as if it never happened, about the way I carried on once I was alone in my room. What I told her about was the way my family acted. About me. My father, who was busy making plans, making adjustments; my mother who didn't seem able to imagine any other kind of life than the one I had used to be headed for; my sister who was so filled with jealous resentment; and the twins, whose polite behavior at the restaurant had been as out of character as their asking me out for dinner. "I don't know, Rosamunde," I finally wound down. "I thought they were taking me out to show me, you know, that it wasn't that bad, that it wasn't going to make that much of a difference. But I got the feeling they were really doing it to show themselves."

"Well, that makes sense, doesn't it?" Rosamunde asked me. I was sitting at the desk, in a chair, with my crutches on the floor nearby. She was lying on her stomach on the big bed, facing me. "I mean, everybody is insincere that way.

Even you. I mean, you act like you're doing so well but . . . you don't look different, but you sort of do . . . and I bet you're still depressed a lot of the time, even though you don't show it."

I didn't admit she was right because—at that moment—I'd forgotten about it. I would have been ashamed to tell her about how I spent some of the nighttime hours, anyway. I was ashamed to admit it to myself.

"Isn't that true, Izzy?"

"Not really," I denied it. That was true, I thought, kidding myself. "So you'd say Francie is just trying to show her sympathy?"

"Not exactly. It's her pity that she's trying not to show. Like the people in the restaurant, the way you said they stared."

"That was *terrible*," I said.

"The trouble is, you're used to people looking at you and envying you, wishing they were you. You're not used to people looking at you and pitying you and being glad they aren't you. But if you look at it from another angle, they're both the same mistake, because people aren't ever seeing *you*."

I just stared at her. Not looking at her either, I thought, but looking at the idea she had just given me.

"Probably, that's why you're dragging your heels about coming back to school. Dragging your heel, that is," she said, and giggled. "Oh, Izzy, I'm sorry. That was sick."

"Yeah, but funny," I admitted. "I'm not, though. I'm just not strong enough, physically."

"That's not true," Rosamunde announced. "I think you're scared. And I don't blame you, not a bit. But you're going to have to do it, sometime."

"You've got gray eyes," I announced to her.

Rosamunde changed to a sitting position. "You're switching the subject."

"No, I've never noticed before—they're gray, with a real

rim of dark gray around them. Let me make up your face, Rosamunde."

"Oh for heaven's sake, Izzy—" She sounded disgusted with me.

"Not much, just to see it—why are you so frightened of makeup. And things?" I asked her.

She smiled at me. "Touché."

"So, will you let me? Nobody'll ever know."

"I bet. This is the beginning of the Improve Rosamunde Campaign. Isobel Lingard, a.k.a. Fairy Godmother, with a touch of her magic wand, or magic blush brush, and suddenly I'll be—all the things I'm not."

"Sorry," I said, sarcastic. I knew that tone of voice was one she'd listen to. "You'll never make a Cinderella."

I talked her into it. We sat on the bed, and Rosamunde held up a hand mirror to watch. I tried the full treatment first, but it didn't look good at all, so she washed it all off and started again, with something very simple, just liner and mascara. Lipstick too, I thought, but I didn't tell her that.

"You really ought to make yourself go back to school," Rosamunde said.

"I know."

"It'll be pretty bad," she said.

"I can imagine. Even if I do decide to work on the paper."

"But what are you really frightened of, Izzy? And why does everyone call you Izzy, anyway. You've got a good name, Isobel."

"In the hospital they called me Isobel. I felt like they were talking about somebody else. I guess they were, weren't they?"

"La Belle Isobel, Best of Breed."

I drew back. I had the mascara in my hand. "You want a mustache?"

"I've already got one."

"You should dye it."

"Dye it?"

"You know, bleach it. I have some bleach. I'll show you."

"Do you?" Rosamunde asked. Her eyes really were neat-looking. They were a great color.

"You really do have good eyes," I told her.

"You really think that," she said. "OK, OK, I'll admit it, so do I, and I have for years."

I did her eyelashes, just lightly. It looked good. "Now, go wash your face and try it yourself."

"Yes, Mommy," she said, sarcastic. But she went off to the bathroom again. I think she was embarrassed to show how pleased she was.

"Anyway," she said, back on the bed, trying to draw a line with the pencil along the edge of her eyelid the way I had. "What is it you're frightened of about school?"

"The people. I really don't want to—face everybody, and all that."

"But it's only the first time that'll be bad. You know how people are, they forget pretty quickly. And most of them are your friends, anyway."

"That's where you're wrong. Most of them are Izzy's friends."

"You're changing your name to Isobel?"

"No, but—you know what I mean."

"OK, I can see it. But there isn't anything for it, but to face it out, is there?"

"I guess not."

"And you've got the courage, Izzy. Or Isobel. Whoever, you've got courage."

I hoped she was right. I wanted her to be right. I knew that in a way she was, and that made me feel good.

"So, you'll be there on Monday? I'll wait to meet you somewhere. You'll need someone to carry your books and all."

"No. Not Monday."

"OK, Tuesday."

"Don't nag."

"Izzy, you can't hide away forever. Even with a pool, and even if your father does get you a special car as soon as you turn sixteen—you're going to have to come back into the world."

"I know."

"So Monday then. Or Tuesday, that would be OK."

I knew she was right.

"I'll tell you what really scares me," I admitted. The little Izzy inside my head had her hands over her face and her words were muffled. "I'm not too eager to see Marco Griggers."

"I can understand that."

"No, I don't know what I'll act like."

"What do you mean? He must know he's not your favorite person."

I shrugged.

"What does that mean?" She glared at me, the mascara brush in her hand. "Haven't you told him what you think of him?"

I shook my head.

"What did you do, tell him it was all right? How nice can you get, Izzy. Honestly. I wonder about you."

"Look, I haven't told him anything, I haven't heard a peep from him, since—"

"He didn't even apologize? He didn't? And you let him get away with that?"

"What was I supposed to do, call him up and yell at him? He just talked to Suzy a lot, and all."

"And now she's dropped him."

"Suzy has? Why?"

"Found someone better, a college boy. But that Marco—he ought to be shot."

"That's what Jack says."

"Jack can't be all bad. What about you? What do you want to say to him?"

"Nothing. I don't ever want to see him again. I don't want to have to see him," I said. I heard the anger in my voice. "So I don't want to go to school."

After a long time, Rosamunde said, "That just lets him make a bigger mess of your life."

That was when I told her what had happened that night. I made her promise not to tell anyone, and then I told her the truth.

Rosamunde had nothing to say. I barely looked at her, and she didn't interrupt me. It didn't take very long to tell. Then she still had nothing to say.

It was depressing to talk about it. I thought I shouldn't have talked about it, because it just made me depressed.

When Rosamunde did speak again, her voice was thick, as if fury choked her—and tears too, that she was trying not to show. "He passed out, that's what happened. You know that. That's why they took so long getting to you."

I said I guessed so.

"Damn him, God damn him." She got up and started pacing the room.

"It's no use, now. It doesn't do any good, Rosamunde. That's what I mean."

"You can't just let him get away with it."

"What am I supposed to do, take an axe to *his* leg?"

Rosamunde stopped, looked at me, and then smiled. It wasn't a particularly jolly smile, but it was an attempt. "I'd like to see that, though. I really would."

"You just have to accept it."

"And there are your parents—"

"It doesn't do any good to—stew and steam. Because it doesn't do any good."

"—they really are something, you know? You're all of you right, of course. That's the only way to handle it without going crazy."

"We don't do crazy, we Lingards," I tried a smart alec remark.

"Snob," she answered, equally smart alec. "No wonder Tony Marcel said he felt guilty."

"It's nothing to do with him."

"I know, but I guess you better work on the paper. I guess that makes that decision for you."

I didn't know about that. I wouldn't have minded seeing Tony every day, even if whenever he saw me I was looking stupid at what I was trying to do, as well as crippled. But I didn't want to be reminded every day that I wasn't normal, didn't have the chances I would once have had. Except, more than anything else, I remembered the way he had said he would feel better about himself if I did. Because I didn't want him feeling badly about himself.

"I think I will, probably. Until they throw me off for incompetence. Or something."

"They'll probably make you editor your senior year, and they'll probably be right. No, I'm not kidding, but—this means you *have* to come back to school, Izzy. And since you have to, the sooner you get it over with the better."

"OK. OK. I will."

"When?"

I didn't know.

"Monday, tomorrow. It's better that way, really it is. I'll meet you at the main entrance, I'll wait for you. Will you be there, Izzy?"

I said I would.

I said I would, but I wasn't. What I did, that Monday morning, was pretend I was still asleep. I heard my mother come into the room and look at me, then she left, closing the door behind her.

Rosamunde called me that night, and I told her I'd slept through. She didn't quarrel with me, just said she'd see me tomorrow, Tuesday, and reported that all of my classes would be meeting on the ground floor.

"Good," I said, agreeing to meet her at about 8:15.

I didn't. I got up in time, and my mother was ready to drive me in, but when she asked me if I was sure I was ready, I said no. Rosamunde called that night, again. She sounded a little put out. "I didn't ask you to wait for me," I told her.

"OK," she said, "but I'll be there tomorrow, and the next day, too, in case. But I won't be pestering you."

"Good," I said.

"But you told me you would, Izzy," she pestered.

I didn't go to school on Wednesday, either, and it wasn't worrying me that much anymore, because I had seen how I could just—not go, morning after morning. I wasn't so bad. I didn't feel so bad about it.

But Thursday morning, Rosamunde was there in the kitchen at eight. She wore her PAL windbreaker and overalls, she had an armload of books, and my mother wasn't any too pleased to have company at that hour. Rosamunde ignored that and ignored me, too.

"I didn't know Izzy had invited you over for breakfast," my mother said, with more than a little edge to her voice.

"Oh, well, she needs someone to carry her books for her, Mrs. Lingard. No, thanks, I've already eaten."

She knew my mother thought she was intruding, and I knew my mother was angry at her being there at that ungodly hour, and even Francie had the sense to stay quiet. But my mother didn't know what Rosamunde was up to; she had sort of judged and condemned Rosamunde as a clinger, and she thought Rosamunde was being rude. So I didn't start any arguments with Rosamunde about her showing up at our house. We rode to town in a thick silence, with nobody saying what she was thinking. It wasn't until I was standing on my crutches beside the car, with people moving around me and pretending they didn't see me, that I realized what I had done. I had stuck by Rosamunde; but I wasn't ready to go back to school. I almost panicked.

My mother came around, to give Rosamunde my books to carry. She was still angry. Rosamunde was ignoring both of us. "Have a good day, Lamb," my mother said, kissing me on the cheek.

"Mom?" I couldn't break down or chicken out with everybody around. "What do you have on for today?"

My wonderful mother knew. She knew what I was asking. She gave me what I needed without making me explain: "I'm going to be at the hospital, until about noon—then we'll probably get lunch, I'm going to make a reservation at Peppers. You know today's my tennis day, so I might be a little late coming to pick you up."

"I can wait," I said. I knew now how to find her, if I needed her.

I didn't watch her drive away. I turned myself around, on the crutches, and made myself start the long, swing-stepping journey back to school.

20

School. It smelled and sounded the same, it looked the same; nothing had changed except me. There's no sense in going back over those first two days at school. The worst was the sudden brittle silence that froze the air whenever I made an entrance. If you imagine it, if you imagine the kind of person who had everything, blonde hair and blue eyes, a good figure, popular with boys and with girls, the kind of person who is always sort of moving around and cheerful and silly, who seems to do everything easily; if you imagine seeing that same person with half of one leg just hanging down inside her blue jeans; if you imagine how you would feel about it, whether you liked her or not, but especially if you liked her; then you'll hear the silence I'm talking about.

The best was the way people tried to help out. For example, John Wintersize. The second day, I made myself go down the long staircase to the cafeteria for lunch, which was hard enough, but when I got up from my table, a few minutes before the bell rang, and went to the bottom of the stairs and looked up—I had forgotten how hard it was to go up a set of stairs on crutches, with a backpack full of books. I knew I'd have to do it, and I knew I could, but—

Somebody grabbed me from behind and lifted me up into his arms. It was John Wintersize, whom I hadn't seen since that night of the party at his house. I'd never noticed how big he was. My crutches clattered to the ground, and he had to shift my backpack around. "Somebody pick those things up," he said. "Hey hi, Izzy. You don't weigh more than a feather do you?"

I was embarrassed, and I was relieved, and I felt stupid being toted around like a baby, and I felt like one of those helpless ladies in a movie, swept away by a rescuing knight. He went up the stairs easily. He set me down gently at the top, helping me get the crutches back in place.

"Thank you," I said.

"No trouble," he said. He stood there, hulking over me. I didn't know why he didn't go away.

"We have the same lunch," John said, "so we could have a standing date. I mean—" He was as embarrassed as I was.

I had a very confused reaction, shame and resentment that he was obviously pitying me, gratitude that he had given me a hand. "That would be a big help," I said.

"Hey, good. That's OK then. I'll see you Monday then."

"Same time, same place," I told him, making a joke out of it.

"OK," he said. "OK then." He moved off, feeling pretty good it seemed. I guessed I felt pretty good toward him, too.

At the end of the day, I was tired. "How was school?" my mother asked, as I got into the car.

"Fine," I answered. "I'm really wiped out."

"I can imagine," she said, and I thought maybe she could.

Rosamunde reassured me, that weekend, "Everybody'll get used to it. People get used to almost anything. The worst is behind you, I bet. Or, most of the worst anyway. You're holding up all right, aren't you?"

I guessed I was.

The first Monday morning, I had to really make myself get going. It had been so pleasant over the weekend, at home. For the first time I could sympathize with those people who simply did not want to go to school, didn't want to enter the big door and the long, crowded corridors, didn't want to sit down at a desk and watch the clock start on its way around to the end of class. I had no trouble during classes. It was getting there that bothered me. I would watch with dread as the minute hand approached the end of the time. I came into classes a minute or two later than everyone else and was given a desk close to the door. For a while, the teachers sort of carefully didn't pay attention to me, not putting any pressure on me I guess. So for most of the two weeks left before the Christmas vacation, I didn't do much in classes except get through them. I saw Marco, a couple of times, from a distance; he kept out of sight, so I knew he was keeping clear of me.

I did tell Tony Marcel that I'd like to work on the newspaper. I started going to the after-school staff meetings that were held four days a week, Monday though Thursday, in the newspaper room. The paper came out every Friday, so there was always something to do, as I learned. We would sit around a long table, and somebody would stand my crutches up against a far wall, because there was no room for them anywhere else. Everybody was there on Thursdays, when the next week's articles were assigned and advertising orders checked in, but the rest of the days only those with work to do showed up. They were too busy to pay much attention to me, once Tony had introduced me. At first, I just sat uselessly beside him, watching what he was doing. He had to oversee the business manager as well as the reporters, as well as write the editorial and do the layout, as well as see that the dummies were taken to the printer by five on Wednesday for that week's paper, as well as pick them up the next evening, so they could be distributed on Friday. I sat quiet while he worked, trying not to be in the way.

The other people on the paper didn't mind me, and I'd watch them do whatever they were doing. There were fifteen in total on the staff: Tony and Deborah, Danny, Pat, Sandy, Susan Hawkes and Susan Wrightson, Freddy, Maureen, Will, Peter, Jason Dooley and Jason Morse and Jason Tellery, and Tag Simmons. Tag was there, as he said, for comic relief—he drew the cartoons and cracked jokes constantly, bad jokes. Deborah was the best writer, but Danny had the best ideas. Jason Dooley, who covered the sports with Susan Hawkes, was a sullen and quarrelsome person, but Susan had a cowlike personality that worked well with his. It was interesting to see all these people working away. I stayed late the first Wednesday, to help with layout, gluing and pasting. When I realized that we would be late, I called my mother to tell her not to pick me up at the usual time. Tony said he'd drop me off home after he took the dummies over. My mother hesitated before giving me her permission. I tried to tell her, without giving anything away, to her or to Tony, that it would be OK, and I guess she heard me.

Newspaper made a big difference to me in school. It was something to look forward to, even though I didn't have any definite job. I fit in well enough and I lent a little bit of a hand wherever I saw anyone needing one. I could look forward to newspaper.

And the truth is, I liked seeing so much of Tony Marcel. I liked working with him, in however unimportant a way. I liked seeing how he made decisions, and how he stood back to let the whole staff decide something. I liked knowing him better. He was always thoughtful 'about me. He always remembered to bring my crutches when it was time to go, doing it as naturally as he handed Deborah a blue pencil and told her to cut a piece by fifty words. I even liked watching him with Deborah, in a way, in a funny way. You can tell a lot about a person by the way he acts toward a girl he is crazy about. I really liked Deborah too, and I liked the way they got along together.

It was an odd time, that time between Thanksgiving and Christmas, at school. I honestly don't think I could have gotten through it without Rosamunde, who was there, with me, whenever she could be. Even though I dropped Latin club, we still had English and Latin together. She always walked with me to those, so I didn't have the feeling of dropping slowly to the rear of the race up the hallways. One of the first days, she met me coming down the cafeteria steps while she was running up so as not to be late. She stopped for a minute to watch. "How you doing? No, don't tell me." She moved back as people surged past us. "I gotta run, but—" I couldn't hear the end of her sentence. The next day, however, she was waiting for me at the top of the steps. She moved down them behind me, not helping me at all as I concentrated on not losing my balance, as I lowered the crutches, hopped down, then lowered the crutches again. "Isn't there an easier way? There must be," she muttered behind me.

"Shut up, I'm concentrating."

"Make way," she called out. "Pregnant woman, make way, please. Please step aside, pregnant woman coming through," she called out.

"Rosamunde!" I protested, stopping on a step and looking back at her. I could have died, but I was laughing instead, as laughter rippled through the surrounding wave of students.

It was Rosamunde I told about the odd thought I had, watching Lauren by her locker one day before homeroom. Lauren was standing, talking to a couple of boys. I saw the tall, stiff way she held her body, a model's pose, and the blank expression on her face. Lauren wore too much makeup, I thought, watching her red mouth move as she said something. She stood as if she was already posing for a photographer. Her glance moved slowly around, seeing who was watching her. When she met my eyes, she gave me a photographic smile.

It was terrible—it was as if she was enclosed in a glass cage, posing for the people who might be watching. The boys didn't notice this, and I wondered who did. With all that Lauren had, I thought, leaning my weight on one crutch while I took books and papers out of my locker—why should she keep herself locked away behind glass like that?

But what did she have? She had her looks. She had friends like me, who had never even looked at her carefully enough to see how . . . separated she was. She had, I thought, as I kept on thinking about Lauren and remembering the years I had known her, a mother who had left her behind when she went out to start a new life, a father who insisted that she had to be a good student so he must not even have known that she wasn't too smart. Why would her father do that? Maybe because he didn't like her, not the way she was. Once I'd thought of that, I thought it might well be true. Nothing Lauren's father had ever said to her that I'd heard, or that I'd heard about, had any affection in it. He set down his expectations and as long as Lauren met them he didn't like her any more than he ended up liking her mother. Lauren didn't even have a family of her own. Poor Lauren, I thought. No wonder she hid behind a glass shield.

I went up to her then, meaning to say something—I didn't know what. To make a new connection to her, to who she really was; because Lauren could really use a friend, I thought. When she saw me coming toward her she smiled her photographic smile and shut her locker. "Izzy, how are you?" she said. She moved away, too fast for me to speak.

Lauren couldn't even risk standing next to someone visibly crippled, as I said to Rosamunde. Rosamunde dismissed her as shallow. "What do you care what a person like that thinks?" she asked me.

"I don't," I told her, which was true. Rosamunde was satisfied, but I wasn't.

The next chance I had to speak privately to Lisa, I tried to tell her. "Lauren won't—can't—talk to me any more, but— No, look, that's OK, I understand," I cut Lisa off before she could interrupt me to reassure me that Lauren didn't mean that at all. It was hard enough having a private conversation with Lisa, who always had people around. We didn't have time for fake excuses, we didn't have the time to waste. "I'm kind of worried about her. We always saw her as just good-looking, Lisa, and I thought you might be able to let her know . . . see, I don't think that's right, I don't think she's happy at all."

Lisa looked seriously at me, and then agreed. "No, she isn't. It's that guy. I didn't know she liked him all that much, but I guess she did. She's really sad about not seeing him this year. I've been trying to think of someone else she might like, Izzy."

"No, I mean, if you think about her looks—"

"Are you trying to say that Lauren's not pretty anymore? Because that's not true. She might even go for an interview with an agency."

I gave up and let the conversation come back to our usual channels. "Of course I still think—Lauren's lovely, you know that. I hope she does gets picked by a modeling agency."

"You know, Izzy," Lisa said, her voice emotional, "I really admire you. Here this thing has happened, and you haven't changed at all, you're just as nice as before. I really admire you."

I was embarrassed in about three different ways. One of the ways was for Lisa, because she didn't know anything about me, or about Lauren, or about people—and she honestly thought she did.

Lisa and Suzy still acted like we were friends, whenever

we happened to be in the same place, and we talked in about the same way. Lisa had no idea of how differently I felt about a lot of things, but she couldn't. Suzy could have but she wanted to maintain the pretenses; she wasn't interested in what was real. I didn't mind; I didn't mind when we met up together and I didn't mind when we didn't.

I could say that to Rosamunde. I did say it to her, indirectly, a couple of days before the Christmas vacation started. "I see what you mean about best of breed," I told her.

Rosamunde never said what I expected her to, and she didn't this time, either. "I never did think you had enough vanity," she said.

Rosamunde was around a lot, at school. She was around when I was standing up or moving, not just when I was sitting down and looking like anybody else except for the crutches parked within reach. She was keeping an eye on me, I knew, although she didn't want to seem to be keeping an eye on me.

She was there when what I had been really dreading happened. The hallways at school are crowded and busy, everybody moving from class to class in the two-minute passing time, some people trying to fit in a quick smoke, or a quick kiss, or a quick conversation. People kind of move along without thinking of much more than what they have in mind. I was making my slow way along the hall to Latin one afternoon, tired as always at the end of a day, looking forward to newspaper, not thinking about much, when somebody cut past me from behind without cutting it quite wide enough. My crutch flew out and away and I lost my balance. I fell down to the floor, on my face. For a long time it seemed a lot of people stood around, and brittle silence was in the air.

I was too tired, I didn't need this—humiliation, and I was sprawled there on the floor, flat on my face. I knew I was going to have to roll over and take the crutch someone would hand to me and heft the weight of the backpack as well as my own weight and get up. I knew what I looked like, helplessly sprawled there, with my jeans leg pinned up with a stupid diaper pin over the amputation. And I suddenly couldn't do any more.

Then Rosamunde was there, telling the people to go away. "Hey, she's fine, she's just doing this for attention." She crouched down near me.

I raised my face and shifted awkwardly to a sitting position.

"We're not going to feel sorry for you," Rosamunde said, looking me in the eye. She had her books in her arms and her hair in those two little-kid pony tails. Her eyes stared into mine.

She had given me something to say. "Well, then, I guess I'll have to try something more dramatic." I smiled up around at the circle of staring faces, as if it was just a joke.

Rosamunde didn't even reach out a hand to help me.

The faces looked a little puzzled, but more relaxed. I grinned around at everyone, whoever they were.

The bell rang, and they hurried away.

Then Rosamunde did put down her books. We were alone in the deserted hallway, the classroom doors closed all along the corridor, the empty faces of the locker doors closed too. Rosamunde helped me up, waited until I had balanced myself on the crutch I held, then passed me the other. "Are you OK?"

Inside my head, the little Izzy was still collapsed onto the floor in a miserable puddle. She was weeping away, and I was weeping away too, leaning on the crutches. "I want to go *home*," I said. Wailed.

Rosamunde took me down to the girls bathroom. She didn't tell me to stop crying, she didn't comfort me, she didn't do anything but sit on a sink and wait. It didn't take all that long.

I washed my face and looked at myself in the mirror. I looked all right.

"Ready?" Rosamunde asked, sliding down from the sink. The sink groaned a little and she looked at it. "Gees— I'm lucky I didn't rip it out of the wall. Can you see trying to explain that to the principal? 'Yes, Miss Webber, how *did* you happen to rip a sink out of the wall and flood the entire first floor of the building? I'm waiting to hear, Miss Webber.' So, are you ready?"

"We're really late. You're late." As we went down the hall, me swinging along on my crutches at a good pace because I could move along pretty fast when the way was clear, I was steeling myself to say in front of the whole class that I had fallen down and Rosamunde had stayed to help me. It wasn't that it was a bad excuse, or that I thought Mr. DePonte wouldn't accept it, or would make a scene or anything. It was just so humiliating to be pitiful and helpless. The problem was that, although I could probably come into any class at any time I wanted without getting yelled at, Rosamunde couldn't.

He turned around from the board as we entered. There were about twenty kids in the room, all looking at us. I opened my mouth.

"I'm sorry we're late," Rosamunde said, "but—I had an emergency and Izzy helped me out."

Mr. DePonte made us stand there while he considered that, the piece of chalk in his hand. An "emergency," as we used it, was a menstrual problem. Everybody knew that, and teachers never questioned it. Mr. DePonte looked from Rosamunde to me and back to Rosamunde again.

"Is this true, Izzy?" he asked me.

"No," I said. I was about to explain what had really happened, but he said, "Rosamunde, sit down. Izzy, take your seat. We've been disturbed enough as it is."

He let everyone else out of class five minutes early and held me and Rosamunde back. They both came to where I sat. I didn't want to have to explain to him, but I knew I could, and I knew I could put a brave face on it.

"Now, ladies. Would you say you had a good reason for being late?" Mr. DePonte asked us both. His eyes were brown, velvety brown, and serious without being angry or curious.

Rosamunde and I nodded our heads.

"All right then," Mr. DePonte said, standing there looking at both of us. "I assume it won't happen often, or even ever again, but don't lie, Rosamunde. When you lie, you insult me, whatever your reason. I'm not asleep up there you know."

"Sorry, sir," Rosamunde said.

"It wasn't Rosamunde's fault," I told him.

"I figured that out." He smiled at me. "I've been wanting to say, Izzy—"

I didn't want to hear his sympathy. I didn't feel strong enough to respond correctly.

"Well, you must know how we feel—"

I nodded my head.

"Because—you had such great legs," he said. He blushed then, looking as young as the twins, and he almost ran out of the room. Rosamunde and I sat there for a long minute staring at each other before we broke into giggles.

"Well," Rosamunde finally said. "Well, well."

"He didn't mean to say that," I told her. I got busy going to newspaper, hugging what Mr. DePonte had said close to myself: because even before, he had noticed me specially, even when there wasn't anything special to notice; Mr. DePonte who made a point of never noticing anything. He hadn't said what he really meant, I knew that. What he really meant had nothing to do with my legs at all.

21

There were so many differences, and some of them were improvements, in a funny way. In a way, it was like my tree needlepoint, compared to the kit I had started out with. I could see in my tree, as I worked on it, something of the feeling the tree itself had given me, even though it didn't have the same professional look the kit had. I had thought the hardest part to get would be the gold of the leaves, but it was the sky that gave me real trouble, that I had to take out after I'd done it, stitch by stitch, for as many long days as it had taken me to stitch it in. The tree needlepoint was my own.

Rosamunde said it was really good, but she couldn't do any sort of handiwork, and besides, her sense of color and design was pretty poor; but my mother said, looking over my shoulder while I picked out the gray stitches, "It has something, doesn't it? I don't know what, and—you know what I'd do with the sky?"

"Don't tell me, Mom, OK?"

She understood. What was different was that I could see her understanding.

Most of the differences were not improvements. If you

think of all the things you can do with two legs, then of all the things you can do with one, all you can do with one leg is hop. Whenever I saw the little Izzy in my head, she was lying flat on her face with her crutches knocked away from under her and her jean leg pinned back with a stupid diaper pin—like a warning.

Christmas was a quiet vacation, and I was glad of that. My mother took me shopping at the mall for the twins and Francie, for my father. But my father wasn't the one who took me out to get my mother a present. My father isn't good at Christmas, or birthdays; he isn't good at presents. He doesn't know what people will want and he hates shopping and he hates wrapping. His presents are the daily and weekly and yearly ones, the whole life that he works to make for all of us. It was Rosamunde who came downtown with me to find something for my mother. I picked out a silk slip, pale yellow, with lace set at the bodice and the hem. I knew how it would make my mother feel to be wearing a slip like that under her dress. It was at the Treasure Trove, of course. Rosamunde was grumpy about it, maintaining that the money could have kept an African family fed for a month and ominously silent when I paid for it by charging it, with a request that the bill be sent to my father at his office. "It's so easy for you," she grumped, once we were outside again. She carried the wrapped box for me while I swung along on my crutches. I wasn't feeling any too cheerful myself, after all the gushing sympathy of the woman at the Treasure Trove, who kept bringing things to show me, as if I couldn't move around on my own, or as if I'd knock something over and not pay for it. Or something.

"Lay off, would you?" I told Rosamunde.

I'd hurt her feelings, I could tell, watching her trudge beside me. I was tired of her cracks about money, but I could sympathize with how frustrated she might feel, even though I thought a lot of her frustration was sour grapes. So

I told her, while we were having Cokes and fries and waiting for my father to pick us up and take us home, what I wanted to give her for Christmas. "A haircut. Oh, it's OK, I won't, but I'd love to see how you'd look with short hair, all over your head—"

"I'd look like a poodle," Rosamunde said. "Like a dog. Like a jerk."

She *was* feeling down.

"I looked up poodles once," I said. "They're one of the smartest breeds, and they're really cute."

"I don't do cute—I leave that to you cheerleader types," but she had started to smile.

"And they're the easiest to train," I finished.

"Isobel Lingard, if you think—you and your mother— you're going to—"

"What does my mother have to do with this?"

"—turn me into one of your—preppy types. Look, your hair looks good short, but it looked good longer, even with that dumb lookalike flip you all wore. Mine doesn't look good any way I wear it."

"Oh yeah?" I said. She just stared at me, her jaw set. "Anyway, I think I'll tell my father to get my mother a piece of nice jewelry. Diamond earrings, what do you think?"

Rosamunde groaned.

"No, they've had—such a hard time this fall. With me. She'd like having them, and he'd like giving them to her, and it wouldn't be hard for him to find some."

"I'm not saying it isn't a good idea." Rosamunde ate a couple of fries, dipping them into the catsup. "I'm just adding it to my list of how I'll know I've arrived—having charge accounts for my kids at the local boutiques, giving my husband diamonds for Christmas."

"That's backwards, he gives you diamonds."

"Not with my luck, with my luck I'll end up with a real failure, a nogoodnik, a cad and bounder, a ne'er-do-well, who—wait, he'll give me diamonds, but they'll be charged to my account and by the time the bill comes, he'll have left me, he'll have run off with my secretary."

I had heard all about Rosamunde's plans for herself, law school and a career in the corporate world. I was a little shocked at her ambitions, and at the way everything she did was aimed at the first step, a scholarship to a top-flight college. That was why she was in Latin Club, to show how broad her interests were. That was why she got ads for the paper, so that eventually they'd have to give her preference when she applied to be on the staff.

"If that happens, it'll be your own fault if he does. Besides, you could have a male secretary."

"Who wants a male secretary? They wouldn't know how to kowtow properly. Do you really think I'd look all right with short hair? Not your mother, what do *you* think."

Rosamunde was fun, even when she disappointed me. I knew she had to be more practical than I did, but I thought that she also took a kind of pleasure in reminding me of how much more practical she had to be. On the other hand, even watching television with Rosamunde was a kick. She muttered a running series of complaints. If a character on the screen said, at a highly sentimental moment, "Together we will find an answer," Rosamunde would mutter, "Together you ought to find a new scriptwriter," and Francie and I would break up giggling. It didn't matter that my mother didn't really like Rosamunde, or that Rosamunde didn't like my mother. I understood why my mother would often tell me that Rosamunde wasn't our type, pointing out how resentful Rosamunde seemed. I understood why Rosamunde said my mother had everything too easy, so she thought she had all the answers, as if cleaning ladies and charge accounts were signs from God that you were doing things right.

I saw a lot of Rosamunde, that vacation. We all did. Jack asked her out a couple of times, to a movie. She had babysitting jobs, though, which she didn't seem to mind. Jack couldn't figure her out: She seemed to like talking with him and arguing with him and playing Trivial Pursuit or just watching TV, but she never went out with him. "What's she got against me?" he asked.

"Nothing that I know of, nothing you don't know about. She just doesn't know she's supposed to be falling under your spell. No, seriously, Jack, she'd probably go with both of us, if she was free, if we let her pay her own way."

"She's weird."

"She's got her own plans for her life. She knows what she's doing."

"What difference would a date make?"

"Jack," I advised him, feeling pretty strange to be talking to him that way, "if I were you I'd try to be friends first. Then see."

"Who cares, anyway," he said.

"Besides, it would probably take a long time," I said, knowing how impatient he is.

He didn't answer, but he did take the two of us to see an adventure film. Rosamunde grumped about how stupid it was, but Jack and I liked it, and she was grumping as much because Jack wouldn't let her pay her own way as because of the movie.

Rosamunde spent a lot of time at our house. She said she wanted me to come to her house once I got my wooden leg. She never would call it anything else, as if keeping it a joke made it not so bad. Well, she was right. "Our house is so small, you couldn't move around on crutches. I don't think you could fit a wheelchair anywhere in it. I don't know what we'd do, if—"

"You know, the thing is going to be fitted onto the stump, and then be held in place with all kinds of straps," I told her. I wasn't looking forward to that, to learning how to strap on an artificial leg and have all that hardware around my hips, all the time. If I thought about it when I was

feeling low, that by itself could bring on one of the weepy
fits nobody but me knew about. The times I was so ashamed
of. I thought it was time I grew up and stopped crying about
what couldn't be fixed.

"But it could, it could happen to any one of us. There's
no guarantee."

"Yeah. I know."

"Straps and all? It sounds pretty bad, Izzy. Like a
girdle." Rosamunde never tried to look on the bright side.

"Adelia says I'll get used to it."

"She should know. Did she like her cookies?" Rosamunde and I had made a big box of Christmas cookies for
Adelia.

"She did. She really did."

Adelia had gotten to like me, and that pleased me as
much as the birth announcement from Mrs. Hughes-Pincke
had pleased me: as if I was a real person, not just a cripple
they had worked with.

"Do you know what I really mind, Izzy?" Rosamunde
asked. I was wrapping my presents in my room, and she
was hanging around watching me. She was staying for
dinner that night, because she didn't have a job.

I thought she was going to give me her little speech about
how if somebody else—another color, another social strata,
another country or even another part of America—had had
my accident, she wouldn't have gotten the same quality of
treatment, and how that wasn't right. "What?" I asked,
getting ready to tune her out.

"I mind . . . I used to really like watching you move
around, because you always seemed so comfortable in your
own body, and it wasn't anything you thought about, or
even noticed; it was just the way you were, that was what
was so great about it."

"You're talking in the past tense," I said, carefully
keeping my eyes on the ribbon I was tying, thinking how
much I'd changed.

"No, that's not true. I mean, I *was*. I mean, it was the past tense, but you still have that way of being—comfortable to be with. Only it used to show, anybody who saw you saw it, just looking at you. Because it wasn't just being comfortable with your body that made you so nice. But I really mind that."

Then I did look at her. "I mind it too," I said.

"For all the good it does, right? Listen, I'm going to go see if your mother needs any help."

"You're going to go see if you can improve the meal," I joked. "Don't antagonize her, OK?"

She stayed out in the kitchen and they stopped talking when I came in, but I ignored that. I don't know what they were saying, but after the twins had driven Rosamunde home that night, my mother said to me: "She's got more depth than any of your other friends, Rosamunde, doesn't she? It's not just intelligence either, is it?" I didn't say anything. She was thinking aloud. "But she's not going to have an easy life of it, she's just not an easy person. I do wish she'd do something with herself, have her hair cut, dress herself . . ."

"I'm working on the haircut," I admitted. "But I figure it'll take months. She's pretty insecure about her looks."

Rosamunde also had something to say. "Your mother puts on a false front. She hides it, but she really has thought about things, did you know that? About how she wants her family to be, what a good mother does—even why she does all that charity work, kind of like some aristocrat with her *noblesse oblige*."

"Princess Di?" I asked her, remembering.

Rosamunde grinned. "Yeah, well I was right, wasn't I?"

My mother gave me a big box of long skirts for Christmas. She made them all herself, one out of black velvet, two out of Indian prints, one denim and two corduroy. She didn't say, and I didn't say, but we both knew that if I wore long skirts it wouldn't be so apparent that there was a foot missing under them.

"Keeping me feminine?" I asked her.

"That's my job," she answered. We didn't need to say anything about how much I liked them and how much she had liked making them for me.

The twins gave me my second favorite present. They had scoured antique stores and found me a gold handled walking stick.

"Open it," Jack said, grabbing it away from me to show me that if I twisted the top I could draw out a thin sword.

"It's only a fencing foil," Joel said. "He told us he wasn't allowed to sell a real blade with it."

"Isn't it neat?" Jack demanded.

"Neat," I agreed.

"I think it's sort of dashing," Joel said, and I knew what he meant. It was like being in an old pirate movie, or a period romance filled with sword fights and damsels in distress. I knew what they meant by the gift.

I even went to a party that vacation, at Lisa's. Not a New Year's Eve party—I spent New Year's Eve babysitting Francie—but still, it was a party. I wore my long velvet skirt and I made myself go. Once there, I made myself talk with people and tried to make sure that anyone who talked to me had a good time. It was harder work than I remembered, being at a party. Rosamunde didn't help—she stuck close, making me feel even more self-conscious, as if we were eighth grade girls at our first boy-girl dance or something. Finally, I turned to her and said, "Don't *cling*, will you, please?"

She moved right off and stayed away. For a minute, I was shocked at myself. You didn't say things like that to your friends, you didn't say the truth like that; but of course you do, to your real friends, you can say the truth. When I saw Rosamunde going with a boy into the darkened living room, where music was playing and couples were dancing, I winked at her. That time, I could see, I surprised her.

Lisa was thoughtful, terribly thoughtful, settling me thoughtfully into a big comfortable chair, coming thoughtfully back again and again to bring me a Coke or someone to talk to, which made it hard for me to have any kind of conversation, with her hovering around being so thoughtful. I appreciated her intention, but she didn't know how she wasn't helping one bit. After a while I just got up on my crutches and started moving around on my own. Suzy hung around for a while, carrying on this disjointed whispered conversation. "You should have warned me about him— Marco," she would whisper in my ear, to give the impression that we were best friends, telling secrets. I thought that was sort of funny and sort of sad.

It was a tiring evening, and I was glad when Joel came to get me. "How'd it go?" he asked.

"All right, I think," I told him, sitting in the car, my crutches propped beside me.

"Life getting back to normal?"

I knew what he was asking, and I knew he would report in to my mother, and I appreciated it even though I minded. "No," I told him, "but it was all right, and that's what I was worried about."

Lauren, elegant in a long black dress, her face a mask, had always been in another room; if I moved into a room where she was, she moved on out of it. Unlike Lisa, who thought I needed special attention to help me through a tough situation, or Suzy who thought I was likely to turn out to be popular again, Lauren thought I was a cripple.

She was right, I was. Am. But that wasn't all I was, I thought, and besides, it was bad enough, she didn't need to add to it by avoiding me that way, even though I thought I could see why she felt the way she did, because she was so frightened of what would happen to her if she wasn't perfect to look at—that didn't make any difference to the way it made me feel, when she—and Lisa being so hatefully thoughtful and—

So it was a bad night. It was bad enough, everything was, without knowing that the brave front I put on was only a cover up. I swore to myself that starting the next morning, I wouldn't ever cry again like that, over that. I promised myself I would stop. But I couldn't even keep my promises to myself, and I spent the small, dark hours of that morning sniveling away in the darkened bedroom and not liking myself one little bit.

22

Going back to school wasn't easy, but I had newspaper to look forward to. I also had—to my surprise, because it wasn't as if I'd been working that much harder—a good chance of making honor roll for the first semester. I thought I would like telling my parents if I made the honor roll.

After the first day things quickly got back to normal, or what had become normal, if being carried up the cafeteria stairs by John Wintersize every day could be called normal. Things in the newspaper room weren't quite the way they had been, though. In fact, between Tony acting strangely out of sorts with everyone and Deborah on a perpetual high because she had gotten into Stanford on early admissions, we seemed always to be on the edge of arguments, and it seemed hard to get even the routine tasks done on schedule. Most of the staff were seniors, and these semester grades were the ones that went to the colleges, so everyone was working hard for exams. That had something to do with it. Tony had most to do with it, though, because he was the one who pulled everybody together to work on a job—and he didn't have his mind on what he was doing, although he never forgot to get up and bring me my crutches when it was time to go. It wasn't as if he had changed or anything. I guessed something was making him unhappy, and I was sorry about that, but there was nothing I could do about it.

Rosamunde made me go to a basketball game. "Just one, you have to." I didn't see why I had to, although I could see why she thought I had to.

"Just once, just to get it over with," she said. "I'm going to nag you until you do, so you might as well give in easily." I considered offering her a trade, her haircut for my attendance at a game, but I decided against that. It was a little too much like blackmail. Besides, if I went along with her, then I could remind her sometime later that I had done this for her, so she should at least just talk to a stylist. That, I thought, might work more effectively. So I went to the basketball game on a Friday night in January, with Rosamunde.

We arrived early, to be sure to get seats on the bottom row of bleachers. The team didn't win. In fact, they lost badly. The stands, however, didn't mind that. People yelled and cheered just as loudly as if the team had been winning. Nobody really cared. Everything was pretty informal, people drifting around and talking while the game was going on. Rosamunde and I talked to a number of people, and Tony and Deborah sat down just behind us, so we carried on a four-person conversation through all the quarters. "Are you enjoying yourself?" Rosamunde said to me.

"It's all right," I said to her, trying to be precise. "Are you?"

"All right, I guess."

When the cheerleaders stepped in front of us, wearing short pleated skirts and enthusiastic smiles, waving pompons, Rosamunde absolutely ignored me, so I knew that this was worrying her. It was worrying me, too. I watched the drills with the close attention you give to somebody else doing something you know how to do. I watched Georgie

Lowe, who even stood in my old place at the end of the line because we were almost the same height. Georgie wasn't as sure of herself as the rest of the squad, but there was something about the way her face was glad as she called out the cheers, or the coordination of her moves maybe, that made her better to watch than anybody else, even those girls who moved with sure, dancer's rhythms, or whose figures were better. Georgie looked at me a couple of times, and I made sure to smile right at her. After the game, I went over to her and told her she looked good.

"You know," Georgie said, her eyes going briefly to where my pant leg ended, "I'd rather have waited another year, if—"

She didn't know how to say what she meant, but she meant what she said, and she had the courage to try to say it.

"I thought she'd put you in to replace me," I said.

"You did?"

"Sure, you were the best choice," I said. "I'll see you, OK?"

Rosamunde and I left right away, with the other people who weren't going to parties afterwards. She was coming back to spend the night, and I was glad of that because if I'd spent the night alone I knew what I would have thought about. If I couldn't control myself, and I couldn't, having Rosamunde there would do the job for me. "How depressing was it?" she asked me.

Turning it into words made it easier to deal with. "Pretty depressing."

"Well, it's behind you now."

The little Izzy in my head was lying on the floor with her crutches knocked away, just weeping miserably, but nobody knew that, and I was going to learn how to make myself pick her by the scruff of her neck and shake her until she stopped that.

As exams came closer, a lot of the staff either cut the

newspaper meetings or left exactly at the end of the hour. The only thing I could think of to help Tony out was to put in a lot of hours myself, doing anything that needed to be done, even writing up articles that were easy enough for me to do, like lunch menus or the calendar of events. Tony worked at his end of the table. I worked at mine. I don't think he even knew I was there. I didn't try to talk to him. He didn't say much to me, beyond, "Proof this, would you, Izzy?"

He drove me home and talked about the next issue. I'd try to help him consider ideas for articles or topics for special reports. He'd park his old Chevy in front of our house, come around to open the door, and hand me my crutches. He never came in with me and I never asked him, but he always stood there, watching until I was safely inside the house. I wished he'd just drive off, but he didn't.

One of those late afternoons, when the whole empty school echoed quiet around us, he passed me the editorial page for a final check. I still had half an hour before my father would come to pick me up. Tony was staying at school to watch a rehearsal of the play, where Deborah had a major role. I read the editorials and letters for a final time, putting in corrections with a blue pencil. Tony just sat at his end of the table, looking tired, twisting a pencil in his hands, looking troubled. I got down to the list of staff members and found my own name there, under Editorial Staff: Izzy Lingard.

"You put me on the staff," I said.

"What?"

"You put me on the staff." I pointed my pencil at the place.

"Oh. It's about time, don't you think?"

I looked at my name for a minute and then I realized what was wrong. I crossed out Izzy and wrote in Isobel. I passed the page back to Tony. He looked over my blue markings.

"Is that your name? Isobel? It's a nice name." He smiled at me then, looking even more tired and troubled.

"It's my name sometimes," I told him. "More and more as I get older."

That amused him. "Nobody ever calls Deborah, Debby—and nobody even remembers that my name is Antony—it's pretty hopeless, isn't it."

He wasn't really asking me, he was just talking. He was thinking, I thought, about how she was going to go out to Stanford, and from there who knew where, or how far, while he was going to go to the state college. He would be living at home so that he could work part time on the local paper, which his uncle owned. It would probably come to him, in time, which he said was all he wanted for his life, to be really rooted in one place and really take part in its history. Yet he was thinking about losing Deborah.

"If it were me," I said, "if I loved her—"

"Yeah, I do," he said, with no expression in his voice.

I had thought about this. "Then I'd try to just enjoy the rest of the year. You never know, anyway, what's going to happen so why not just—make the most of the time you have? If it were me," I finished clumsily.

Tony just stared at me and stared at me. "I've been acting like a jerk," he finally said, but his voice sounded pleased. "Haven't I?"

I didn't answer, because I didn't know what was true.

"I have," he assured me, his smile showing his crooked teeth. "But you're right, Izzy, you're pretty sharp after all, aren't you?"

I didn't know what to say to that, either. He kept on looking at me until it made me uncomfortable.

"I just had a crazy idea. Listen, I think we should really be friends, you and I. Isobel Lingard, let's be friends all of our lives. What do you say?"

"I wouldn't mind that," I answered, smiling back into his eyes.

"Good. That's settled then. I've got to run, take these to the printer, and get back in time to apologize to Deborah—if she hasn't written me off entirely as a jerk. Your father's coming to get you, right? OK, then, I'll see you tomorrow. OK?"

I watched him leave the room and listened to his footsteps hurrying down the hall. I could feel the smile lingering on my face. Then I got ready to go myself. That was when I noticed that Tony had forgotten my crutches, that they stood leaning against the far wall, down the whole length of the room.

I was glad I was alone as I stood up on my one leg and started hopping over to where the crutches were. When I had them under my arms, I suddenly realized—

Tony Marcel had forgotten my crutches.

Inside my head, the little Izzy gathered herself up and did an impossible backflip, and then another and another. I knew how she felt.

After exams, everyone seemed to settle down again. The seniors, especially, relaxed. For better or worse, the first semester was finished, and now they just had to get through the rest of the year until graduation. The newspaper was running smoothly again. Although Deborah was still strung up high with excitement, Tony was serene, contented, and he managed to spread that mood around the newspaper room.

Life was going along and I was going along through it— on crutches now, but Adelia had started me in the swimming pool and Dr. Epstein said I was ready to be fitted for an artificial leg, if I was ready. I was about ready, I thought. I had learned how to make myself change into a bathing suit and get into the hospital pool: It was a matter of concentration on the task at hand, which was not that easy, since I had to swim awkwardly to keep myself from going around in circles. Then, I would concentrate on other things as well, irrelevant things, like the idea of getting Rosamunde over for regular swimming, once our pool was built. She needed exercise, but she lacked the kind of physical discipline that would enable her to do that herself. With just the two of us in the pool, I was pretty sure I could get her swimming laps. She trusted me—in a way, more than she trusted herself. Thinking of those things, I could stand up on the crutches, with my amputated leg hanging down naked, and move over the distance between the changing room and the pool.

In time, I thought, I would be able to do something about the slides into depression. I thought maybe. In time, I would outgrow the stupid, hopeless longing for the things I had lost—for dancing to soft music—and all those things. It was only at nighttime, alone, that I wasted my time wishing, or dreaming. During the days, I moved around home and school on crutches, doing all right.

One mid-February day I was moving down the hallway to my locker to get my books for the afternoon classes, when I saw Marco Griggers talking with Georgie Lowe. I slowed down, and people moved around me, but I only saw the two of them. Marco sort of leaned towards Georgie, who was looking up at him through her lashes, her cheeks a little pink. Marco grinned at her.

He was asking her out, and she was flirting at him, pleased to be asked out by a senior.

And I was angry.

Marco had always pretended he didn't notice me, whenever we came anywhere near each other, which wasn't often, and I had pretended he didn't exist; so he was surprised to see me come up to the two of them.

"Izzy," he said. He looked furious and nervous.

"Hi, Georgie. Hey, Marco," I answered. I leaned on my crutches and smiled at them, a big fake smile. "I don't mean to interrupt anything," I said, repressing the anger I could feel burning up from my stomach.

"Yeah, well," he muttered, his eyes going to Georgie to make an I-don't-know-what's-with-her expression.

I didn't let him finish. "So. Are you going to go out with him?" I asked Georgie. "I only went out with him once, but it was quite an experience." I kept on smiling.

Georgie was looking at the two of us, back and forth. I don't know what she was thinking, but I knew what I hoped she was thinking about. I was glad I was wearing jeans that day.

"You have to look out for Marco," I told Georgie, as if I was making a joke. "You know his reputation." After a long minute, I added, "Marco's such a flirt, everybody knows that."

Marco had stopped wavering between being furious and nervous. He was just furious. He glanced at me, so mad that his nostrils flared, and I had to bite on my lip to keep from giggling. I had taken over all the nervous.

When he could finally speak, he just had one thing to say to me. The bell rang and the corridor emptied quickly, and he glared at me: "Bitch."

Then he walked away.

Georgie didn't know what to say. She felt sorry for me, although she quickly disguised that, and she was puzzled at my interference. "You'll be late to class," I reminded her.

"Oh—you're right," she said. "I've got to run."

Run she did. I watched her sprint down the empty hallway and up the stairs—it was lovely the way she moved, the way her body worked, it was so perfect, she was. With the long lines the bones gave and the curves of flesh over it. I had never realized.

Georgie turned at the landing to look back and wave, smiling.

I watched the places where she had been, after she had disappeared from sight. I envied her her perfection and her gladness. Envy ran through my stomach like an ice cold sword. I didn't think I could breathe in, because my whole body was curled up around that envy's edge.

I could breathe, though, because I breathed in all of what I had seen, all I had just done. I breathed in as if I'd never breathed before. That's what it tasted like, that breath. It was like one of the old movies, where the homely girl in glasses is made over and looks at her new self in the mirror for the first time. She just stares at herself, not saying anything. If she were to say anything, all she could say would be, "Oh." I stared at myself, thinking, "Oh. Oh my. Oh, wow."

I had seen Marco and Georgie talking and understood what was happening. I had done something, which nobody at that party had done for me. I knew that however much Marco's intention was to hurt me, you wouldn't call someone a bitch if you just dismissed her as crippled. I knew also that I could never before—and maybe not for years, under ordinary circumstances—have seen how perfect Georgie was, I could never have understood that: how lovely it was when someone was young and perfect. And I knew that I would weep that night, alone in my room. I would weep, but that was all right too. I couldn't help but wish. I couldn't expect myself not to.

"Oh, wow," I thought. It was the richness of it, the richness in me; there was so much more than before. Better, too, I had to admit it, although if I could have gone back and changed things I wouldn't have hesitated for one minute to do that.

I didn't know what to think, but I wanted to stand there, for another minute or five, just being myself. Inside my head I saw the little Izzy. She was standing alone, without crutches. She wore her black velvet skirt and a silky white blouse. Her hair was feathered gold all around her head. Her arms were spread out slightly. She looked like she was about to dance, but really her arms were out for balance. I knew, because it was true even though it didn't show, that underneath the long skirt one of the legs was flesh and the other was a fake. The little Izzy balanced there briefly and then took a hesitant step forward—ready to fall, ready not to fall.

ABOUT THE AUTHOR

Cynthia Voigt is the author of fourteen previous novels, including Newbery Medal winner DICEY'S SONG and Newbery Honor Book A SOLITARY BLUE. She currently lives in Maine with her family and their dog.